Had a great Fall

SHAWN McGUIRE

Shawn McGuire 2015

ISBN 978-0-9961035-6-5
ISBN 978-0-9961035-7-2 (ebook)

Published by Brown Bag Books

www.Shawn-McGuire.com
www.Facebook.com/ShawnMcGuireAuthor

Cover Design by Karri Klawiter
www.artbykarri.com

Titles by Shawn McGuire

THE WISH MAKERS Series:

Sticks and Stones
Break My Boncs
Never Hurt Me
Had a Great Fall

For Mom and Dad

Because you gave me the gift of knowledge and empathy.
Everything really does work out for the best.
Ibble dibble.

Chapter One

Robin

Maybe I could call in sick. With something fatal. Something so contagious the entire high school would contract it just by looking at me. Was there such a thing? I took out my phone. "Okay, Google. What is visual contagion?"

"Good morning, Robin."

For half a second I thought my phone had learned my name. And started speaking in my mom's voice. I entered the kitchen and found Mom standing by the stove, dunking a tea bag in her cup.

"Morning." I set my messenger bag by the back door and took a seat at the kitchen bar.

Google had only come up with only one direct hit and was now blinking at me, waiting for something that would challenge its storage banks. The 'contagion' it offered wasn't even a disease. It was some company in Vancouver that spread positive messages on organic hemp or bamboo T-shirts. Great. I ask for science, I get hippies.

"Do you think Visual Contagion would be a good name for a band?" I asked Mom as I scrolled through a few of the T-shirt pictures.

"Hmm," Mom said, tapping her fingernail against her teacup. "A band that plays music?"

My turn to sit and blink. "What other kind is there?"

"Plenty. A wrist band. Hairband. Wedding band. Waistband."

"Okay, okay." She'd go on and on and then open the thesaurus app on her tablet if I didn't stop her. It's her marketing background. Details were very important. "Mom, guys don't think about hairbands and jewelry. Yes, I mean a band that plays music."

"Then I'd say no. Visual Contagion, great a name as it is, would not work for a musical group." She took a sip of her tea, Irish breakfast according to the tag hanging from the string, as she contemplated. "Auditory Contagion could work. Audio? Audial?"

Auditory Contagion would indeed be a damn cool name for a band. Almost made me want to form one. Except I couldn't play a single instrument. Not even that plastic flute thing they made us play in elementary school. I might be able to compose something on my computer though. I needed music for my video game anyway.

"Okay, Google. Popular music software."

"Would you like some breakfast?" Mom asked. "Or are you just going to play with your phone until it's time to leave?"

My mom wasn't the most domestic person. She did like to feed people though, and when she took the time to make an actual meal, she was a great cook.

I set my phone in my lap and analyzed my hunger level. "Juice and toast with butter and jam. Two slices."

"Two? You're hungry today. What kind of tea?" She held up her Irish breakfast to me with a questioning look and wiggled the box as if that would lure me to the Celtic side.

"*English* breakfast, please. With cream and two sugar cubes."

"Off to the range," my dad said as he entered the kitchen and set a black case—smaller than a briefcase, larger than a lunchbox—on the gray marble counter.

"Before work?" Mom asked. "You'll be late."

He was never late. Being at his desk before those he supervised got there was a must for Dad. He insisted, "The boss should set the example."

"I'm taking a couple of personal hours," he said, as he plugged the first of two coffee pods into the machine to fill his travel mug. "My first meeting isn't until ten today. I want to try out my birthday present. Want to come with me, Robin?"

Despite his many attempts over the years to lure me to *the range*, I didn't share my dad's enthusiasm for guns. His new one came with a built in laser site, though. The gun I could do without, but present me with a laser infused piece of technology, and I could understand his excitement.

"Thanks, but I *do* have a meeting before ten," I said. "I have that test first thing today."

"Finally," Dad said. "I don't understand the holdup on allowing you to take a placement test. You studied?"

"Of course he studied," Mom said as though nothing could be more unthinkable than me *not* studying.

"I did," I told them. "Don't worry, I'll pass."

"They should put him directly into Calculus and Differential Equations," Dad said.

"He could handle it," Mom agreed, "but AP Calculus will be an easy A for him."

"Good point," Dad said and clapped me on the back, nearly knocking me off my stool. "Build that killer GPA. Get into the college of your choice and accumulate academic scholarships as well."

Which college was still undecided. Dad wanted me to go to MIT, his alma mater, or UC Berkeley. Currently, my only plan was to survive high school.

"Don't pressure him," Mom said, setting a plate with my buttered and jammed toast on the placemat in front of me.

"I don't need to pressure him. He's a self-starter. Puts adequate pressure on himself." Dad had his coffee mug in one hand and his new present in the other. "I'm off."

"Don't forget your briefcase," I said and nodded to the dark-brown leather satchel sitting on the stool next to me.

"Ah, yes. I do need to go to work at some point today, don't I?"

Mom stood by the door and watched as Dad drove off. Then she turned to me and gave me the look that said a discussion was coming.

"I assume you'll tell me if anything is wrong, but I know how shut-mouthed teenagers can be, especially boys, so I'm checking to be sure." She paused, steeling herself. "How have things been?"

Her eyes were bright and shining. Tears were ready to fall, but whether happy or sad depended on how I responded.

"Oh, you know." I took a big bite of my sprouted wheat toast with huckleberry jam, samples from one of Mom's clients, and gave her a closed-mouth smile and a thumbs-up.

She exhaled like she won the lottery. "I knew this move would be good for you."

A little spot in my chest warmed at that sigh and then immediately fizzled. The nutty-buttery-sweet flavor that filled my mouth turned to cardboard. How could I possibly tell her that after all we'd gone through, things were only different, not better?

I'd get through this. I made it through my first nine years of school, I could make it through the last three. I needed a person. There had to be one person in this school I could consider a friend. Sitting alone in the lunch room every day, too afraid to risk further harassment, was only enhancing the loner nerd reputation I just couldn't shake.

While Mom studied her calendar, I finished my breakfast and put my dishes in the dishwasher.

"Hope you have a good day, sweetie," Mom said. "I'd wish you good luck on your test but I know you don't need it." She glanced at the microwave clock and jumped. "I've got a video conference in an hour." She looked down at her pink bathrobe with the tea stain down the front. "I should probably put some clothes on."

She gave me a quick hug and shuffled off to get ready.

"Good luck," I called, but she was already half-way up the stairs.

I hitched my messenger bag over my head and tugged on a stocking cap. It was chilly enough this morning for a hoodie, but it would warm up in no time. The hat would be good enough.

As I started the six block walk to the bus stop, I remembered that I never checked the results of my 'popular music software' request. I pulled out my phone and found a lot of options. I studied them as I walked, glancing up every few feet so I didn't do something stupid like step into the pathway of a bicyclist. I'd only needed to do that once to learn my lesson. No, today my mistake was that I didn't look behind me.

"Morning, Tweety."

I stopped breathing and my gut tightened. I knew who it was without looking: Zane Zimmerman.

Zane was the school's star athlete. I didn't pay attention to sports, but even I knew Zane killed it on the pitching mound. He was about five-seven, an inch taller than me, and a good twenty pounds heavier. All muscle.

I was about to put my phone back in my pocket when I got bull rushed. He didn't actually tackle me, this time, but did hit me hard enough to knock what little breath was in my lungs out of them and send my phone flying. It landed six feet away and slid down the sidewalk another two or three feet before coming to a rest, teetering on the curb like a jumper about to leap from a bridge.

"Careful, Tweety." Zane said. "You should watch where you're going."

My breath returned as a gasp and I rushed to retrieve my phone—bent at the waist, duck-walking with my hands stretched out, dorky as hell—before someone stepped on it or kicked it out into the street. The screen had cracked. Great. Maybe I could convince my parents to upgrade to a phone with gorilla glass instead of just replacing the screen. Again.

"Oh, snap," Zane said, making a dramatic aw-shucks motion. "Tough luck there, dude."

Zane wasn't just a bully. He was the really dangerous kind, in my opinion, because he was smart. Not just book smart but street smart, too. He knew when he could get away with stuff and when he had to wait to dole out his attacks. As far as the teachers and any other adult were concerned, Zane was a dream kid.

"Yeah," I said. "Tough luck."

Unfortunately, I was used to being harassed. It started years ago, in fifth grade, back in Wisconsin. I made the mistake of laughing at Cole, a meathead of a kid. He thought he was the greatest thing to ever attend Cleveland Heights Elementary. He was a boy's boy. He played tackle football and the other roughest of the rough sports at recess. He also had an older brother that beat on him every chance he got. I'm talking bloody noses, black eyes, and bruises all over his body. It made him, justifiably, angry. A cork ready to pop.

We'd all been walking to our classroom first thing one morning. It had been snowing hard and the hallways were wet from everyone's boots.

"Careful, kids," the janitor told us as we walked past. "The floor is slippery."

No sooner had the words come out of his mouth than Cole's feet went out from under him. His backpack went flying one direction, his lunchbox the other. It was funny. So I laughed.

"Shut up, ass-wipe," Cole snapped as he picked up his backpack and lunchbox. His face bright red.

A bunch of other kids were laughing, too, but I had started it and I was closest.

He started swinging, using moves he'd surely learned from his brother. He was the same size as me and not much stronger so the punches didn't really hurt. The problem was, I took a defensive swing just as our teacher came out of our room to see what all the noise was about. All she saw was the back of my fist connecting with Cole's jaw. I got suspended for two days because no one would come to my defense.

When I got back to school everyone was on Cole's side. He was more popular than me. He was funnier. He had a big brother who would defend him to the death in public even though he pounded the snot out of Cole at home.

The harassment got so bad I started having nightmares, got headaches, and lost weight. We moved to a nearby town as soon as Dad's promotion and raise went through. The harassment from Cleveland Heights stuck to me like a bad smell and I became everyone's target at my new school, too. Then came Dad's transfer to Colorado.

"You'll have a fresh start," Mom said, fully believing her own words. "You can reinvent yourself, be whoever you want to be."

That sounded like a good idea and during the two-day drive I decided I was Robin the technology dude instead of Robin the un-athletic, scrawny, bullied wimp.

"The bus is here," Zane said and ran the last half block to the stop. "Better fly fast, Tweety."

Because we went to a private high school, transportation was up to the parents. Most of the kids got rides. If I asked, my dad might drive me the five miles. It was on his way. For that to happen, though, I'd either have to get to school super-early or Dad would be late to work. Well, late by his standards. Mom almost always had early-morning calls and was already in work-mode by the time I came down to breakfast. If I made a big deal out of it she'd probably take me. It would only be twenty minutes out of her morning. But she'd want to know why I was making a big deal about riding the bus.

During the Cole incident, Mom tried to fix things by calling and talking to his mom. When that didn't work, Mom went to the principal who dragged Cole and me into her office and gave us a lecture about staying away from each other. Things got better for a while but as soon as everyone forgot to pay attention to us, things got way worse. I didn't want to risk a drama like that again so just took the city bus.

I got in line behind Mrs. Richards, a tiny great-grandmotherly looking woman with leathery, wrinkled skin and pure-white hair.

"Good morning, Master Robin," Mrs. Richards said, happy like always. "Oh my. What happened to your phone?"

I glanced up at Zane who was moving to the back of the bus with his minions Thad, Wayne, and Ben.

"I dropped it," I said and frowned at the splintered screen. "My parents are going to be so angry."

"Pish-posh," Mrs. Richards said with a swat of her hand. "Accidents happen."

I helped her climb the bus stairs, scanned my pass, and looked for a seat.

The front seat was full. The next three rows were full. Along with the perceived protection of the driver, the other reason I preferred to sit up front was that I got motion sick in the back of the bus. Today I ended up in an aisle seat in the middle, right on the fringe of the danger zone.

I stared at my worthless phone during the ride, trying to concentrate on anything other than Zane's group behind me. For a few minutes the smell of the guy next to me—body odor covered up by too much cologne and lingering cigar smoke—distracted me. Then Zane and the Minions started talking louder, a sure sign they were building up to something. Birdcalls were their favorite torment. *Tweet, tweet. Sing for us, Tweety.* I expected the performance to start any second.

Why hadn't I included adopting my middle name as part of the Reinvention of Robin? A crucial mistake on my part. I could have been Alexander. Or better yet, Alex. A strong name. Not a little yellow bird name.

We were over halfway to school and still not a single *chirp*. It was Monday morning. Maybe they were talking about stuff that happened over the weekend. As the bus came to our stop, Zane's group jumped up first. As he passed me, Zane smacked the back of my head and simultaneously snatched my cap.

"Hey!" I called out then bit back the other words that wanted to follow it. Not worth the retaliation. Not even for the cap my grandmother had knitted for me with her crooked, arthritic hands. I thought of throwing my phone at the back of Zane's head. My pulse raced as I imagined suddenly having enough strength in my puny excuse for an arm to pitch that phone so hard it would connect with him better than any flaming fastball he could ever dream of throwing. The baseball coach would hear about the kid with the miraculous arm. He'd beg me to take over as the team's star pitcher. Zane would go down, humiliated at being bested by some unknown, un-athletic, computer geek.

As I followed them down the aisle, I went through the full cycle of emotions starting with pissed off to high on fantasy to afraid of what was coming next all within a few seconds. An adrenaline letdown would come next, but first my fear turned to energy and I started to bounce as we waited for the bus door to open. Why couldn't he just leave me alone?

"Tweety's jumpy today," Minion Thad said.

"Maybe he's trying to fly," Minion Ben said.

My first day at Woodland Academy had been the first

day of the fourth quarter of my freshman year. It had been five months and I hadn't made a single friend. I barely knew anyone's name. Despite Mom's best efforts, my clothes hadn't, and still didn't, come from the right swanky store. My book bag wasn't quite expensive enough. My phone wasn't quite new enough. I wasn't quite enough. *I* never would be.

The school's policy was for new students to wear a nametag. Theoretically this was so everyone would be nice to me. They'd offer me assistance if I got lost or help me with the daily routine. The secretary handed me my class schedule and that nametag—*Hi, I'm Robin* written in hot pink ink because that was the first pen her hand touched. A bull's-eye in the center of my chest wouldn't have been more obvious.

It started my first day, between second and third period. I was standing in line, waiting my turn at the drinking fountain. Out of nowhere everyone burst out laughing and started fist-bumping each other. Zane was at the center of it. A replay of Cole slipping on the wet floor flashed in my mind like a sickening premonition. Zane's moment of embarrassment had quickly turned into humiliation. He looked around in a panic, desperate for someone or something to rescue him. His eyes locked on me, the new face in the crowd, and then darted to the nametag.

"Hey, Tweety," he had said in a sneering tone that made my guts drop to my feet. "You gonna teach us all to sing a pretty birdie song?"

It was so stupid. A really lame-ass thing to say. But it had the effect he wanted. Everyone turned and laughed at me. I hadn't even made it to lunch on my first day and I was a target. An outcast. A freak.

Again.

Chapter Two

Desiree

For the new genie home, I chose the most spectacular place. I'd dubbed it Mystic Lodge. It was huge with more than enough room for all two hundred, give or take, of the Guides now under my supervision. The central commons area had floor-to-ceiling windows that looked out on mountain peaks and a glacier lake. A massive circular fireplace occupied the center of the room, its hearth large enough to perch upon and chase away the chill of the cool alpine mornings.

Each Guide got her own bedroom, bathroom, private balcony, and jaw-dropping view. They could swim in the lake when the weather was warm. Swoosh down the ski runs when the snow fell. There were woodland paths to wander and wildlife to appreciate. Anything else they wanted or needed, they were free to manifest.

Their unhappiness had nothing to do with the location though. They weren't happy with me and they didn't hesitate to let me know that.

Newsflash: With the exception of the location, I wasn't happy either. Being the leader of the genies had never been in my plans. Now I was stuck for the next two hundred years or so with a group of Guides that couldn't stand me.

The little disco ball hanging from the roof of my renovated school bus started to spin and strobe, as it had been off and on for hours. A deep, reverberating gong sounded periodically, vibrating my brain. I really should change it, maybe to a soft chime.

Or you could go see what they want, a voice in my head scolded.

"They want to yell at me," I told the scold.

A soft knock sounded on the door of my bus and Indira poked her head in.

"Checking to see if you're alive."

"Still here," I said from my bed at the back of the bus.

She stepped all the way in and pointed at the disco ball. "That will stop if you answer the summons. *My* summons."

"I'm working on it," I mumbled into my pillow.

"You'll never get over him if you lay there and wallow all day."

"I'm not wallowing."

"What would you call it then?"

I pulled my blankets up to my chin. "You're not the boss."

"Exactly!" Indira said, throwing her hands in the air, her dozens of bracelets jingling. "*You're* the boss. I'm happy to have helped where I could, but incoming wishes are your responsibility. You've got to make decisions about them soon or you'll have such a backlog you may never catch up."

"But I don't—," I started and was immediately silenced by Indira's arched eyebrow.

I'd been putting off assigning wishes. Not because I

12

didn't want to grant them, but because I didn't know who to assign them to. Indira had done a bitchin' job filling in for me while I tried to find a level of comfort with my new job, and dealt with the fact that Kaf was gone. But Indira was starting to look frazzled. I couldn't be sure from across the bus, but it looked like she was wearing two different shoes. Groovy if chosen purposely. Concerning if due to stress.

"It's been two weeks." She was practically on her knees begging. "I have requests of my own that need attention."

"All right." I kicked my blankets off. "Let's go see what they want to harsh my mellow about today."

I flung my legs over the side of my bed, then stood, straightened the covers, and smiled. Two and a half months ago, Ritchie the Hitchhiker had hijacked my bus. The police found her, defaced with graffiti and stripped of everything inside. One of the nifty things about getting my powers back was that I was able to get all my stuff back, too. Wish I could have seen the look on his face when the crushed velvet comforter, tin ceiling tiles, and miniature crystal chandeliers suddenly disappeared from wherever he'd taken them.

"I'll meet you at the Lodge," Indira said and vanished.

The second, I mean the absolute instant I appeared in the commons area, I got swarmed like a snack vendor at a 420 gathering.

"Why couldn't we stay where we were?" a Guide named Amber asked. Amber had big, frizzy, white hair and even bigger boobs that strained the limits of her shirt buttons.

"Sometimes a change in management calls for a new location, too," I said. "A fresh start. You can't get much fresher than a mountain valley.

I took in a breath that filled my lungs with crisp, clean air.

"So this is a dictatorship now?" Amber asked. "Kaf never told us where we had to live."

"Actually," I said, "he did."

Amber tilted her head to the side in the questioning pose

of a confused Golden Retriever.

"Did he ever give you the choice to live anywhere other than that castle?" I asked.

"No," she said, tilting her head the other direction. "But we got to choose what our rooms looked like."

"I told you"—I closed my eyes and went to my mental Woodstock—"you are free to do *anything you want* with your personal space."

How many times had I said those words in the last two weeks? Don't like the cabin-style interior? Go gypsy or Victorian or modern or whatever floats your boat. Don't want a private room? Find a roomie or move walls around and make bunk rooms. They're genies. They could manifest anything they wanted to make them happy.

Apparently what made them happy two weeks into our journey together was bitching about everything that had anything to do with me or any decision I made. The more Amber complained, the more other Guides gathered around to join in pelting me with words of dissent and dissatisfaction.

What they didn't understand was that it wasn't just the desert location I couldn't tolerate. (Some might consider mile after mile of sand beautiful. I found it mind-numbing.) It was the constant reminder of Kaf there that made my heart ache.

Two weeks and not one word from him. He handed the reins over to me without even so much as a nod toward the path I needed to follow. Then he left. If any good came from the Guides' constant harassment, it was that it kept my mind off of him. As angry as I was that he was gone, I also missed him so much that when I did have quiet times, late at night or first thing in the morning, I almost couldn't function.

"Desiree."

A new voice in the mix. This one, with its odd dash of southern twang and a hint of Scottish brogue blend, was familiar. Lately, it was also whiny.

"I *need* to see Wyatt," Dara said, tapping a message into

her phone.

"Not right now," I said.

"But I'm bored," Dara said. "I rearranged my room six times. I know all of the girls on my floor. I went for a three-mile hike. I even sat by the fireplace and read a whole book. Can't I go just for an hour?"

"Desiree, I need a different room." This from a tiny Guide with dark, short-cropped hair who barged in front of Dara. She spoke broken English with a heavy Asian accent. I could never remember her name.

"Adellika," Indira whispered in my ear.

"What's wrong with your room, Adellika?" I asked, sending appreciative thoughts to Indira.

"It does not face east." The girl looked like an elf with her softly pointed chin and little turned up nose. Even though she was the exact opposite of Kaf—massive, muscular, and all hard edges—her Asian features made it impossible for me to be around her without thinking of him. "There is no feng shui. I must wake each day with my face in the sun. How I am to Guide wishes when feng shui is no good?"

I couldn't argue with her. Of all the guides, she was the first to speak my language. Not literally. I barely understood her sometimes. But the way she appreciated nature and how it affected our well-being, that I could understand. Living for two months in San Antonio, surrounded by nothing but concrete and steel had made me uptight and stressed. I loved it there but needed to commune with Mother Earth, too.

"Have you asked if anyone will trade rooms with you?" I asked.

"No." She crossed her thin arms over her chest, her mouth turned in a frown. "My room in castle face east. All wishes ended happy."

"I'm not arguing with you," I said, hands up in surrender. "One of the Guides must prefer a room that does not face east."

"All should," Adellika said. "Good feng shui."

I closed my eyes and exhaled. Clearly she just wanted to be mad at me. Like the other Guides. This wasn't my fault, though. Kaf backed me into a corner and gave me little choice but to agree to become the Wish Mistress.

"I'm sure it is," I told Adellika. "But that's their choice."

"Desiree." Another Guide came up to me with the same want-to-be-mad expression. "There are no kumquats in the kitchen."

I stared at the girl then blinked once. "You're kidding me, right?"

"Kumquats are a part of my daily diet. There are none in the kitchen." She jerked a thumb over her shoulder to the galley-style kitchen that ran the length of the commons area.

There were six industrial-sized refrigerators and six professional-quality ovens spaced evenly along the kitchen. Pantry cabinets of dark-stained wood, filled with every cooking gadget imaginable, were placed between the cooking stations. If, somehow, something was missing, there was one easy fix.

"You're a genie," I told the girl. "If you want kumquats, manifest all you want."

"Desiree…" The next girl in line started in on me.

"Enough!" I shouted and squeezed the bridge of my nose. My head had been throbbing with a dull ache for days. It was stronger than ever today. I held my hands out in the traditional meditation pose—palms up, thumb and pointer finger touching in an O. Immediately the gong boomed and the Guides fell silent. "Everyone, please report to the commons area." My voice rang out, as though over a loud speaker, to every corner of Mystic Lodge.

Five minutes later only half of the Guides had gathered. I placed my thumb and pointer finger together again. A much louder gong sounded and I called out, "Report to the commons area now!"

The room started to fill with the remaining one-hundred, transporting Guides like popcorn filling a bowl. I climbed on top of the kitchen bar so everyone could see me. I magnified my voice so everyone could hear me. I used my magic so all the Guides heard me in their native language.

"Get comfortable, please," I said. "We're going to be here for a little while."

This, as I expected, caused grumbling and protestations. They forget, I'm a hippie. Not one of them could protest like I could. I placed my fingers together again. Another, still louder gong.

"I can do that all day if I have to," I said. "The sooner I say what I need to say, the sooner you can get back to your day."

"I have wishes to attend to," someone shouted.

I pointed in the general direction of the voice since I wasn't sure who had spoken. "You are the first to acknowledge that in nearly two weeks. I hope you all have been checking in with your charges because that is your first responsibility. Making your rooms perfect and arguing about living among Ponderosa pines instead of sand dunes should be the last thing on your priority list. As I just pointed out to Miss"—I almost said *Miss Kumquat* when Indira whispered *Mae* in my ear—"to Mae, you can all perform magic. This is the last time I'm going to say this. Manifest whatever you want. Fix up your room however you want it to be. This is where we're living now, make it yours. We're not leaving the valley."

This resulted in moans and sighs and eye rolls and even a "This stinks" from the crowd.

"You don't get it," said Olanna, a tall woman with the longest neck I'd ever seen. She had flawless skin the color of chocolate pudding and wore a gorgeous printed turban around her head. "None of us understands why you were chosen. You are only nineteen."

"But I've got a lot of experience being nineteen." Well, I'd only been nineteen for two weeks. I had forty-five years of being eighteen though, thanks to the generosity of the

Great and Terrible Kaf. I'd be wrinkled and saggy right now if he hadn't allowed me to remain ageless throughout my indenture.

"You lived apart from us for forty-five years," Olanna said. "You only joined us when Kaf required it for gatherings such as this. We barely know you, and now we are expected to obey you?"

"How well did you know Kaf when you agreed to be indentured to him?" I asked. "You obeyed him."

She crossed her arms and turned regally away.

Olanna was the first Guide Indira had warned me about. She was strong and determined, Indira said. She was considered the alpha Guide. And she had been in love with Kaf for nearly ten years. Her anger had more to do with him being gone than about me stepping in. We were more alike than she knew.

"Look," I said, "this wasn't my idea. Kaf chose me for this gig and I had little choice but to accept."

"You could have said no," Olanna said, holding her head high, her Nigerian accent growing stronger along with her indignation.

Then Kaf would still be with us, was what she didn't say.

I motioned for Dara to join me on the counter.

"Many of you have already met Dara," I said as she climbed up. "For those of you who haven't, allow me to introduce you."

Dara stood there, plucking at the string bracelets running up and down her arm. I nudged her with my elbow and she gave a little wave.

"Dara was the last person Kaf saved."

They all knew what that meant. With the exception of Indira, who had wanted to escape a potentially bad situation, every single one of the Guides had been in a life-threatening situation when Kaf appeared and gave them the choice to live or die. I'd been in a car accident and he found me lying in a ditch. Olanna had been stumbling through the rainforest in

Nigeria, slowing dying from injuries she'd suffered during a gang rape.

"What does Dara have to do with you being in charge?" Olanna asked.

I crossed the bar until I was directly in front of Olanna. I stood there, silent, until she met my eyes.

"Dara was minutes from death," I said, remembering the night along the Riverwalk. "Kaf gave her the option to live but, being the groovy dude he is, put a condition on it."

Murmurs rose from the group. They all knew what that meant, too. Kaf rarely granted something without putting his own little spin on it.

"The condition was that she had to agree to a fifty year term. During that term, she had to serve me." I was starting to feel a little like a preacher as the murmurs grew more intense. "And I couldn't just return as a Guide. Dara couldn't just be an apprentice. In order for Dara to live, I had to return and take Kaf's place." I turned to Olanna. "How was I supposed to say no?"

She broke eye contact with me. Hard to be hard once you knew the truth.

"As for us not knowing each other," I said, "you're right. We don't. But that should work in your favor. If I don't know any of you, I can't play favorites."

"You know Dara," Olanna said. "She has privileges the rest of us do not."

Angry murmurs this time.

What could I say? Dara refused to agree unless I said she could see her family and boyfriend anytime she wanted. I couldn't let her die, of course I agreed to her request as long as she agreed that her parents and Wyatt were the only ones she would see. What's the worst that could happen?

I looked out at the sea of faces before me, all ages and ethnicities, and spotted a little elfish one.

"I've got one more thing and then you're all free to go and check on your charges." I motioned to Adellika to join me on top of the bar. "I assume you all know Adellika. She has a request. If anyone has an east-facing room and would be okay with one that faces…"

I gave her with a questioning look.

"North," she said quietly, as though embarrassed.

"If you'd be okay switching for a north-facing room, please come see her." I looked over at her again. She looked slightly less angry now. "It's important to her to have the sun greet her each morning."

She actually offered me a smile then, and something inside me melted.

"Okay," I said and touched my fingers together. Instead of a booming gong this time, a soft chime sounded out. "Thanks for your attention. Disperse and do good."

Some of the Guides transported away immediately. Some hung out for a few more moments, studying me. Trying to figure out if I'd be okay or if I'd be the downfall of this society. A few stayed in the commons room, gathered around the fireplace talking and laughing, occasionally shooting looks of varying intents at me. *What a joke.* Or, *I wonder if she has any clue what she's in for.*

The latter was my biggest fear. Thank the cosmos I had Indira.

"Nice speech," she said as if reading my mind. "Good that you talked to everyone. But we *really* have to address the waiting wishes now."

"Gypsy V?" I asked.

"I'll meet you there," Indira said.

"Desiree," Dara came up to me again. "Please? One hour?"

I had more important things to do than get into a discussion about Dara's aching heart.

"Fine. One hour. But get ready. Once you have a charge assigned to you, he or she will be your prime concern."

She jumped up and down and squealed. "I promise." And she disappeared.

Chapter Three

Robin

What I wouldn't give to get through one day without drama. This wasn't going to be that day. Our principal, Mr. Service, stood by the front door to greet us every morning. His quality time with the students. That was the only time we saw him except for on the classroom monitors when he read the morning announcements.

Today, instead of a robotic "Good morning" Mr. Service stuck his arm out to stop me as I walked past. "You need to get a haircut, Mr. Westmoreland."

Even though our school was private we didn't have to wear uniforms, but there was a dress code. Khaki pants or nice jeans (or skirts for girls) and either polo or button-down shirts. Boys were supposed to be *clean shaven and clean cut*, meaning no beards or moustaches (not an option for me yet) and our hair couldn't hang past our collars or in our eyes.

Mine did both but I'd gotten away with it because I hid it under my cap as I walked in each morning. Few of the teachers cared so they mentioned the rules but never did anything about violations.

Mr. Service did care, however, and this morning he wrote me an actual demerit ticket which stated I had one week to correct the offense listed—*hair below collar, covering ears, and hanging in front of eyes*—or the demerit would count toward a detention. Three demerits resulted in one afterschool detention.

"One week, Mr. Westmoreland."

"Yes, sir. It's Westmore, sir."

"Excuse me?" he snapped, already having moved past me to the next person in line.

"My last name. It's Westmore."

He placed a hand on my shoulder, surely a contact violation of some kind, and pushed me along.

A kid would be justified in thinking that school, especially one that his parents paid a boat load for him to attend, would be a fairly safe place. That kid would also be very naïve, and very wrong. All the way down the purple and white hallways, Zane and his three minions tormented me. They followed me to my locker, kicking the bottoms of my feet and pushing the backs of my knees trying to trip me up and make me fall. Little did they know, my coordination was actually getting better because of their attacks.

They whistled, making birdcalls, and said clever things like, "Why don't you fly, Tweety?"

"Someone must've clipped his wittle wings."

"Why are you here? It's fall. Shouldn't you fly south?"

Good question. Why was I here?

At least today I'd get to disappear into my placement test first thing. The school had insisted on putting me into Honors Algebra even though my grades indicated I should be well beyond that. Because I had transferred at the end of freshman year, the school claimed they didn't know me well enough to advance me, regardless of what my transcript said. My parents fought all summer with them to let me take the placement test to bump me up to Calculus and Differential Equations. Dad wanted me taking college-level courses next year, my junior year. Finally, the school agreed to put me in AP Calculus as long as I did well on the test.

They wanted me to perform for them. Fine. If it meant I could be in a math class that didn't bore me, I'd jump through whatever flaming hoop they wanted me to.

As instructed, I reported to my math teacher, Mr. Emerson, before first bell.

"Are you sure you want to put yourself through this?" Mr. Emerson asked. "This is a tough test. At best you'll probably end up in Honors Algebra. I can put you there without you having to suffer through this test, Robert."

"It's Robin, sir. I'm already in your Honors Algebra class."

He checked his notes and verified that yes, I was in his class.

"That's already impressive, uh, Robin," he said, double-checking his class list. "A very small percentage of tenth graders end up in Honors math classes."

"I understand," I said. "I'd like to take the test anyway."

"All right," he said in a warning tone and escorted me to the front office.

We stopped in front of the administrative assistant's desk. He gave her the test papers and told me to go to whatever class I should be in once I was done, no need to report back to him. The admin lady took me to a room that was used for in-school detentions. It was empty except for a chair-desk, a clock, a bottle of water, and one purple wall. I thought the water was a nice touch until I realized it had already been opened. Whoever was in the room before me must have left it behind. I set it in the bookrack beneath the chair.

There was no window in the closet-sized room which

was fine by me. Nothing to distract me. I could disappear into the test and do what I did best. Math. And science. I planned to test out of Honors Chemistry into AP Physics next week. If only I could test out of sophomore year altogether.

I finished the test with thirty minutes remaining on my time. It was a snap. Still, I sat in the little room for that last half-hour, safe from the rest of the school. I thought about the video game I was designing and what I wanted to work on tonight. The initial setup had been easy, your basic drag-and-drop program, but I started playing around with the code to make it more dynamic. I'd done basic coding, HTML and Javascript were easy, but I wasn't an expert yet. Now that I was at the point where I could start testing it for bugs, I knew there would be some.

When the clock's alarm sounded, signaling that my time was up, I gathered together the papers and took them to the admin assistant. She wrote the end time in the bottom right corner of the top sheet.

"Your teacher will grade this later today or tomorrow," she said in a droning tone as she scribbled out a hall pass. "You will be informed of your score and class assignment at that time."

My English teacher didn't even pause to acknowledge me when I walked in with only ten minutes left of the period. He was in the middle of talking about *The Chocolate War*, the novel we were supposed to read and write an essay about. I tossed the pass on his desk and took my seat. When I went up to him at the end of class to find out what I missed, he hadn't even realized I'd been gone.

"What, did you fall asleep? Are my lectures that riveting?"

"No, sir, I was—"

"I'll be emailing the homework reminder later today. If you have any questions, the best way to reach me is through an email."

Could he possibly give me a more canned response?

"You should move along to your next class now, Mr. West."

"Westmore."

He looked up from whatever he was tapping into his computer. "I'm sorry?"

"Nothing. I'll look for your email, sir."

What was wrong with the teachers in this school? They chose the profession. Why did it seem like they hated being here as much as the students did?

Because I'd missed my first period to take the test, I had to check in with my History teacher during lunch to find out what I'd missed. That meant I only had a few minutes to eat. I settled on a giant pretzel. It was the last one so it was dried out from being under the heat lamp for so long and only lukewarm because they'd shut the heat lamp off ten minutes earlier. At least it filled my stomach.

Then, because I was distracted by all that had happened that morning and wasn't thinking clearly, I made the mistake of stopping in the bathroom next to the lunchroom.

"Well look who's here." Thad, the head minion, was standing there. He wasn't tall, but Thad was big. He was famous for holding the bench press record: two-hundred-thirty-four pounds.

"Is it Tweety?" a voice from one of the stalls asked. "Wait for me, I'm almost done." Cigarette smoke rose to the ceiling followed by the sound of the toilet flushing. Then Wayne, another minion with white-blonde hair, stepped out.

I'd learned the first week that the bathrooms were only safe from about five minutes after each class period started until about mid-way through each period. In between classes and especially right after lunch were the danger times. This particular bathroom was the single worst place in the school. It was rarely monitored so it was the favored hangout of Zane and his minions.

I turned to leave. I could hold it until I got home if necessary. But Thad stepped in front of me and blocked my exit.

"What's up, Tweety?" he asked.

"Nothing," I said looking at the floor.

"So you just came in here to hang out with us," Wayne said, breathing his cigarette breath in my face. "Is that it?"

"That's so nice," Thad said. "We don't get to hang with Tweety often enough."

"Come on, guys," I said and my voice cracked.

"Come on guys," Thad said, imitating me. He put a hand on my shoulder and my guts turned to water. I thought for sure I was going to shit myself. "I'm glad we ran into you, Tweety. You make me laugh."

"Yeah," Wayne said. "You're a funny guy."

Then Thad pulled back his fist, middle knuckle sticking out like a bayonet and slammed it into my right shoulder. On the other side, Wayne did the same thing. Pain shot down both arms and my instinct, of course, was to grab my shoulders. I didn't dare though. *Flinching gets you three*, they told me the last time I met up with them. The bruises on my shoulders that time covered my entire upper arm. That had only been ten days ago. They hadn't fully healed yet so the pain this time was even worse.

"He's getting better," Thad said, waiting with his hand pulled back for me to give him a reason to let it fly.

The warning bell for class sounded then and I said a silent thanks. They'd leave now. Like Zane, they knew not to draw attention to themselves with the teachers so they wouldn't risk being late for class.

"Good job, Tweety," Thad said.

He bent to grab his backpack and I figured I'd gotten out of it with just two knuckle punches this time. But when he stood up he grabbed my arm with one hand and punched me again with the other.

"One more to remember me by," he said with a wink, then they left.

I locked myself in the first stall and bent over, leaning

my butt against the wall and my hands on my knees. I didn't dare react while they were in front of me, but now, behind the safety of the stall door, I stood there shaking until I threw up. I didn't dare cry, no matter how scared, humiliated, or in pain I was. Walking into class with red just-been-crying eyes would only make it worse the next time. They'd push it to see if they could make me cry in front of them.

Once I'd gotten myself back together, I stopped in the nurse's office and asked for an ice pack.

"Are you okay?" she asked.

"Yeah," I said. "I turned and ran into my locker door."

"Should I take a look?" she asked, reaching for my shirt sleeve.

"No," I said too quickly. If she saw the bruises on my arm she'd start asking questions. She'd probably assume there was something going on at home. "Really, it's not that bad. Just trying to prevent a bruise. You know?"

"I do. I've done that same thing with my closet door at home," she said and got a chemical ice pack from the cabinet. She smacked it with her fist—the sound causing a twinge of pain in my shoulder as if it had received the blow—and squeezed it a few times before handing it to me. "Do you want to sit here or take it to class?"

"I'll just head to class." If I stayed much longer I'd want to hide there for the rest of the afternoon.

"All right. If you're sure."

"I am."

She wrote out a pass and told me to come back if I wanted another icepack.

"Could I just take another one with me?" I asked. My right shoulder got the worst of it, but the left was starting to hurt, too.

She studied me for a little longer than was comfortable and then got another pack for me.

The day continued as it had started, teachers getting my name wrong and birdcalls in the hallway. There was a single bright spot, though. I got to see Brianna.

Usually I saw her at the bus stop, but she hadn't been there this morning. Sometimes we walked a few blocks together, talking about nothing in particular. During the day I was usually only lucky enough to catch a glimpse of her from down the hall or across the lunchroom.

Brianna was easily the prettiest girl in the school. She was there the day Zane first called me Tweety. She'd been standing at the back of the group and was one of the few who hadn't laughed at the nickname that refused to go away. As she passed me that day, she touched my arm softly and handed me a little piece of paper with her phone number and a note that read, "I'm new here, too. Give me a call if you want someone to talk to." Her smile was so sad as she walked past. That was the only time I'd seen that smile. Every other time it was bright and beautiful and lit up her entire face. I looked for her smile the way a drowning person looks for a life preserver.

Today I got to see her in the hall just before last period. She was talking with some of the cheerleaders. They had circled her, probably trying to convince her to join the squad. I imagined her in one of those little skirts and tight sweaters, her long honey-blonde hair pulled up into a ponytail. I pictured her bouncing around the field or court, doing her pompom routine just for me. Of course everyone would think she was performing for the crowd, but she and I would know the truth.

That was the moment she glanced over at me. Our eyes met and she held the gaze for a few wonderfully long seconds.

I swear, Brianna saw me. The real me.

On the ride home that afternoon the bus was packed. All of the seats in the front were taken. So were the ones in the middle. I had to go all the way to the back.

Zane never rode the afternoon bus. He always had baseball or some other extracurricular thing going on. The

Minions did though. They didn't bother with me when I sat in the front, another bonus to sitting there. Thad, Wayne, and Ben all sat three rows behind me.

"How's the arm, Tweety?" Thad asked.

"I missed it?" Ben asked in his high-pitched voice. "Did you guys give him his love taps again?"

"Took it like a man," Wayne said, running his hands through his white hair over and over. "I'm proud of the little bird."

That started a round of non-stop birdcalls. The glares from the other passengers said they were bothering everyone. No one said anything though.

I managed to keep the motion sickness under control all the way to my stop by sitting with my eyes closed and taking long, deep breaths. As soon as I stepped off the bus and the fresh air hit me, I puked all over the sidewalk.

Of course they all saw it. The calls turned from birds chirping to birds puking, which was impressive really. They all had their phones out. Taking pictures to send to Zane. Most likely they were posting to every social media site out there, too. God only knew what nickname they'd have for me by tomorrow.

I walked the six blocks to my house with my head down. To nearly every teacher in the school I was invisible. To Zane and The Minions I was anything but. Why couldn't the teachers see me? Why couldn't I be one of the neutrals that the kids ignored? That's all I'd ever wanted. What had I ever done to deserve this?

Mom was home when I got there. Most of the time her working from home was cool. She was clueless to my real life, but if I wanted to I could tell her, she'd listen. Of course she'd probably go straight to the principal and try to 'fix things' like she had at my other two schools. No way was I going through that again.

Right now, she was uber-focused on trying to build her client list for her new business. Her job in the marketing department at some big company had been eliminated a few years earlier. She bounced right back and looked at it as a chance to do something new. She enrolled in culinary school, but before she graduated Dad's company promoted him and transferred him to the Denver office.

On the drive to Colorado from Wisconsin, Mom decided to combine her two loves. Once the house was set up well enough, she opened *Marjorie Westmore Marketing and PR*, specializing in food-related businesses.

The downside to Mom working from home was that the house was never empty. I followed the path around our house to the backyard where I could be alone for a while before going in and putting on my *life is great face*. I lay in the grass and looked up at the sky. Bright blue. The color of Brianna's eyes.

I'm not sure how long I laid there, thinking about her in a cheerleading uniform, but long enough that I'd seriously cut into my homework time. Which really meant I'd cut into my game development time. I already didn't sleep much. Missing another hour or two wouldn't be a big deal.

I sat up, ready to go in and get to work when I noticed a single dandelion off to the side of the yard. A dead one. The puffball kind that you make a wish on.

I crawled across the yard and picked it, planning to just toss it in the garbage can on my way inside. Before doing that, I took a good long look at it. Most people just thought of the dandelion as a weed. The gossamer seed ball was really beautiful though. When held up to the backdrop of the Brianna-blue sky, the fluff looked like tiny, bright stars connected to a soft, fluffy web.

What if they really were little wishes, ready to be blown into the world to see if they could stick to something and come true?

"Can't hurt to try." I closed my eyes. "My parents are too busy to see me. My teachers don't see me. The kids who see me, harass me. I wish I could make it all stop and just be myself."

Then I took a deep breath and blew my wish into the world.

Chapter Four

Desiree

By the time I got back to Gypsy V on the far side of the lake, my headache had intensified again. It couldn't be good for brain cells to have that kind of pain coursing through them.

Indira was waiting outside of my bus. She followed me in, sat in the threadbare wingback chair across from my desk, and glowered at me as I changed clothes—my body could be comfy even if my head wasn't—and manifested tea.

"What have we got?" I finally asked while sitting cross-legged in my desk chair. Nope, not going to work. I tapped my thumb and pointer finger together and a hanging hammock chair, like the one hanging from the rafters in Mandy's barn, appeared. Hers was canvas. Mine was macramé with a soft-n-cushy pillow to cradle my backside. I climbed in and pulled my legs into crisscross again. "Oh, much better."

Indira shot me the kind of look a teacher would give a hyperactive kindergartner.

"Are you ready now?" she asked.

I folded my hands in my lap and looked down, duly scolded. "Yes, ma'am."

She placed her hand on a stack of papers sitting in her lap. "These are the wishes that made the cut. There are five thousand of them. I eliminated ten thousand."

"You denied ten thousand wishes?" My heart hurt with that news, but not as much as my head. I figured it was the stress of the Guides, but maybe I was just hungry. I manifested a cheese stick, an apple, and a handful of nuts. "The wishes that come to us are from the soul. That means they are truly and deeply desired, not just some spur-of-the-moment, greedy want. Why shouldn't all fifteen thousand be granted?"

"You know the rules." Indira slapped her pointer finger to her palm. "First, we can't bring people back from the dead." A second finger slap. "We can't change a person's feelings or beliefs, which means we can't make anyone fall in or out of love. We can't make an enemy sudden be an ally. Third—"

"I know the rules." I squeezed the bridge of my nose, my head nearly bursting now with the drone of a million bees.

"I turned them back on," Indira said.

"What?" I squinted at her. Even my eyes ached.

"I turned the requests back on. Your head is buzzing, right?"

I nodded, which made things worse.

"You are the Wish Mistress," Indira said. "All wishes now come to you for distribution to the Guides. That's what you're feeling."

"How do I shut it off?" I asked. "The buzzing. Not the wishes."

"Distribute the wishes," Indira said as though that should

be obvious. "You could also create a buffer."

"A what?"

"You remember the cloud that always floated around Kaf?"

I was about to nod again but caught myself in time. "What about it?"

"That was Kaf's buffer. When it was smaller it indicated fewer wishes awaiting distribution. When it was bigger... well, you get the picture. Same with his throne of clouds. Think of it as a holding cell for the wishes until he could tend to them."

"So it's either constant buzzing or constant smoke?" I pressed on my temples. The wishes were getting louder.

"Smoke and clouds were what Kaf chose," Indira said. "You can choose whatever buffer you'd like. It does need to be independently portable and external from you."

"Independently portable?"

"It needs to follow you on its own."

I wasn't a smoke and clouds kind of gal. Too intrusive and overpowering. Not to mention cliché. I was more about swirls and nature. What in nature could hold...? Got it. I touched my fingers together and opened my eyes.

Gypsy V was full, I mean absolutely filled with tiny swirling, undulating, brightly-colored lights, like thousands of little Aurora Borealis streamers following me around. Through it, I could just make out Indira still sitting in the chair, her hand over her eyes.

"Can you turn it down the wattage?" she asked. "Maybe go with pastels instead of neon?"

I tapped my fingers together again and the bright light turned to the muted pastels of a watercolor sunrise.

"Better?" I asked.

She peeked through her fingers and then pulled her hand away. "Much. Is your head better?"

Slowly, I tilted my head side-to-side. Then I got brave and shook it hard. No more buzzing.

"Much. Thanks."

"Can we get to work now?" she asked, placing her hand on top of the stack again.

"One last thing," I said for which I received an aggravated sigh from my second-in-command. "We're going to be denying people's wishes. I don't want to bring all that negativity into my home."

Gypsy V had been my sanctuary since the day I moved into it over forty-five years earlier. No matter what was going on in the outside world, no matter how hard the wishes I guided became, my bus was a place where I could disappear and let my hippie-self be free.

"Desiree, you really need to get serious about this," Indira said.

I held one hand in the air and crossed my heart with the other. "This is the last thing. I swear on Mandy and Crissy that I won't stall any longer."

Indira knew that since I'd guided their wishes, Mandy and Crissy had become my best friends in the world. A vow on their names could be taken as gospel.

"Come with me," I told her.

We walked about a hundred yards from my bus to a little alcove nestled into the base of the mountain next to the lake. It was surrounded by pine trees and had a straight-shot view of Mystic Lodge.

"Does this look like a good place?" I asked.

"For what?" She was still irritated, but intrigued, too, if the way she was checking out the area meant anything.

I manifested a small log cabin. It was about twice the size of the *vardo* Indira used for her beauty salon. Large windows covered the walls and allowed for panoramic views. Comfy rocking chairs and warm wool blankets waited for the Guides beneath a covered porch. Inside, next to a big stone fireplace, was the macramé butt hammock for me and a few overstuffed leather chairs for the Guides.

"Sit," I told Indira as I climbed into the hammock.

"What are you waiting for? We have a lot of work to do."

She made a face at me, but then smiled. "I admit it, this is better. Good to keep your home private."

Finally, after days of waiting, wishes were about to come true for five thousand people. Probably half of those wishes were for people to recover from illnesses. I never realized how many sick people there were. Some had minor, constant aches and pains that made day-to-day life hard. Many had fatal illnesses such as cancer or Alzheimer's. There were lots of wishes for friends or loved ones to recover from accidents of one kind or another.

Hours later Indira was still reading wishes. "This one is from a seven-year-old boy who wants his brother to recover from a skiing accident. He wasn't wearing a helmet and ran into a tree. The brother is expected to be fine. The boy is just scared. We could reject this one."

I shook my head. "No, the boy just needs a little courage. Learning to be courageous at seven years old will help him throughout his life. Who's the best Guide for him?"

"We've gone through more than two thousand wishes," Indira said while rubbing her eyes. "You've assigned multiple wishes to every Guide. You tell me."

On top of working with Indira, I'd been studying Kaf's compendium every night. In it were not only notes from every wish he had ever granted, but also bios. There was a page for each Guide, written in surprisingly neat handwriting, that explained what her life had been before she became a Guide, how she became a Guide, and what her strengths and weaknesses were. It would take me a while before I knew everyone, but those who had exceptional strengths stood out to me.

Adellika, my feng shui genie, was the first one to come to mind. I closed my eyes and pictured her bio page.

"Adellika's strength is empathy," I said, "especially when it comes to comforting small children. I'm guessing that's because even though she's seventeen, she's not much bigger than a child herself."

Indira nodded and yawned. "She'd be my choice as well."

"Have we done more than half of those yet?" I asked, fighting an echo yawn. The aurora level in the cabin had decreased dramatically.

Indira flipped through the stack. "Almost. Now that you know the Guides better these will go faster."

We'd been at it for more than ten hours. I'd manifested lunch and then dinner but I couldn't manifest sleep.

"How about we pick this up in the morning?" I asked.

"Good plan. I'll meet you here at five?"

"Sure. We can have tea and watch the sunrise."

She smiled as she adjusted one of the many rings she wore. "For the record, I never doubted that you were the right one for this job."

I placed my hands in Namaste and bowed my forehead to my fingertips.

"Thank you. It means a lot to know I have someone on my side."

"Give them time," she said of the Guides. "They're a little shaken up. Some were like you and were more frustrated than satisfied by Kaf. Most adored him though. You were not the only one he left without warning, you know."

True. But how many had the added conflict of being in love with him? Then I remembered Olanna and realized I truly wasn't the only one grieving.

Indira transported to her quarters at Mystic Lodge for the night. I walked the hundred yards to Gypsy V, Kaf's compendium clutched to my chest. It was simultaneously comforting and heart-wrenching to possess an item that he had touched, held, and left his aroma on. If I inhaled deeply, I could still smell his sweet-and-spicy, bitter-and-sour warmth. It was like he was right there with me.

When I let myself think of him, emotion would catch in

my chest and I'd have to fight back sobs. Inevitably it would all burst free, first as overwhelming loneliness then, slowly, my sorrow would turn to frustration and finally betrayal. Ever since the reality that he really was gone had fully registered, this was the routine every night as I tried to fall asleep.

I entered Gypsy V to find Dara sitting in my wingback chair.

"You can't keep coming here," I said, wiping my eyes with the back of my hand. "The other Guides are going to catch on and they'll accuse me of favoritism."

"I know," she said quietly.

"How's Wyatt?" I asked, setting the compendium on my desk. I'd smell Kaf later.

"He's good," Dara said and burst into tears.

I held my arms out and she threw herself into them.

Dara was still getting used to her new life. She was homesick and lovesick. Her parents had needed numerous displays of magic to accept the truth of what had happened to her. Once they did, they didn't understand why I couldn't just save her or why an indenture as a Guide needed to be a part of it.

I explained that those were the conditions Kaf had laid down and the ones Dara agreed to. What was done, was done. They relented only after I explained that death was the only other option.

Wyatt had been much easier to convince. Dara transported him to the top of the Eiffel Tower and back to her balcony overlooking the Riverwalk and he was a believer.

"You can do magic," he had said. "That's hot."

"You can't tell your parents," Dara said.

"Like they'd believe me," he said and grinned. "Unless you do a trick for them."

"She's not a carnival act," I said, peering over my blue granny glasses at him. "I've agreed to let you two keep seeing each other, but you have to keep quiet about it. I can wipe your memory at the touch of a finger." I tapped my fingers together and the gong sounded. "Don't ruin things."

"Okay, got it," Wyatt snapped, looking annoyed for the first time since I'd met him.

For these first two weeks I hadn't seen any signs of him going back on his word. Everything was daisies and rainbows in the Dara and Wyatt realm. How long until the spell broke and reality set in?

"What's going on?" I asked Dara as she sobbed into my arms now. "You're wigging out. More than usual, I mean."

"His mom... said... I can't... come over... during the week," she said through her sniffles.

"Why?"

"He has... to study," she said, trying to control her breathing.

"Um," I said cautiously, "that's not exactly unreasonable."

"I know. But this weekend he's going on a campout with the Boy Scouts." Her tears started again. "That means I can't see him until Sunday night. That's six whole days!"

While I understood her pain, she was able to see the love of her life. The only thing worse than being here with a bunch of Guides who didn't want me, was being in the genie world without Kaf.

"You'll live," I said. "I promise."

"It's so long."

"Sounds like it's time for you to take on your first charge," I said. "Guiding someone through a wish will keep you busy."

She sniffed and wiped her nose on her sleeve. "Yeah? I guess that could help."

"I'll find a charge for you tomorrow." With all the drama going on around here, I hadn't thought to assign a charge to Dara. She was new. Kaf never made a bio page for her. "Maybe you can have dinner with your mom and dad one night this week, too."

Just saying that made my guts twist with jealousy. I would love to have dinner with my parents one more time. Especially if my mom made that salmon loaf thing she used to make every Friday night. Back when I still lived with them, I hated it. Now, I'd give anything for one more spoonful.

"Why are you surrounded by light?" she asked of the aurora following me.

"It's a containment system for the wishes so my head doesn't pop off."

She didn't ask for any more explanation. Instead she dried her face and went back to Mystic Lodge to have cocoa and girl talk with the other Guides. They all knew, as well as I did, how hard it was to leave the world you'd always known. They'd take good care of her.

My guts twisted once again. Never thought I could be jealous of cocoa and girl talk.

☮ ☮ ☮

Normally I started my day by sitting on top of my bus with a cup of tea, staring at the mountains and meditating. But I stayed up late studying the Guides' bios, and Indira arrived at the stroke of five, which meant I didn't have time for meditating. I'd only slept for four hours, herbal tea wasn't going to do anything to help jumpstart this day. I manifested a big mug of coffee with a triple-shot of espresso instead.

"What's the matter with you?" Indira asked as we settled into our spots in the cabin.

"Nothing," I answered before the question was fully out of her mouth. "Why do you ask?"

"Because you haven't blinked in nearly a minute and I know Chihuahuas that aren't as jumpy."

"I may have over-caffeinated."

"You think?"

I expected day two would go faster since I knew the

40

Guides better after my late-night cramming sessions. Instead Indira and I argued even more over who was the best Guide for each wish. I relented a few times to Indira's *gut feeling based years of living with the Guides*. A few times I overruled, using my Wish Mistress status and proclaiming my own gut feeling.

Before we knew it, we'd been going at it for another ten hours. It was late, nearly dinner time, and we were both getting crabby. I was ready to call it a day.

"We only have a few left," Indira said, pointing at the few tiny swirls by my feet. "Let's just finish this. Then you're on your own and I can catch up on makeover requests that have been waiting for two weeks while I did your job."

Normally, Indira was as mellow as I was. Maybe even more so. I needed to do something to thank her for filling in for me. A few times she'd quietly mentioned that she wished she had an apartment in Mystic Lodge rather than just a bedroom and bathroom. Someplace she could hole up and do her own thing without having to be with the masses.

Indira wasn't a Guide. She didn't have charges assigned to her. Instead, the Guides' called her to help with wishes when necessary. Indira's gift was the ability to make a person look and feel beautiful by enhancing what was already there. She could perform minor magic such as transporting herself and her *vardo* wherever she needed to go. She could manifest the products she needed to do the makeovers. She couldn't manifest anything for herself, though. Like an apartment. Kaf had offered the ability to her. She refused it, saying she did what she did to help others, not benefit herself.

Giving her a place to escape was the least I could do. As my second-in-command, she deserved it. I closed my eyes, touched my fingers together, and gave her the apartment of her dreams on the top floor of the Lodge.

It took another ten minutes and we were done. Or so we thought. Before she could leave we noticed one last blood-orange aurora. Neither of us had seen it come in. Her shoulders slumped and she sat back down.

"No. You said the wishes were mine now. You can't have it." I placed my hands in Namaste and bowed my thanks to her. "Go home. I'll see you tomorrow."

She stuffed the compendium into my arms. "It's all yours," and left with a grunt of goodbye.

The book was ridiculous, bulky, heavy and cumbersome. Not to mention it was impossible to actually find anything in. Time to leap forward and enter the modern era.

I held out my hand and manifested a computer tablet in a leather case that resembled Kaf's compendium. He had used a feather quill to record the granted wishes. I preferred a more high-tech, friend-of-the-trees manner of record keeping. The old-looking leather cover was cool though.

This would be a much more efficient way of sorting and assigning wishes. It did mean that Kaf's carrier pigeons would be out of work. It also meant I'd have to manifest tablets for all of the Guides and some of them were about as un-techie as Kaf. Teaching them would be a good assignment for Dara. She was great with computers.

First, I had to take care of this lone wish.

I scooped the little orange light into my hand and set it on the tablet. Immediately a picture of a thin, sad-looking boy filled the screen. His voice filled my ears: *I wish I could make it all stop and just be myself.*

Information about him began to populate the screen next. He was getting picked on at school, had been for years, and felt ignored at home. Sounded to me like he needed to find the confidence and courage to stand up to his tormentors and ask his parents for their attention. This would be a fine first wish for Dara. She knew all about trying to get parental attention.

On my tablet I created a new folder labeled "Dara MacDonald" and slid the wish from Robin Westmore into it. I'd discuss the wish and tablet responsibilities with her first thing in the morning.

"I'm just not sure this is the proper wish for her to start with," Indira said after reviewing Robin's file on her own tablet the next morning.

"I'll keep an eye on it," I told her. "Kaf hawked me so closely for my first few wishes he was practically guiding them himself."

"But this boy is getting bullied," she said. "You know how bad things can get with stuff like that."

"Look," I said, leaning forward in my hammock chair, which wasn't a good idea as I almost fell out. I needed a more traditional chair. Didn't want any embarrassing spills in front of the Guides. "Dara is a very empathetic person. I saw her deal with people for a couple weeks when we worked together at the soup kitchen. She understands that everyone's life takes a different path and she respects that."

"It's just—"

"Indira, please. You pushed and pushed for me to do this. Now that I'm ready to fly, you're trying to pull me back into the nest."

She gave me that look. The one with dual raised eyebrows that caused shivers to run up my spine. It said, *okay but don't come crying to me when it turns out I'm right.*

"Just stay on top of this one," she cautioned once she realized I wasn't going to back down. She placed her hand on top of the tablet in her lap. "I do like this idea. The carrier pigeon method of communication was..."

"Archaic?" I offered.

"And messy," she said.

"Time to shake things up and bring the mystical world into the twentieth century," I said.

"It's the twenty-first century," Indira reminded me.

"I know. That's how out of touch Kaf was." Time to steer us away from the topic of Kaf. "How are your new-and-improved quarters?"

Her smile was immediate and huge. "It looks like my *vardo* in there."

Her gypsy wagon salon was a lot like my bus. Full of gorgeous silks and lace and furniture that was beautiful in its less-than-perfect state. While I decorated Gypsy V in muted pastels with a few deep jewel tones mixed in, Indira preferred her surroundings bright and loud. Surprising because while Indira was vibrant and full of life, she was not at all a loud soul. She surrounded herself with bright turquoise, hot pink, lime green. And she loved plants. Like the jewelry she wore anywhere she could attached a piece, I put plants all around her new apartment.

"Thank you," she said with a slight inclination of her head. "I appreciate having such beautiful surroundings."

"I can change anything you're not happy with," I said. "Just say the word."

The cabin door opened. First a carrier pigeon flew in and dropped a message from a Guide onto my lap. Then Dara poked her head in.

"Can I come in?"

"Of course," Indira answered for me. "Your timing is perfect. Desiree needs to talk with you. And I have appointments that have been waiting for days."

Then she disappeared, off to whichever makeover was first on her list.

"What's up?" Dara asked and flopped onto one of the big, cozy chairs I'd set up for the Guides.

"I have a wish for you."

"Aw, that's nice. I'm not sure anyone has ever made a wish for me before." She bounced in the chair. "What is it?"

Her phone buzzed before I could answer. She looked at the screen and let out a little squeal. Had to be from Wyatt.

"Dara," I said.

She held up a finger, indicating I should wait.

A little tremor of trepidation skittered through me. Dara

could be so scattered sometimes. Maybe being a Guide wasn't right for her. Maybe something more like what Indira did. Something that didn't require her constant attention. I pushed the worry away as fast as it had arrived. Everything would be fine.

She hit send and sat back with a happy wiggle.

"I meant," I said, "that a wish has come in that I think will be a good one for you to start with."

She frowned for a moment. I knew that look. It said she didn't want to work, she wanted to play. Another text buzzed through. As she was responding to that one, another carrier pigeon flew in. Enough of this. The Guides needed tablets sooner than later and I might as well start with Dara. I manifested one and handed it to her. That caught her attention.

"What's this?" she asked, her eyes shiny with excitement.

"How do you feel about teaching?"

I could magic the knowledge into the minds of everyone who didn't know how to use the tablets, but this would give Dara something to do. Guiding Robin and teaching the Guides would fill her days and keep her from being bored. That was crucial. A bored Dara wasn't good for anyone.

"Cool," Dara said of the instructing. "Can I make tweaks?"

"To individual tablets, sure," I said. "To the network, no. You have to run that past me first."

"Listen to you." Dara leaned back, impressed. "I didn't know you knew what a network was."

Up until a day ago, no. Then I *taught* myself all about computers for this exact reason. Being able to infuse my brain with knowledge on any topic necessary was a Kaf-level skill and really quite handy. The only thing worse than a bored Dara was a Dara who knew more about something than you.

"You can focus on teaching later, though. Open the file

labeled Robin Westmore," I instructed. Dara tapped the screen and a picture appeared of a thin, sad-looking boy with a slouchy gray hat and bangs that swooped in front of his eyes. "That's Robin. He's your first charge and your first priority."

Dara's face fill with compassion as she studied his file. "Why is he so sad?"

"He's being bullied."

Right in the middle of my explanation, another text came through. Before she could answer, I leaned over—and fell out of the hammock, but at least I did it gracefully—and put my hand over the screen.

"Hey," she complained and tried to swat me away.

"This is important," I said, nodding at the tablet.

"So is this," she insisted of the text.

"Fine. Answer this one and tell him you're busy. Isn't he in school?"

"At lunch," she mumbled as she responded to him.

"Tell him you can talk after school."

Cosmos help me, I sounded like a mom.

She hit send again, stuck her phone under her butt, and said, "Well what are we waiting for?"

I manifested a meditation chair—it had an extra thick cushion and wide seat to accommodate crisscrossed legs. I sat down and pulled into full lotus position.

"Desiree—"

My turn to hold up a finger. I closed my eyes, breathed deep, and imagined I was perched atop a mountain peak. No, it's cold on top of mountains. I imagined a mountain meadow and the peace of nature surrounding me. My brain calmed as did my breathing. Now I was ready.

"Robin is being bullied," I said, "and his wish is for it to stop. Read his file. Learn as much about him as you can. Find out what's important to him. Remember that the wishes we grant are life changers. We don't give people a pile of money or a new car. We help them find their proper life path."

"So what am I supposed to do?" she asked.

"Wish journeys don't always take the expected route," I said. "Sometimes things get really bad before they get good again." I thought of Crissy. Her wish journey almost got her killed, but her future looked very good now. "Once started, a wish can't be stopped. They have to see it through to the end. Sometimes they need a little moral support to do that. That's your job. Keep reassuring them that they will make it to their satisfying ending."

"What," she laughed, "we don't give happy endings?"

Same thing all of my charges asked me.

"Happiness has a different definition for everyone," I said. "What one person will be delirious over, another will consider a disappointment. So for us, a wish is considered fulfilled when the charge finds their new life path. They've still got a lot of life to live at that point so no happy *endings*."

Instantly one of my charges from decades earlier popped into my head. He was riddled with cancer. There was no hope of survival. He was in constant pain and unable to do anything but lie in bed day after day.

"I take that back," I said. "Very rarely a wish for life to end will come in. Usually they're from people with fatal illnesses who have no hope of getting better and want to die in comfort and dignity."

Dara frowned. "Did you ever have a wish like that?"

"Once." I told her about my charge. As I did, my eyes welled with tears. "He was in so much pain. He died peacefully when the nurse accidentally gave him the wrong medicine."

"You switched it?"

"Something like that." I stared into the flames crackling in the fireplace next to us. "It was really hard and really easy at the same time. It was satisfying for his family in the end, too. That's our goal. Satisfaction."

Dara sat quietly for a minute then said, "Learn all you can and figure out what was important to them? That's how

47

you used to do it?"

How I *used* to do it. "Yep."

"The other Guides say you had the best satisfaction rating of all of them."

For a moment, the universe paused. They said that about me?

"Well, I had high standards," I said, trying to disguise the gushy feeling warming me.

A pigeon flew in with a message from Mae complaining about her assignment. Guess that was better than complaining about kumquats, but it still harshed my gushiness.

"Anyway," I said, "yes, that's what I used to do. I'd learn every detail about my charges that I could. Knowing what makes a person happy is great, but knowing what they're afraid of is where their wishes usually lie. They're unhappy with something and either they don't know why or they're afraid to face it. Many times putting them face-to-face with their fear is what ultimately helps them deal with it and find happiness again."

Dara looked at me like I was the wise elder and then she turned on her tablet.

"He's genius-level smart," she said, reading out loud. "He likes computers. Just like me. He's moved around a lot over the last few years."

She frowned.

"Hitting a little close?" I asked.

Dara nodded. "My home doesn't move, but I never get to stay in one place."

Private high school in Scotland. School breaks spent at friends' homes in different countries. A few months a year in her 'home' at the hotel in San Antonio. Dara's life never had a sturdy base.

"The similarities between you and Robin," I said, "are why I thought you'd be a good Guide for him. Finding common ground with your charge, no matter how small, is how you can truly help."

She read the rest of his file, out loud, as I tried to read the pigeon messages that had been dropped off all morning. Of the two hundred Guides, ten were displeased with their assignments. How often did they complain to Kaf? I knew what his reaction would have been. *I have made my decision.* He had never granted a re-assignment. Not for me at least. No matter how difficult a few of them had been.

"He's fifteen and in tenth grade," Dara said, spitting out a new detail about Robin every few seconds.

Just because Kaf was unyielding didn't mean I had to be. We were all adults here. Well, Dara wasn't. At fifteen, she was the youngest Guide. Still, even Dara could act like an adult when she wanted to. As adults, we should all be able to make our own decisions. If these ten Guides were this upset about their assignments, they should be able to make changes. I didn't want to dictate how their lives should be lived.

I manifested ten identical responses and directed the pigeons to deliver them to the dissatisfied Guides.

If between the ten of you, you can come up with a mutually agreeable trade of wishes, I am fine with that. The only requirement is that all ten wishes must be granted. I trust you all to make the right decisions.

"So what do I do?" Dara asked, snapping me out of my thoughts of The Man and dictatorial societies.

"Tell me what you think he needs. What do you think will help him get to that satisfactory ending?"

"Well," she pulled up his picture again and studied his face. "He's alone and kind of feels like an outsider. I know what that's like."

I did, too.

"He needs to get involved with something," she said. "He likes computers. Almost to the point of obsession. Maybe there's a computer club at school he could join. Or he could start one if there isn't one."

"So you think being with other people will help with him getting bullied?"

"I think it's easier to ignore or stand up to bullies when you've got your own people. Friends with similar interests are the best."

"Sounds like a great start," I said. "Remember, with almost every wish things get worse before they get better. You can't decide for him which choices to make. Things need to happen organically. Just be the shoulder he'll need when things take a bad turn. Like a supernatural psychiatrist."

"That's it?" Dara said, clearly not thrilled with her new role. "I just listen?"

"You get to do some magic, too," I said. "You can put people or things on his path that will help him. What one of my last charges needed most was for her imaginary friend to come to life. I gave her Lexi."

"That's cool," Dara said. "So I need to create something for him."

"Only if it will help with his wish," I cautioned.

"Something computer related."

"What?"

"Nothing," she said with a little head shake. "Just a thought."

"One last thing." I held out my palm and a Zen stone appeared there.

"What's this?" Dara asked as I handed her the flat, oval emerald.

The stones used to have a Zen circle engraved on them—a circle with a slight opening. I always saw a circle as a representation of life. In this case, the circle wasn't fully closed because until we died and moved on to whatever comes next, our life journey wasn't complete. When I took over Kaf's position, I altered the circle by adding a peace sign.

"I call it a Peace Zen," I said. "You give one to each of

your charges when you explain that their wish has been granted. You then explain the terms."

As I did with my charges, I waited until I had her full attention.

"This part is super-important," I said. "You gotta listen close, you dig?"

"You're doing the hippie speak thing again."

I couldn't say this part any other way.

"Every now and then a wish takes on a life of its own. Regardless, once a wish has started, no matter what happens, no matter what path it follows, it cannot be stopped."

"What do you mean, once started?" Dara asked. "Doesn't it start when you grant it?"

"Nope. You give them the details and if they're cool with the deal they just have to touch the circle." I nodded at the stone in her hand. "One last thing. You cannot, under any circumstances, alter the course of the wish. Even if the turns out to be one of those wishes that goes dark before it gets light, the charge has to follow it to the end."

Dara stared at Robin's picture again. She nodded like she understood.

"Any more questions?" I asked.

She shook her head.

"Study him a little more," I said. "Do whatever you need to do to make sure you know him really well and what will get him that satisfactory ending. When you're ready, go tell him his wish has been granted."

Chapter Five

Robin

My game was full of issues. It froze in some places. The graphics pixelated in others. It took me until eleven-thirty to finish my homework and then I stayed up way too late working on the game. Now Mom was yelling at me, for the third time, to get up or I'd miss the bus. Things like being late for appointments or missing the bus turned her from her usually easy-going self into one crabby-ass woman.

"I'm up," I called before she could yell at me again.

A glance at the clock told me I didn't have time for a shower. Great. Now I'd be Stinky Puking Tweety. I took thirty seconds to take what my grandma called a birdbath. Ha! Tweety takes a birdbath. Oh, the irony. I filled the sink with warm water and soaped up my pits and chest. That, and a fresh shirt, would have to do for today.

I walked into the kitchen to find mom standing by the

sink, arms crossed, fingers drumming on the opposing biceps.

"I can get my own breakfast," I said, trying to keep the attitude out of my voice. Attitude definitely wouldn't help right now. "Go on to work if you need to."

"Which tea, Robin?"

She was so stubborn.

"I'm thinking maybe coffee this morning. I can—"

"Robin, what kind of tea do you want?"

I didn't understand why she was making such a big deal about tea instead of coffee, but I knew better than to push my luck after three "get out of beds."

"Some of that super-caffeinated stuff," I said. Then quickly added, "Please."

"You stayed up late again?" she asked as she took a box of tea from the back of the cabinet.

"Lots of homework," I said. She knew I'd spent my summer developing the game. She didn't know I still spent at least two hours a night, after homework, working on it.

She never protested when I said the dark circles under my eyes were study related. Usually that was the case. Sometimes, though, Zane's harassment got really intense and the circles came from lack of sleep due to nightmares.

There were days when he would stop in the middle of whatever he'd been doing and charge at me from across the lunchroom to slam into me or sneeze on my lunch. He was careful to never touch me though so the monitors brushed it off to joking around. Once he even stood in front of me flapping his arms and making birdcalls. In the middle of the lunchroom. Why didn't someone record that and put it up on the web? He looked ridiculous. Didn't anyone else see it?

"Are you feeling all right?" Mom put the back of her hand to my forehead and I resisted the urge to swat it away. It was a caring touch. One of the few signs lately that someone gave a damn about me.

If I told her what was happening, would she do

something? I didn't want her to talk to my principal or Zane's parents. When she tried to talk to Cole's mom back in Wisconsin, it only made me look like a mama's boy and the harassment got worse. Cole left me alone for two weeks, until the attention had died down, and then one day he tripped me in the bathroom in retaliation. I fell and hit my face on the sink. Because Mom decided to help, I got eight stitches. He didn't even need to tell me that if I said anything again it would be worse. I'm a smart guy. I figured it out on my own.

If I told her what was happening and asked her to not to go to them, would she respect that? Did I dare take the chance?

Maybe I could do online schooling. She knew I was self-motivated. She never had to check to see if I'd done my homework. Grades were everything to me. I'd never had less than a 3.8 GPA. The only reason it fell below a 4.0 was because of gym class. I could barely lift my backpack let alone do a pull-up. Maybe online school was the answer to my problems.

"Mom—"

Her phone rang just as I was about to ask.

"Hello… Oh, I'm so sorry." She glanced at the clock on the microwave. "I was thinking there was a one hour time difference. Five months and I'm still adjusting to being in the Mountain Time Zone. Let me get to my office and I'll call you right back."

She was already heading out of the kitchen when I said, "Bye."

"Oh, sweetie." She came back and kissed my forehead. "If you're not feeling well you can stay home. Or call if you need to come home early. I'll give permission for you to leave."

She knew I got motion sick on the bus. If I said I was nauseous, would she still make me ride the bus or would she take twenty minutes off of work to come and get me?

54

I toasted a piece of cinnamon-raisin bread and spread on a thick layer of butter. Then I tugged on my coat and headed out the door. With every step I thought of how Zane would be waiting for me and that single bite of toast turned into a little rock in my stomach. I paused at the garbage can next to the garage and lifted the lid to toss in the barely-eaten piece when someone came around the corner, making me jump.

"Robin?" A girl with long dark hair that looked kind of like dreadlocks but kind of not stood at the corner of my garage. "Wait. You're not throwing that out are you? That's so wasteful. There are hungry people who would gladly eat that."

I looked from her to the toast and then shoved it in my mouth. I couldn't handle a lecture right then.

"Who are you?" I asked through the mouthful of bread-covered raisins.

She made a disgusted face. "Manners. Heard of them?"

I chewed, swallowed, and brushed the crumbs off my hand. "Sorry. Yes, I'm Robin. Who are you?"

She smiled then. She had a great smile, one that made her eyes crinkle at the corners. "I'm Dara."

"Nice to meet you. Can I help you with something?"

"I don't know. Possibly." Dara put her hand to her mouth and tapped a navy blue-painted fingernail against her blindly-white teeth, like she was contemplating the question. "Teasing. Nothing you can do for me, thanks, but I can sure help you."

I shook my head. "You've got the wrong person. I don't need help." At least none that she could give. I doubted she could take on Zane.

"You're Robin Westmore."

She knew my name. Whatever that meant.

"You just moved here from Wisconsin."

"Five months ago. So not *just* but yes, I'm from Wisconsin."

"You're being bullied by some kid named Zane and you

want it to stop."

I stood there, next to my garbage can, wondering who this girl was and what she was up to. It was common knowledge that I was Zane's favorite target. Of course I wanted his harassment to stop, anyone would, but what could she possibly do about it?

"Look, I don't know who you are but if Zane sent you—"

"Zane didn't send me." She paused, just for a beat. "I guess you could say the universe did."

I didn't need this. I had enough drama in my life. I didn't need this chick adding crazy to it as well. Marijuana was legal in Colorado. Maybe she'd been dining on pot gummies or something. The universe sent her. Yeah, right.

"I've got to get going," I said. "I'm going to miss my bus."

"Don't worry about that," Dara said. "I can take care of it."

I started walking. I had to go six blocks in about two minutes. If I wasn't there I'd have to either wait for the next bus, which wouldn't be for half an hour, or beg my mom for a ride during which I'd have to listen to her chew me out about responsibility.

Dara followed, her arms wrapped tightly together. She wasn't wearing a jacket.

"Let me try again," she said. "This is my first time and I'm not sure how to do this."

What was she saying? "Your first time? Are you a prostitute?"

"What? God." She made a face. "No, I'm not a prostitute. What kind of hooker comes up to someone by their garage first thing in the morning?"

"I wouldn't know. I'm not privy to the methods of the, uh, working class."

She said nothing for half a block and then started laughing. Probably at the thought of me soliciting a hooker.

56

"Let me try this again." She cleared her throat and squared her shoulders. "Yesterday afternoon around three-forty-five you made a wish."

"I did what?" Then I remembered, the dandelion. "Do you live next door or something? How could you know that?"

"I told you, the universe sent me. Your wish has been granted."

She gave a low, sweeping bow.

"Zane did send you," I said. "I admit, this is better than breaking my phone or stealing my hat, which I'd like back by the way. My grandmother made that hat."

"He stole your Grandma hat?" she asked. "That's just wrong."

I stopped walking and stared at this odd girl. I'd never seen her before. My parents had made it their mission to meet every neighbor on the street when we moved in. If Dara lived close enough to us to see me blowing dandelion fuzz around my backyard, I would've known about her because Mom would've gone on and on about the cute girl who was about my age.

Dara didn't go to Woodland Academy either, I'd never seen her there at least, so she either went to a public high school or was homeschooled.

I blinked and realized she was staring at me.

"Checked out there for a sec, didn't you?" she asked and my face went hot. "Let's see, how can I make you believe?"

She was shivering hard by this point so I took my coat off and put it around her shoulders.

"Oh, you're so sweet," she gushed and slumped at the warmth of the wool. "Okay, we've still got a lot to talk about and since I don't know how to pause time, you'll most likely be late for school." She held up a hand to stop me from responding. "Don't worry, I can transport you."

Great. I'd just given my coat to a mentally ill person. How was I going to explain losing both my hat and coat within two days to my mom? This is what I got for talking to strangers. If I hurried, maybe I'd still make the bus.

"Come," she said, putting a hand on my back. "Let's keep walking."

"What, exactly, do we need to discuss?" I asked, taking a step away from her.

"Your wish," she said like this should have been obvious.

Okay, if she'd seen me blowing on a dandelion it would be a safe bet that that I was making a wish. But how could she know what I'd wished for? Had I said it out loud? Maybe she'd been hiding in my backyard at the time or on the other side of the fence. Was she homeless and living in our shrubs?

"The universe and Desiree have decided that your wish is grant-worthy. My job is to guide you through it."

"The univ... Who's Desir...? Look, this isn't funny." I was so tired of getting picked on.

"Take a breath, macho man." Dara nodded at my hands.

I looked down to see my hands tightly clenched into fists.

"Oh. No, I wasn't going to hit you," I said, horrified. I stretched my hands open wide and shook them out at my sides.

"I know that," Then more to herself than me Dara said, "I'm not doing this right. How did Desiree convince me?" She glanced up, as though looking into her brain for the answer, and let out a short laugh. "Oh yeah, she stopped me from bleeding to death. Don't worry. I won't take things that far."

She took off my coat and held it out to me. When I protested that I was wearing a sweater and she only had on a T-shirt—gray with *Wild Child* printed in big black letters— she silenced me with an upheld finger. She closed her eyes and held her arms out straight in front of her as though waiting for something to be set there. A second later, a long, thick, black cardigan started to appear, like a slow-fade in the movies.

"How did you do that?" I asked, freaked out now.

"Magic," she said while slipping on the sweater.

"That's a great trick," I said, seriously impressed.

"Not that kind of magic." She took a deep breath. "I'm a genie. My official title is Guide which I don't understand because no one knows what a Guide is. We have to explain that a Guide is like a genie and then people are like *oh, you're a genie*. Desiree should just change our title to genie."

"You're a genie?" I looked up the block. Zane, Brianna, and the rest of the regulars were still waiting at the bus stop. It must be running late today.

"What would it take to convince you?" Dara asked.

To convince me that she was a genie? Was laughing at Cole in fifth grade seriously a bad enough offense to sentence me to a life of this crap?

"Do that thing you just did with the sweater except get me my hat back." That would end this because I'd be able to tell immediately if it was the hat Grandma made.

"Okay."

She closed her eyes and held out her hands. I didn't take my eyes off of them. I didn't even blink. If she had the hat tucked into that sweater somewhere, I'd see her reach for it. But as I stood there, the slow-fade thing started to happen again. A hat, one that looked exactly like the one my grandmother spent two weeks knitting, started to appear.

I took it from Dara and inspected the top. There, about an inch down from the center, was a small, round burn mark. I'd been using a wood-burning tool to solder wires on my headphones and I accidentally touched the hat with it. It was quick, just a touch, but enough to burn the little hole.

"I believe you," I told Dara as I put the hat back on my head. As illogical as it was, there was no other explanation.

"Cool!" She wiggled happily and took me by the arm. "Come with me. Let's find a quieter place to talk."

We took a right one block before the bus stop. There was

a bench around the backside of a church on the corner and we sat there.

"Your wish has been granted," she said again, all official and genie-like.

"Yeah, you said that before." I didn't want to believe her, science told me this wasn't possible, but I did. Maybe because I needed to so badly. I needed to believe that I wasn't destined for life of constant hell. "So life will be good now. They're going to leave me alone."

"Well," she said, "it's not that simple. See the wishes we grant, they're not like an immediate gratification thing. Desiree says they're like journeys meant to help you for life, not just for the moment."

"Being left alone would help me for life."

"And what happens the next time?"

I could tell by the way she asked that she somehow knew I'd been a target for a while.

"Can't you fix it so there isn't a next time?" I asked.

She shrugged. "Even if I could, don't you think you should figure out why you're letting it happen and how to deal with it?"

"Letting it?" I jumped to my feet, furious at the implication that I somehow invited the Cole's and Zane's of the world into my life.

Dara placed a hand on my arm again and I instantly calmed. Almost like her touch was magic as well. "You haven't told your mom about Zane."

"She's busy," I said, unsure if I was defending myself or my mom.

"Your mom loves you. So does your dad. If they knew this was happening again, I'm sure they'd do anything to help you." She looked me in the eye. "See, you are kind of letting it happen. If you're not standing up for yourself, that's practically saying it's okay."

Dara was very direct, a trait that could be rude. On her it was simple honesty.

"What's going to happen?" I asked.

She pointed at the pocket of my jacket and I felt something heavy appear inside. I reached in and pulled out a flat, green stone. A partially drawn peace sign was etched into it.

"Don't touch the circle," she cautioned. "The wish will start if you do and I'm supposed to explain some stuff first."

I set the stone on my knee and held my hands away.

"Like I said, this wish will help your life, not just your current problem. That's pretty cool if you think about it." She took a moment to either allow me to think or to do so herself. Maybe both. "The wish may take a little while. A day or two. A week or two. A month or two. We won't know until we're into it. You wished for the bullying to stop. If you accept this wish, that will happen. But the wish will lead you on a journey first to make sure the end result sticks."

"So what are the side effects?" I asked.

"Side effects?"

"Yeah. If I have to decide whether I want to accept my own wish or not, what could happen?"

"Well sometimes… no, oftentimes things get worse before they get better. I guess the universe likes to test us, to make sure we've learned our lessons."

"Okay."

"Once you decide you want the wish and you touch the circle," she said, "the wish can't be stopped. You can't go back to the way things were. You can't pause things to catch your breath. You're in it to the end."

"What if I say no?"

"Then I have to summon my boss and she'll come and teach me how to wipe your memory."

"She'll teach you?" I nearly choked. "Oh no, you're not practicing a memory wipe on me."

I picked up the stone and before I touched the circle she said, "Don't you want to think about it?"

"There's nothing to think about," I said. "My life sucks.

The only time it doesn't suck is when I'm locked away in my room. That's not a life. I'd rather be dead. So, I accept the wish."

Before she could say another word, I pressed my palm against the stone. And waited.

"I don't feel anything," I said.

"I don't think you're supposed to."

"Don't you know?"

"I've never done this before." She batted her eyelashes at me and said, "You're my first, darling."

"I'm your...? Wait. You *are* practicing on me. You didn't tell me that."

"Don't worry," she said. "I have a supervisor. She's been guiding wishes for forty-five years. No one knows the wish business better than Desiree. You'll like her. She's nineteen and a hippie—"

"Wait," I said and held up my hands. "She's been doing this for forty-five years but she's nineteen years old? Are all genies this bad at math?"

"Ha ha," Dara said. "Basically she almost died when she was a teenager. This other genie, Kaf, saved her and said she could live as long as she became a genie for fifty years. She agreed as long as she could remain a teenager and get a second shot at life once her contract was fulfilled."

I blinked and waited for Dara to continue.

"Anyway, she'll be watching your wish, since you're my first"—another flirty smile—"and everything will be fine."

I nodded, like one of those bobble head dogs. Genies will be watching me. Everything will be fine. Right.

"If you need me," Dara said, "touch the circle again. That will summon me. Like I said, I can't do anything about what's happening with your wish, but I can be a shoulder to cry on if you need one."

"I'll be fine."

"Probably," she said. "The offer is there, though."

I tried to read the time through the cracks on my phone.

"I think I'm late for school."

Dara held her hand over my phone. When she pulled it away, the screen was fixed.

"I'll transport you. I'll also fix the record to show that you were there on time. I imagine you've got a perfect attendance record going?"

I nodded proudly. "Haven't missed a day since I had strep throat in kindergarten."

She smiled and bumped her shoulder against mine. "You're such a nerd."

Then she touched her hand to my shoulder and the next thing I knew I was sitting at my desk in World History.

Chapter Six

Robin

No one reacted. Granted, I sat toward the back of the room in history, but how invisible was I that not even the people in the desks next to mine reacted when I suddenly appeared in my seat?

It took a good five minutes before I was sure the teacher saw me there. Guess he hadn't realized I'd been missing either. For all of second period, I kept expecting the office to call me in wanting to know why I'd been late this morning and how I got past them without detection.

Magic, I'd tell them.

Who was I kidding? This wasn't magic. This was my life. I could walk in naked, slamming cymbals together in front of the entire administration department and none of them would notice.

Maybe this was how *the universe* was going to help me

survive high school. Cool. I could handle being invisible. Especially considering the alternative. I took my seat in third period Honors Algebra and had just taken out my notebook when Mr. Emerson appeared at my desk.

"What are you doing here, Mr. Westmore?"

He got my name right.

"Sir?" I asked.

He smiled at me. Well, a small smile appeared on his face while he was standing in front of me. I couldn't prove that smile was for me.

"What are you doing here, Mr. Westmore?"

He had almost the same tone as Mr. Smith in that old movie, *The Matrix*.

Why are you here, Mr. Anderson?

Maybe that's it. I've been stuck in a matrix where the bullies live this whole time. *The universe* was going to pull me out now and send me back to Zion.

"Didn't the office contact you?" he asked.

Damn. They did know I got here late.

"I can explain," I started to say, but he cut me off.

"I owe you an apology," Mr. Emerson said. "I gave you a hard time about taking that placement test yesterday. In my defense, we get a lot of parents who insist their kid is a genius and should be in the advanced classes. About ten percent of the time they're right. The other ninety percent of the kids stay in the class they were assigned."

He paused to answer a quick question from another student. This gave me a moment to process what he'd said. *I owe you an apology.* I had never heard those words come out of a teacher's mouth before. Mr. Emerson held up a hand to a second student with a question and returned his attention to me instead.

"You can only imagine what I thought when I received notice that a tenth grader wanted to test out of Honors Algebra, an already great achievement, with the hopes of placing into AP Calculus." He paused and gave me another smile. It was starting to creep me out. "Mr. Westmore, not only did you pass the test, you got a perfect score. You might be able to test into—" He stopped himself from completing the thought. Instead he took my algebra book from me and handed me a hall pass. "We've rearranged your schedule. Report to your science class for third period and then come back here after lunch, for AP Calculus."

In Honors Chemistry, Ms. Rolfing indicated I should take any open seat I wanted. Before I could choose one she said, "I understand you're moving up the food chain. Robin."

She added my name like it was a foreign word and she wasn't sure of the pronunciation.

"Yes, ma'am," I said.

"You're planning to test out of this class into AP Physics?"

I looked at the class out of the corner of my eye. Their thoughts pummeled my brain. *Not good enough for us, hey. Think you're so special.*

"I'd like to try, ma'am," I said quietly, hoping she'd follow my lead.

"If you're as gifted in science as you clearly are in math then I'm sure that won't be a problem," Ms. Rolfing said loud enough for people in the hallway to hear. "I'll schedule the test for next Monday. That'll give you the week and weekend to prepare."

I nodded and turned to find a seat. Not only had the class been in session for nearly ten minutes by the time I'd walked through the door, the dynamics had been developing for two weeks. Everyone knew each other and their place within the group. I was an invader. A mutant cell worming my way into a fully functioning organism. Even if they welcomed me, I'd be sitting in another classroom by this time next week, being the invader all over again. Why did I do this to myself? Why couldn't I just leave things alone and be happy with what I was given?

The stone that Dara had given me was in my pants

pocket. It bumped against the desktop as I grabbed the first empty seat I came to. Almost like a nudge, it reminded me that the universe had granted my wish. I couldn't be happy with what I'd been given because I didn't have to be. I was entitled to better.

"We're studying the same thing in this class as we are in the other, Robin," Ms. Rolfing said. "So you shouldn't feel lost. Not that you would, I'm sure."

As frustrating as it was to have everyone ignore me or get my name wrong, being singled out for positive reasons was just as embarrassing. This is the brain I was given. My parents pushed me to use it to its full potential. Why couldn't people just accept that?

Finally, Ms. Rolfing turned her attention away from me, thank god, back to the current curriculum topic, atomic structure.

Once class was underway again and everyone had forgotten about me, I looked around to see who was in here. I counted fifteen and as I focused in on the girl sitting next to me, all the cells in my body froze. Brianna. Without looking up, she reached around her head, gathered her long, honey-colored hair into her fingers, and pulled it over her left shoulder. She had filled the margin of her notebook page with atoms, each fully complete with electrons, neutrons, protons, and nuclei. She had completed two more atoms when she must have sensed me staring at her. She turned and offered me that smile. The one that lit up not only her face but everything around her. Impossibly, she'd gotten more beautiful since yesterday.

The period passed in a blur and before I knew it, class was over. I hadn't had a single class with Brianna last year. It looked like my luck was changing. Maybe I wouldn't bother with AP Physics. Maybe I'd stay right here, next to Brianna, for the whole year.

My parents would have a meltdown.

"Do you have any idea what an MIT education costs?"

Dad was fond of asking me. "You need to get as many college credits in high school as you can."

Guess I could take the test and not pass it. It would be worth it to sit next to Brianna for eight months. I could do AP Physics over the summer and be back on track once school started in the fall.

Things returned to what more closely resembled normal for me as soon as class was over. I made it to my locker and once my back was turned I heard a chorus of birdcalls behind me.

"Tweety missed the bus this morning," Zane said.

I literally had to bite my tongue because "I'm touched that you missed me" almost came out of my mouth. I knew it would be the last thing I'd ever say if it did.

"You need to flap harder," Minion Thad told me. "Such a puny bird needs to fly faster if he wants to make it to the bus."

They were close enough that I could actually feel their body heat radiating onto my back. If I took one step back I'd bump into them, and they'd pound me. If I looked back at them, they'd pound me. If I acknowledged them in anyway, they'd pound me. Ironic that I needed to act as though my tormentors were invisible to keep invisible me from getting pounded.

Okay, truth time. I knew they'd never lay a hand on me right now. The teachers might see. Say anything you want. Post anything you want on social media. Do anything you want to another student off of school property, but if you so much as laid a pinkie on anyone while inside the school, even in self-defense, you would pay the price. They called it zero tolerance. The aching bruises on my shoulders reminded me of what Zane and his minions could do. They wouldn't risk taking me out now, but sooner or later they'd find a way to make sure I suffered.

I kept my eyes focused on my locker as I switched my math and science materials to their appropriate new slots. I liked to keep my books and folders lined up by period.

The birdcalls continued as I stalled, praying they'd go away. When one of them blew on the back of my ear—"Did Tweety go deaf? We're talkin' to you, little birdie."—I carefully pulled my phone out of my pocket. The school had set up a text number for emergencies, like an in-school 9-1-1. If any student needed to get a message to the front office and couldn't get to one of the classroom phones, they could text a message. I typed in *problem by the sophomore lockers* and was about to hit send.

"Tweety's no fun today," one of them said. I think it was Wayne "Let's go."

Just that fast, it was over. I wasn't sure if I was more shocked or relieved. My knees were a little rubbery, but I didn't feel the need to rush to the bathroom and throw up. I felt like I should get a gold star for that achievement.

My aunt swore there was good to counter everything bad in the world and vice versa. That way balance was maintained. If that was true, then the locker incident was the balance for my excellent morning. At least it had only lasted less than a minute. And they stayed at my locker instead of following me down the hall, like usual, where everyone could hear and watch like we were a parade passing by. It was like The Minions got bored. That's what the experts suggested, *Ignore it, they'll get bored and move along.* Maybe that's what happened. Or maybe Dara really had worked some magic for me.

During fourth period I helped Miss Clark in the computer lab. It was supposed to be a study hall but my parents complained long and loud to the school about it. "He can study at home. He's in school to absorb knowledge."

The school finally agreed to the lab position once Mom and Dad pulled out the "we could easily pay tuition to a different school" threat. I liked the position because it gave me a chance to learn from Miss Clark. She wasn't so much a teacher as she was an IT genius. Fourth period was her free period so we could talk as geeky as we wanted and usually there wasn't anyone around to hear us.

"Where's Miss Clark?" I asked the substitute reading a novel at Miss Clark's desk today.

"At an off-site meeting," the woman said. "I assume you're Robin. She said you should defragment the computers today."

A cushy assignment. Punch a few buttons and let the computers do their thing. One of Zane's Minions could've done that. Hell, Zane could have done that. If the instructions were written out.

"Is there anything else that needs to be done?" I asked the sub.

"You can fill the printers with paper. Miss Clark is supposed to be here to supervise anything more technical," the woman said and returned to her book.

A shadow on an otherwise sunny day.

Dara's magic seemed to be wearing out by the time I got to lunch. I filled my tray and headed straight to where I always sat, at the table closest to the door. But someone was already sitting in my spot. A Goldilocks-style breach of protocol. Regardless of when a person got to the lunchroom, their seat was their seat.

I was about to point this out to the invader, a girl in a white polo, a long skirt made up of multi-colored layers of ruffles, and black combat boots. I'd seen her in the halls, she had to be pushing six feet, so she was pretty hard to miss. Honestly, she scared me. I decided things were going so well today, I'd let the breach go and find a different seat.

Our cafeteria had the standard long tables down one side and up the other with aisles at the center and edges. There were only a handful of empty seats, all at tables where I wouldn't dare sit. I'd never open myself to the humiliation of the athletes' table. I might be okay at the musicians' table. I had zero skill but plenty of interest. I could tell them about my Auditory Contagion idea.

The deeper into the cafeteria I went, the more I felt like everyone was staring at me. I needed to just pick a spot. Not with the stoners, although they probably wouldn't even know I was there. There was a seat open at the moody table, I might fit with them. Nah. They'd depress me and ruin my good day.

I needed to quit analyzing and just sit. So I took the first seat along the outside aisle I came to. A casual sideways glance showed me that this group was made up of three guys and two girls and, unbelievably, they seemed to be geeks. I didn't even know there was a geek table. They hadn't acknowledged me yet, but I felt like I fit with them. They weren't beautiful people, but not ugly either. They did fall to the ends of the spectrums though. They were either really skinny, like me, or pretty heavy. They were either dark skinned or, like me, so pale they'd disappear in a snowbank. One guy was tall, skinny, and pale—the trifecta of nerdom—and talked a lot while the others listened.

"Trust me," he said. "You just gotta try it. It'll blow your mind."

"The guy developed it himself," one of the girls said. She was like the leader's shadow—tall, skinny, and dark. "How great can a game be if it's indie?"

"How great?" the guy asked, grabbing a fistful of his own yellow-blonde hair. "How great are indie bands? How great is Apple? Which, I apparently need to remind you, was started by two indie guys in their garage. Some of the best books being written are by indie authors who dare to be a little different."

"All right, all right," she said. "I'm just saying that the mega-developers have about a bazillion dollars behind them to make their graphics primo." She gave a succinct, finger-and-thumb-together okay sign.

"It can be done," I couldn't help but say. Holy crap what was that? I dared to speak to a tableful of people I didn't know? They lured me in with their geek-speak, but still.

"I'm sorry?" the second girl asked. She was the polar opposite of the first girl—short, chubby, and pale. "Are you talking to us?"

I know she didn't say it in a threatening way. She was the size of a fourth grader, after all. Still, I heard a mobster voice come out of her. *Are you talkin' to us? 'Cause if you're talkin' to us then we need to step outside and have Vinny the Enforcer explain to you that you don't talk to us unless we say you can talk to us. Capisce?*

"Hello?" The girl said in a friendly and distinctly non-mobster voice. It was tiny, like the rest of her, and high-pitched. "Did you say something?"

"Sorry," I said. "I heard what you were talking about. Not that I was eavesdropping or anything like that."

The guy looked at the girl. "What did he say?"

"I don't know," she said. "Something about it being done, I think."

"I'm designing my own game," I blurted. "And it's turning out pretty sweet."

Once again, words were slipping out of my mouth without permission. I hadn't told anyone about my game. My parents only knew because they bought me the software.

"You're designing your own game?" leader-guy asked in this tone that said he assumed it was something on par with Pong.

"I started over the summer," I said cautiously. I was probably setting myself up for more humiliation.

"Is it any good?"

"What's the game?"

"Will you show us?"

The five of them bombarded me with questions and while the leader was obviously skeptical, the rest of the group wanted to hear more.

The tiny girl held her hand up in a wave. "I'm Emily."

"Jeremiah," the biggest guy in the group said while jutting his chins at me in greeting. "'Sup?"

"Pranav," the third guy in the group said. "Nice to meet you."

"Who are you?" the first girl asked.

"I'm Robin," I said. "Who are you?"

She narrowed her eyes, analyzing me. "Tabatha. Do you always listen in on conversations?"

"No," I said. "I wasn't listening in. Sorry. I'll just eat my lunch and go."

"Don't be a nerd," Tabatha said, turning away, bored with me already.

"She's just testing you," Emily said. "To see if you're worthy."

"What's the game?" the first guy asked. "I'm Ivan, by the way."

"I call it *Pharm Runner*," I said. "As in pharmaceuticals. That's the working title right now. I'll probably change it."

"That's not bad," Ivan said. "Tell us about it."

Really? He wanted to hear about my game? The warning alarms weren't going off in my head yet, but I could feel them charging up, ready to blare at a moment's notice. Mom always said it was best to give just enough information to raise curiosity and get them to ask questions.

"Well," I said, "my mom was telling my dad and me about some flower in the rainforest that can cure cancer. Dad said the pharmaceutical companies would fight a miracle cure because it would eliminate the need for some of their biggest money-making drugs. I decided to make a game out of it."

Ivan nodded, like he was with me so far.

"So how do you play it?" Emily asked.

The alarms charged a little more. *Tread carefully, Robin.*

"You start out at a hospital," I said, pushing down on my knees to keep them from bouncing. "There's a group of doctors talking about this flower that's a wonder drug and how it could cure half of their patients if only they could get their hands on it. They leave and then you have to make your way from the hospital to the rainforest and to the top of this super tall tree to harvest this little orange flower and bring it back to these doctors.

"Along the way you can choose your routes. The harder the route the more points you earn. You have to fight off jungle creatures, work with a team of scientists already there looking for the flower, or you can go solo and look for it yourself, and you have to stay away from the dudes from the pharmaceutical companies there to stop you."

They all stared at me. I was sure I'd said too much.

"I like it," Jeremiah said.

"Is it 2D or 3D?" Pranav asked.

"It's 3D," I said. "The graphics are pretty nice."

"What software are you using?" Ivan asked.

"It's called Consensus," I said.

"I've heard of that," Pranav said, nodding in approval.

"Free or pro version," Emily asked.

"Pro," I said.

Tabatha let out a slow whistle. "Cha-ching. That's a serious chunk of change."

"That's how my parents kept me busy this summer," I said with a smirk. "It was that or send me to a camp somewhere. The software was cheaper."

"I've heard Consensus tries too hard to do everything though," Ivan said. "Jack of all trades, master of none."

"It's easy to use," I said, defending my software choice. "I'm happy with the results but I can mess with the code if I want to change things. I do have a few bugs to work out but it's mostly a hobby anyway."

"What about sound effects?" Tabatha wanted to know. I'd already figured out that any question Tabatha asked would sound like a challenge.

"I do a lot of them myself," I said. "I record different sounds and play around with them until I have something I like."

"Do you do your own birdcalls?" Ivan asked.

The table went silent and one of the guys quietly said, "Ivan. What's the matter with you, man?"

I think it was Jeremiah. Don't know for sure. I stared at my lunch tray. They knew who I was, that kid who got targeted and harassed every day. They'd probably witnessed the birdcall parade making its way down the hall.

"Sorry, man," Ivan said. "Really."

He held his hand out to me in truce. I stared at it and finally shook with him after Emily said, "Don't mind him. He was raised by wolves."

There were only five minutes before class started and the lunchroom was emptying.

"Do we have any classes together?" Pranav asked.

"I'm not sure," I said and quickly listed my afternoon lineup.

We had French II together. Funny I hadn't notice him before. It was a full class though and I tried not to look around at people too much. I'd pay attention now.

"You'll join us again tomorrow, right?" Emily asked.

"Yeah," Tabatha said, again with a challenge. "I want to hear more about this game."

Ivan paused, letting his gaze settle on one person at a time, then nodded. "That would be cool."

Cool indeed. For the first time in a very long time, I'd been invited to something. It was only lunch, but I was good with baby steps.

Chapter Seven

Desiree

I was sure the magical world had started to find its balance again. I thought everyone was accepting our new home. Some even seemed to be accepting me. I thought the tablets would be a fun thing for them. Who didn't like getting a new toy?

Then one crisp early-fall morning as the sun glinted off the lake, frizzy-haired Amber wanted to know, "What's wrong with carrier pigeons? Everything was fine. We were happy with the messaging system. Just like we were happy with our home." She gave me a stone-cold stare. "And our boss."

I held out my hand, manifested my granny glasses, and plugged them onto my face. "Seems to me our boss wasn't diggin' us anymore though."

"How would you know?" Amber asked, throwing her

hands angrily into the air. "You were never there."

What I'd learned about Amber was that she would blindly defend Kaf to the death.

According to her bio, Kaf had found her lying in a big cardboard box in an alley. She'd been roofied by this guy she met at a club and he dragged her out back to do... whatever it was he was going to do to her. She was completely out of it but still made a wish that had come from her heart. Her parents had abandoned her at a shopping mall when she was eleven and she had no other family, none who would take her in at least, and had been living in a series of foster homes. Her wish was for a permanent home. Kaf gave her one, and now she was the best Guide for dealing with foster and adopted kids.

"Kaf cared about me when no one else did," Amber said. "He gave me a home."

"I hate to break it to you," I pushed my glasses back up on my nose, "but Kaf didn't take any of us in because he cared about us."

"That's not true," she said in a softer voice.

"Look, a home isn't about the place," I said. "It's the people. You're still with your people. Don't fool yourself about Kaf. He was looking out for exactly one person and that was himself. Think about it. Do you really believe there weren't any men out there who could have become Guides? He chose women because he thought he could manipulate us into doing what he wanted."

"Remember, my dear hippie-child," Olanna said, looking down at me as she walked past, "you are no different."

"Never claimed to be," I said, ignoring the stabbing shock of cold her words caused in my chest. "Look, we're starting to come together. We could become a force rather than the obedient mass Kaf thinks we are. He's probably out there laughing at us right now."

"Those are big words," Olanna said, turning toward the group gathering in the commons, "from someone who does not really want to be here."

"Why would you say that?" I asked, stung again but hiding it behind my blue-tinted lenses. "What makes you think I don't want to be here?"

"You left," Olanna said. "You did your time and left."

"I was on my own wish journey." The microscopic slump of her shoulders said she hadn't known that. "Kaf didn't tell you that part, did he?"

"He shared no personal information with us," Olanna said, her voice breaking just a bit.

Did she mean about other Guides or himself?

"He told me," I said, "that my time as a Guide was a part of my own journey. I wished for a second chance at life because I'd made such bad choices the first time."

"No surprise there," Olanna said with a lift of her chin.

I wouldn't let her bait me. "He said that I had to successfully put my past in the past before I could move forward. All the wishes I guided were supposedly helping me with that. Then he released me from my indenture and allowed me to return to the real world for that second chance."

If you love something, release it. If it returns, love it forever. If it does not, it was not meant to be.

Was that what he had done? Had he released me to see if I'd return? I had. Was it my turn now to release him? Would he return?

"You all refuse to believe that I'm not responsible for this," I said as I climbed on top of the kitchen bar. "Maybe you will if you hear the words directly from The Man himself."

Olanna, surely expecting I'd humiliate instead of redeem myself, summoned all of the Guides to the commons.

I cupped my hands and created a ball of light, similar to the aurora swirls that followed me like obedient pets. I threw the ball toward the ceiling and it started to grow until it was the size of a screen at a movie theater. There I projected the

78

moment Kaf told me what he wanted from me.

"This was about a month ago," I told them. "The eve of my birthday. After being frozen at eighteen for forty-five years, it seemed I was about to get a year older. I had summoned him to ask if that was true."

No one spoke. All eyes were directed at the screen of light as though the truths of the universe were about to be revealed. In a way they were. Some truths about their universe at least.

Slowly, the screen revealed an image of Kaf and me in my bus.

"I have always found it ironic that you labeled yourself the Wish Mistress," Kaf said. "My own title has always been Wish Master. As I mentioned, my term ends when I find a suitable replacement. I believe that person to be you."

"Kaf—" I started.

He held up a hand. "I do not want an answer now. This is not the moment for you to choose. That moment will come soon, however, and you will know when it is here. At that point, I would like you to consider this option along with the others."

He stepped closer until we were barely an inch apart then placed a kiss on my forehead and said, "Happy birthday, Desiree."

And then he vanished.

Gasps rose from the gathered Guides at the moment of the kiss. Kaf never allowed anyone to get closer than two feet to him. That he stepped so close to me was unthinkable. And the kiss? Some of the gasps were the *oh, how sweet* type. Others clearly said *I want to gouge her eyes out.* Truthfully, I could have stopped the image before the kiss, but part of me wanted to claim him as my own. I wanted them to know I'd had something special with him.

There had been something special between us, hadn't there? Olanna hadn't reacted to the kiss. I never took my eyes off of her, she didn't even wince. Either she was a pro at

hiding her feelings or this didn't bothered her because...
why? Did she have something *special* with Kaf, too? More
special? Cosmos help me, he hadn't been playing me all
along had he?

"There's more," I called out, my voice a little shaky
now. "Keep watching and then tell me I'm lying."

The scene on the screen changed from inside Gypsy V to
the Riverwalk in San Antonio. Dara was lying on the
sidewalk in a pool of blood. I was kneeling on the ground
next to her. Kaf stood nearby.

*"She understands the conditions now," Kaf said,
crossing his arms over his chest. "She either agrees and lives
or does not and dies."*

"Can I still see my mom?" Dara whispered.

"Really?" I asked.

*"We were going to try and fix things," she said. "I want
to do that. And I want to see Wyatt."*

I groaned.

"I love him, Desiree."

"You agree to the conditions?" I asked.

*"Fifteen for fifty," she whispered, "if I can still see my
parents and Wyatt. If I can't, what does it matter if I die?"*

"She agreed," I told Kaf. "Save her."

*"And what about you?" Kaf asked me. The look on his
face was an emotional mix of anticipation and pain. "What is
your decision?"*

*I stared at Dara, as I said, "Yes, Kaf, I agree to be your
replacement."*

"So tell me," I said, "what would you have done?"

The commons had gone silent. Some stared in shock.
Others in disbelief.

"That's the last time I saw him," I told them. "As far as I
know, he left all of us at that moment. This is how much our
great and mighty Kaf cared." I tried to push down the pain
that surfaced every time I talked about him. That pain of not
knowing where he was, what was happening to him, and

most of all, if I'd ever see him again. "This is why I've changed a few things. You might feel differently, but I don't want to be surrounded by the memories of someone who would do that to me."

I turned to Dara. She was pale and swaying a little.

"Are you okay?" I asked, standing close, ready to catch her if she went down.

She nodded. "I don't remember any of that."

She had been so close to death she could barely understand what she was agreeing to, which was the case for almost all of us. We'd all been beyond vulnerable when Kaf came to us, offering exactly what we wanted in exchange for what he wanted.

"I'm sorry," I said. "I hadn't thought about that. Do you want to forget again? I can wipe the image from your mind."

"No, I'll be okay." Then she hugged me. "Thank you for what you did for me."

I hugged her back even tighter. "I meant what I said. You're like a sister to me. I'd never let anything happen to you."

"I'm going to go call Wyatt."

Before I could remind her that she had Robin's wish to tend to, she vanished and Indira had come up to me. "May I offer a word of caution?"

"Could I stop you if I wanted to?"

She shook her head and the mass of gypsy coins on her long gold earrings caught the light. "Don't change too much too quickly. I know you're angry and hurt by Kaf right now—"

"Why should I be hurt? Kaf decided that his path lead in another direction. That was his choice, just as each of us have chosen our own paths. How could I be angry about that?"

If I kept telling myself that, maybe I'd believe it.

The smile Indira offered me said exactly that—*keep telling yourself that*. "All I'm saying is that he ruled this world for two hundred years. Some of what he did may have been chauvinistic and self-serving, but consider that it may also have been for a reason." She turned, her long layers of skirts flaring slightly. "I've offered my warning. Heed it if you choose."

Why did I feel like Indira the Gypsy had just placed an evil eye curse on me?

"Did I understand correctly? You're giving us freedom to trade wishes?" asked Sarah, an older Guide with a gentle demeanor and beautiful salt-and-pepper hair woven into a long braid.

Indira's warning immediately pinched at me.

"Within reason," I said. "Our purpose is to insure that wishes go smoothly. As long that happens, how it happens is not a huge concern to me."

"What if we choose not to?"

"Not to what?" I asked, suddenly distracted by a flurry of wishes that made the light around me pulse.

"What if we've had enough?" Sarah asked.

"Of being a Guide?"

She nodded. Sarah had chosen to continue aging during her indenture. The soft lines on her face showed she'd been a Guide for about as long as I had. Her bio stated that she had told Kaf, "My parents are already gone. My husband will be too when my time here is done. He is the love of my life. Continuing without him is nothing to look forward to."

She still accepted the option to become a Guide rather than to die in a fiery car crash. Her condition was that she be allowed to insure her husband and three young children had happy lives. Kaf agreed, but she could only see them, never go to them.

Now, she wasn't just asking a random question. She wanted out.

"What happened," I asked, "to make you decide you've had enough?"

"My husband died yesterday," she said, tears filling her pale blue eyes. "As I wanted, he had a good life. My children are happy and successful with their lives as well. I have guided hundreds of charges over the years. What more do I need to do?"

Sarah had agreed to be a Guide until she reached eighty years of age at which point she would die peacefully in her sleep. She had known her destiny all along.

"You still have two years to go," I reminded her.

"I'm tired, Desiree." She seemed to deflate a little just saying the words. "What will happen if I just stop?"

"Stop fulfilling your duties? You'll be breaking your contract." She knew this. My heart started to race. Was she asking me for permission to die? "Your contract, everyone's contracts, state that you will return to the condition you were in when Kaf saved you."

She nodded, as if accepting a fatal diagnosis from a doctor.

"You heard what I said?" I asked, trying to keep the desperation out of my voice. It would be up to me to implement the punishment. I would have to proclaim her contract broken. I would be the one sentencing her to a fiery, agonizing death.

"I heard." An eerie sort of peace washed over her that chilled me to the core. "I also heard you say that things were going to change now."

My breath caught as Sarah walked away.

A lineup of Guides had formed behind her. Most of them only wanted to apologize for being hard on me about Kaf. Others wanted to understand what exactly the rules were now. Indira's warning about change rang in my head.

"For now Kaf's rules are still in effect," I said, "but I will alter them if I think they aren't right for us anymore."

"What does that mean?" Amber asked. She wasn't as hostile toward me this time but it was clear that I wasn't her favorite person.

"It means that you have more freedom," I said. "I'm not in favor of either charges or Guides learning lessons the hard way. If a lesson is to be learned, the universe will see to it, not any of us. If I assign a wish that you don't feel you can properly guide, switch with someone who can. If you don't like your room, change it. If you want kumquats, manifest them."

As I spoke, thoughts of Cliff—the self-proclaimed ruler of the commune I had lived on with my best friend Marsha, my boyfriend Glenn, and anywhere from thirty to fifty other people at any given time—filled my head. Cliff had lured us to the commune proclaiming a lifestyle free from the iron fist of The Man and society's rules. At first he didn't believe we needed anyone in charge. Insisted, in fact, that the group's personality would form naturally the longer we lived together and learned each other's strengths and weaknesses. After a few weeks he had risen to the top, like the rich fatty cream in a jug of milk. He decided who was best suited for each job, while sitting back and watching his hive buzz around him.

Few of us were happy. If he would have left us alone to live our lives, to do what we wanted within the group, everything would have been fine.

I climbed on top of the kitchen bar so everyone could see me and sounded the gong.

"I will not run this group as a dictator. I trust you to all do what you agreed to do without me hovering like a shadow." Indira shot me a pleading look from a few rows back. I held up a hand, showing I understood, then locked eyes with Sarah. "Remember that there are consequences if you do not uphold your end of the agreement. Many of you are not happy that I am changing Kaf's rules. One that I will not change is that if you do not fulfill the agreement you entered into with him, to honorably guide our charges' wishes, you will suffer the *or else* clause."

A soft murmur went through the crowd.

"Let me remind you in case you've forgotten," I said. "The *or else* clause not only returns you to the place and time where Kaf found you, it also negates all that you have done as a Guide. The wishes you guided, the charges you so painstakingly cared for, will be guided by another and the results may not be the same."

This was the condition Kaf had put on me. I could move forward with my life or I could go back to 1969 and try again. If I went back, all of my wishes would go to another Guide. I'd taken too much pride in guiding my charges. Risking things not turning out well for them wasn't an option. I hoped the other Guides felt the same way.

Sarah nodded. She understood the consequences. What would she do?

"I do not know what kind of hold you had over him," Olanna said to me once I'd come down from the bar, "but he was wrong. You are not the one to lead us."

As she stood before me, all I could think was, did he kiss her? If he did, was it more than on the forehead? Did he have feelings for her? He said my time as a Guide had been my wish journey. Had I simply been a charge to him? Was his only concern for me that of a Guide? I felt nauseous with all the thoughts spinning in my head.

I had to let it go. There wasn't anything I could do about what had or had not happened. I placed my hands together in Namaste and lowered my head to her. "Peace, my sister. Remember, one small crack can bring down the dam."

Cliff had been the crack in our dam. Every time he spread his arms wide to gather his flock together, the crack widened. Dissention seeped in. Some were happy with Cliff's commandments. Some left because things weren't any better on the commune than they had been at home. They were, in many ways, worse.

We had wanted a community where we all lived together equally instead of where a ruling body demanded obedience with an iron fist. Was there any way that could have happened on the commune? Was it possible here?

Olanna opened her mouth to say more, but instead held my gaze as she slowly turned and disappeared into the crowd.

"I sure hope you know what you're doing," Indira said.

"Haven't got a clue." I held my hands out, until I realized the similarity to Cliff and then clasped them in front of me. "I'm trusting the universe will light a path for me."

Chapter Eight

Robin

For the first time in years, I was excited to go to school. Since the Lunch Bunch—my label for them, not that I let them know that—invited me to their table the second day, I didn't even ask on the third. I was part of the group. I'd never been part of a group. Except for that month of Cub Scouts in second grade. I guess math camp could be considered a group. We were all equally geeky and while it got competitive at times, no one bullied anyone. It was nice. I liked that camp.

"You're up early," Mom said. "I saw your light on past midnight again. Lots of homework?"

"Yeah," I said, "but I had that done by ten. I was working on my game."

"Your game? The one you started over the summer?" She got out a cup and saucer and held up two tea options. I pointed to the English Breakfast. Like I did every morning.

"Same game. It's got a few bugs, so I've been working on them."

"You shouldn't stay up late on a school night for that," she said and poured hot water over the tea bag. "It's one thing if it's homework—"

"I'm fine, Mom. I wasn't up that late." I went to bed at two o'clock, but if I admitted that the lecture would be ridiculous.

"How's the new math class going?" Dad asked as he charged into the kitchen and set his gun case down on the counter.

"Fine," I said. "Calculus is nothing."

"They should put you straight into the highest level class," Dad said with a look of disappointment. "It would challenge you. Challenge is good. Maybe I'll give them a call about the math placement again. The sooner we get you into college level courses and earning credits the better. You're going to take the science test this week, right?"

"Don't push him so hard," Mom said, plugging a coffee pod into the machine. "He pushes himself hard enough. He can take a couple classes this summer."

"Summer is for extracurricular activities," Dad said. "Got to pad those college apps. They want to see well-rounded citizens. He needs to get involved with community activities."

"Why don't I just shoot myself?" I said and pointed at his gun. "It would be far less painful."

The only sound in the room was coffee dripping into Dad's mug. Wow. Suddenly I had their full attention.

"That's not funny," Mom finally said, but I wasn't sure if she meant the shooting me thing or the insinuation that community involvement would be painful.

"Sorry," I said. "Wasn't trying to be funny."

She scowled at me then motioned to the gun case. "Are you going to the range again?"

"After work," Dad said. "I've got meeting after meeting today and if I was a betting man I'd guess that I'm going to want to blow off a little steam by the end of the day."

Mom handed him his mug of coffee and gave him a kiss. "Just keep it aimed at the targets."

"Yes, a few of my coworkers will make fine targets," Dad said. Mom scowled at him this time. "Fine. I'll just write their names on the targets. Right smack over the bull's eye." He sighted his finger at the clock on the wall. "Damn, gotta go. Gonna be late."

He flew out the door, forgetting his gun, and a second later came back for it.

"All right," Mom said, "I need to get to my desk. I've got three new client calls today."

"That's great," I said. "Your business is really taking off. You're going to need to hire an assistant soon."

She came to kiss my cheek and looked down at the placemat in front of me. "I didn't make your toast."

"That's okay," I said. "I can do it."

"No, that's my job," she insisted and set down her cup and phone. As soon as she did, the phone rang. "Darn."

"Mom, really, go to work. I can make toast."

She picked up the ringing phone. "Marjorie Westmore Marketing, can you hold please?" She nodded and held her hand over the receiver. "Everything's okay? Anything I need to know?"

"Everything's great. Promise." I nodded at her phone. "Your customer is waiting."

She studied me for a second, blew a little kiss at me, then grabbed her cup of tea and went into business mode. "How can I help you today?"

I checked the first item off my mental daily to-do list: communicate with parental units. Nice chatting with you. Let's do it again tomorrow.

I made it to within half a block of the bus stop when I heard the birdcalls start behind me. Zane. My shoulders tensed. I wanted to punch him. Just pull back my fist and let it fly. I could already hear the crunching of the cartilage as my fist connected with his nose.

"Hey, Tweety!" he hollered. "Haven't seen much of you this week. How's it hanging, my little birdie friend?"

Little old Mrs. Richards was already in line for the bus. It was sad, absolutely pathetic, but I went directly to her side. Zane was a jackass, but he never harassed anyone in front of adults and he never harassed adults. One of the Minions made a rude comment to Mrs. Richards once and Zane smacked him hard on the back of the head as soon as Mrs. Richards' back was turned. A bully with standards. The world gets a little shinier every day.

"Good morning, Robin," Mrs. Richards greeted me. She cocked her head to one side and gave me a scrutinizing look. "You look different. What is it?" More scrutiny. "I know! You've got a little gleam in your eye." She nudged me with her elbow and whispered, "Is it a girl?"

She nodded at something behind me. I turned to see Brianna a block away. My face went hot.

"Only in my dreams," I said quietly, hoping she'd follow my lead. Mrs. Richards had a really loud voice. Zane and The Minions had to be hearing every word she said.

"Nonsense," Mrs. Richards said. "I notice the way you look at her."

"Yes, ma'am, but she's not interested in me."

"Oh, don't be so sure." She gave me a little wink that made me laugh and wonder if she had a sixth sense she hadn't told me about. "If it's not our Miss Brianna, what is putting the bounce in your step?"

"Well, I tested into a higher level math class."

"Goodness, such a smart boy," she said. "That's not it though. What else?"

"I made some new friends," I admitted. Why was it so much easier to talk to Mrs. Richards than my own parents? I met the Lunch Bunch on Tuesday. It was Friday and I still hadn't mentioned any of them to Mom or Dad.

"New friends," she confirmed with a head nod. "That will do it every time."

The bus pulled up to the stop then. I held my hand out for Mrs. Richards to get on first and glanced over my shoulder. Brianna had to run the last half-block. She laughed the entire way. That was Brianna, always happy.

I scanned my bus pass and started the hunt for a seat. Mrs. Richards had saved one next to her for me. Why not? I'd already proven I was willing to use a little old lady as a bully shield.

Mrs. Richards told me about her upcoming day: a doctor's appointment, an eye appointment, and then lunch with her daughter.

"Sad to say that doctors' appointments are a highlight," she said, "but they get me out of the house."

"Lunch should be nice though," I said.

"It should be, as long as she doesn't bring the little one. What a whiner."

I looked at her in shock. What kind of grandmother talked about a grandchild that way?

"Oh," she said, "not my grandson. He's a little dolly. I mean that dog of hers. Whiny, yippy, annoying little thing. Dogs shouldn't be allowed in restaurants. This is my stop. Have a grand day, Master Robin."

"You too, Mrs. Richards."

I'd survived another morning without major incident. Brianna was sitting next to Zane this morning though. That was almost like harassment. She was on the inside seat next to the windows. He was turned to face her, one arm on the back of their seat, the other holding the seatback in front of them. She was trapped.

I imagined charging back there and demanding he let her go. I'd challenge him to a duel if necessary. That, actually, was something I could do. Math camp also offered fencing classes.

Idiot. She got on last. She chose the inside seat.

I tried not to look but every time she laughed my eyes shot directly to her. Watching her sit there talking and laughing with him was like a fencing foil to my heart. Watching him tuck a strand of hair behind her shoulder made me want to jab that foil into his heart. Longest bus ride ever.

At school, classes were uneventful, except for science. Brianna distracted me the entire period. Not that she purposely did anything. She had this habit of twirling her pencil between her fingers. I don't know how she did it without dropping it. I tried it at home and the pencil flew out of my hand, bounced off my computer monitor, and landed in my glass of milk. The twirling mesmerized me. She had little hands but long fingers. I imagined her running those fingers through my hair—another reason to not get a haircut—and then down my chest towards my…

Ms. Rolfing asked me a question then, which I had to ask her to repeat.

Okay. Maybe I should take that test and transfer. Except that meant three weeks of lessons to catch up on. What a nightmare. I wouldn't have any time for my game.

At lunch the topic, as it had been all week, was my game.

"I finally figured out the pixilation problem," I told the Bunch. "I was up until two in the morning but everything looks good now."

"What was the problem?" Pranav asked.

A wave of embarrassment washed over me. I stared at my chicken nuggets as I said, "I had the bit rate set too high."

"Seriously?" Tabatha laughed and shot Ivan a look that said I was a moron.

"That was the *last* thing you checked?" Ivan said, reveling with Tabatha at my stupidity. "That's like the most obvious thing."

"I know," I said. "I guess sometimes the most obvious is the last thing you'd expect."

"Might be the last thing *you'd* expect," Ivan said while polishing an apple on his sleeve. "I always start with the easiest item on the list."

"Lesson learned," I said, putting my hands up in surrender.

"On to a new topic," Ivan said.

"Tell us more about the game," Jeremiah interrupted him.

Ivan cleared his throat loudly and Tabatha smacked Jeremiah's arm.

"What?" Jeremiah asked. "I want to hear more about how to play. We haven't talked about that yet. We've been analyzing design problems all week."

"Yes, we have," Ivan said, his jaw clenched.

Pranav shook his head and dug around in the chicken curry he brought from home. Emily, the pacifist, sat with wide eyes, silently looking from one to another of us. Tabatha crossed her arms and stared at me like I was clueless, but I didn't get it. What did I do? Jeremiah kept pushing me for more details and that's all I'd been doing, giving him details.

After a few uncomfortable seconds, Ivan sighed and held a hand out in a *go ahead* gesture.

"We can talk about this later," I told Jeremiah.

"Robin," Ivan snapped, "say what you gotta say."

It was like an invitation and warning in one. This was ridiculous. Was there some rule I didn't know about that stated we could only talk about one thing at a time?

"You leave the hospital," I said, "and have to get to the airport. I set it in Chicago, so you can pay a cab, but you only get minimal points for that. You can sneak onto the 'L' train, the elevated trains—"

"We have those here," Ivan said.

"Yeah, but they're called light rail here," I said. "Anyway, you catch an 'L' to O'Hare airport. Sneaking onto the 'L' is a higher risk level so you get more points. Or you can take a cab and then run without paying. Cabbies tend to be crabby and some carry guns so that's the highest risk and the highest point value."

Jeremiah nodded, over and over like his head was on a spring. Then he settled back with his arms crossed over his big belly and closed his eyes. "Cool. Keep going."

"You bored already, big guy?" Ivan asked. "You gonna fall asleep?"

"No, I'm not going to fall asleep. I'm envisioning the game. Go on, Bird Man." Eyes still closed, Jeremiah patted for his French fries, grabbed three, and tossed them in his mouth.

Tweety. Tweety Puke. Fly Boy, although that never really took hold. Insig, as in some unknown superhero's insignificant sidekick, was the favorite in Wisconsin. No one had ever called me Bird Man before. As though it was cool. I liked it.

"So once you're at the airport," I said, cutting Ivan off from whatever he was about to say. "Sorry. Let me just explain a few things quick. You have to get through TSA and on a plane. There are different ways with different point values there, too. You fly to South America and have to find transportation to this base camp that this group of scientists has sent up. You can convince someone to give you a ride, stow away in a Jeep, or steal a Jeep. Again, different point values for whichever option you choose."

"What," Ivan asked, "no bad guys?"

"Of course there are," I said, surprised by the question that should have been obvious. "I told you before, the pharmaceutical people are after you. Remember? They know what you're up to and they don't want you to find that flower."

Ivan sat back and glared at me. Sorry, but where's the excitement if there wasn't an antagonist?

"Once at the site," I continued, "you can follow the scientists to the spot where they're searching for the flower and go it alone or team up with them." The five-minute bell sounded. I hadn't touched my lunch yet so I quickly took a huge bite of my burger. "If you're going it alone you have to find supplies. Then while you're trudging through the jungle there are animals trying to attack you and pharma dudes shooting at you."

"Eat your lunch before you choke," Jeremiah said. "It sounds like a cool game. I'll be a beta tester if you want one."

"That would be great," I said through another bite of burger.

"Gross, Robin," Tabatha said. "Didn't your parents teach you any table manners?"

Ivan stood and shoved his chair into the guy behind him.

"Watch it, jackass," the guy said.

Ivan flipped him off and stomped away.

"What's his problem?" I asked.

"He wanted to tell us about this new monitor he's got his eye on," Pranav said. "And you took over."

"I didn't take over. If Ivan wanted to tell you guys about his monitor, why didn't he just tell you? Or is there a rule that only one of us can have the conch at a time?"

"What are you talking about?" Pranav asked.

"Nothing," I said. Guess they hadn't been forced to read *Lord of the Flies* in middle school. "Jeremiah asked about the game, so I told him. That's it."

"Dude, you talk about your game every day," Tabatha groaned and rolled her eyes. "Today you didn't stop talking long enough to even eat your lunch."

"The game sounds really cool," Emily said, placing a placating hand on my arm. "But maybe we should talk about something else."

Everyone scattered, leaving just me and Jeremiah.

"Did I do something wrong?" I asked.

"Nope," Jeremiah said. "If you haven't noticed, Ivan thinks he's our leader. Like we need a leader. Guess I could've stopped asking questions, but your game sounds cool. Besides, it was fun watching Ivan get silenced for once. No, the only thing you did wrong, my friend, was intimidate him."

"Me?" He could have said I'd just been nominated King of the World and I wouldn't be more surprised. I'd never intimidated anyone in my life.

"True statement. He never sits back and lets someone else talk when there's something he wants to say. I think the group is in shock. I, on the other hand, am amused."

"What should I do?"

"Keep being yourself, Bird Man. I got no problems with you."

Great as it was to have Jeremiah on my side, I wasn't sure his advice was solid. In French, Pranav completely ignored me. Punishing me for what must've seemed like a mini-coup but was just me being excited to have people to talk to.

Things had been going so well. Then again, the odds of me having a good day or even two were high. Luck had to swing my way at some point. Maybe that's all this week had been. The one good one after years of none.

☮ ☮ ☮

There's chicken cordon bleu in the freezer. Pop it in around 6:15 for me? Or you can order a pizza. Mom had left a sticky note and a twenty-dollar-bill on the refrigerator door, the message center in our house.

Chicken sounded good. I set a 6:15 reminder on my phone and went up to my room to study. Mom had converted the empty space over the garage into her office and I could hear her on the phone, talking about a marketing plan for a bakery. That meant we'd probably start getting regular deliveries of breads and baked goods, one of the perks of working with customers in the food industry. This was why we had really good chicken cordon bleu in the freezer.

I closed my door, sat at my desk, and turned on my computer. My *Pharm Runner* game was still on the screen. I could have sworn I turned it off before going to bed last night.

The stone that Dara had given me, the one with the partial peace sign carved into it, sat on my desk between my desk lamp and a UW-Madison mug filled with pens. She said I could summon her if I needed to talk.

I held the stone by its edges and checked it over again. It was just an emerald-green rock, nothing spectacular. The chances of this stone having any magical capabilities were slim to zero. To test this belief, I placed my thumb over the circle.

Two blinks later, my laptop pinged and Dara appeared. Her eyes sparkled, as bright as her smile.

"Hey, Robin! How's it going?"

"Could be better." I held up the stone to the laptop's camera. "This thing is just a pager or something isn't it? I thought summon meant you'd actually appear."

Another two blinks later, Dara was standing in my bedroom. She seemed distracted, like there was something else she'd rather be doing.

"Did I bother you?" I asked.

"Not really," she said. "I was teaching some of the other Guides how to use their new tablets. What's up?"

I told her about how things had been going really well and then came lunch today.

"You need to step it back." She smoothed out my comforter and had a seat. "It's awesome that you have new friends and I know you're excited to have computer people in your world, but you can't talk about yourself all the time."

"I don't."

She nodded and winced. "You kind of do."

"What am I supposed to do?" I asked, feeling frustrated. "I thought friends share."

"That's it exactly," Dara said, twirling a lock of hair around her finger. "You're not sharing, you're dominating. You have to be a friend to make a friend. Talk a little about you, then ask them about what they're doing, and let them talk."

"But Jeremiah—"

"Dude," Dara said, holding up a hand in stop position. "I don't make the rules. I'm just telling you that if you don't back off they'll get tired of you."

Honestly, I hadn't had a real friend since fifth grade. After the Cole incident, I never got invited to anyone's house or birthday party again. Not only had I forgotten how to be a friend, I was the most socially awkward person I knew. Put me in a gamers' or programming chat room and I could hold my own just fine. Put me face to face with actual people, I collapsed.

"Be a friend to make a friend?" I asked.

Dara nodded.

"How do I do that?"

She laughed like I was joking then realized, probably from the frustrated tears filling my eyes, that I wasn't. She frowned and her voice softened. "You really don't know, do you?"

I shook my head.

"Well, you're partway there already," she said with a bright smile. "You found people who like what you like. You've proven that you can be one of them."

"I went too far."

"Yeah." She wrinkled her nose when she said that. It was kind of cute. "So on Monday when you get there, just listen. Sit down with your lunch tray, say hi, and then listen. If someone asks you a question, answer it but don't go on and on with details. They'll ask if they want to know more."

"That's it?" There had to be more to it. Then again, that's exactly what Mom said about how to win a client.

"That's it. You can laugh at their jokes, that's always

good. You can complain about a teacher or the amount of homework you have. But keep it short. Don't hog the conversation. No matter how excited you are about something." She kicked the toe of my shoe with hers. "Do you think you can do that?"

"I think I can."

"Great." She came over to my desk then and motioned for me to get out of my chair. When I did, she sat and started playing around on my computer. "I knew you were a gamer. Sweet setup."

It was a sweet setup. It had taken me years of birthdays and Christmases, odd-jobs for the neighbors, and saving my allowance to get it. There were three twenty-four-inch monitors side-by-side to give me a miniature IMAX feel. Speakers perched on the corners of my gray-glass desk provided surround-sound audio affects. My headphones, keyboard, and mouse were top-rated in the gaming world. I had a desktop computer, my prized possession, for developing and playing and a cheaper laptop for email and homework. I couldn't ask for much more really.

"Thanks," I said. "I like designing more than playing."

"Cool. I do a little of that myself."

"You do?"

"I do," she said. "I'm sort of technology freak. That's why I get to train the Guides on the tablets."

Never would have pegged Dara as a techie.

"It's easy to get lost in the cyber world sometimes, isn't it?" she asked.

"Yeah. Get lost, forget about the rest of the world and whatever is bothering you."

Dara nodded then held one hand over my mouse and the other over my headset.

"What are you doing?" I asked.

"A little favor for a fellow geek." At my panicked expression she said, "Chill, dude. I just upgraded your software. Made it a little more responsive I guess you could say. Now you can design like the big boys." She stood and took out her phone. "Give me your number."

"Why?"

"In case I'm busy. I can text you right away and come see you when I'm not busy. Cool?"

"Sounds fair."

I liked that she was here with me. It was nice talking face-to-face with her. Still, I gave her my phone number and she tested it by sending: *Feeling better now?*

I texted her back: *Yeah. Thanks.*

"Hang in there," she said. "These things take a while. You're on the right path though."

Chapter Nine

Desiree

Dozens and sometimes hundreds of wishes came in every day. As I went through and assigned them to the Guides, I thought a lot about Kaf and wondered how he chose the pairings he did. I didn't know how methodical he'd been with everyone else, but he very specifically chose which wishes to give me. It was all a part of my own wish. Some of the charges given to me were intended to force me to deal with mistakes I'd made and move past them.

That's what Mandy's and Crissy's wishes were supposed to do. At the end of Crissy's wish, when I was, supposedly, finally ready to accept my new life path, Kaf gave me the choice to move forward with my current life or go back to before I ran away from home and get a do over. I chose to move forward, but now I felt like something was missing.

Maybe I should have gone back. Since the day I agreed

to become a Guide, guilt gnawed at my insides because my parents never knew the truth about what happened to me. I started thinking more and more about that other option. Going back. If it had been possible for Kaf to send me back, maybe there was a way I could send myself.

I stayed up each night until I was bleary-eyed, scouring Kaf's compendium for clues. He'd left notes throughout the book, details about everything that had anything to do with wishes.

It wasn't witchcraft, this thing we did. It didn't involve spells or herbs or eyes of newts. It was us connecting with the universe and using the natural energy around us to get the results we wanted. The only difference between Guides and non-magical humans, was that the universe bestowed us with the ability to use that energy. I decided to call it I&R: Imagine and Request. Manifesting was simply the ability to imagine an object and then request that it appear. Transporting was the ability to imagine oneself somewhere and then request that the universe place you there.

This was why it didn't work on emotions. Emotion wasn't an object that could be manifested or a place to be transported to. I couldn't make Kaf fall in love with me. I couldn't make myself fall out of love with him.

"Whatcha doing?"

I looked up from the compendium to see Dara standing in the cabin doorway. She was bouncing in place which told me she was bored. Eager to be entertained.

"I'm looking for a... spell."

"I thought we didn't do spells," Dara said, dropping onto one of the chairs.

"We don't," I said, flipping through compendium pages for the hundredth time. "I'm not sure what else to call it. A rule maybe? That's basically what we do. We follow the rules of nature and the universe but in a way that normal people can't."

"So anyway," Dara said with a sigh. I was boring her.

Again.

"When my wish was coming to its end," I said, "Kaf gave me two choices. I could move forward or I could go back. That meant he could either send or take me. Now that I've got his powers, I'm trying to figure out a way to send myself back."

"You mean to 1929?"

"I'm a hippie, Dara, not a flapper. It's 1969, not '29."

"Wait. You want to time travel? Oh, that would be so cool. Can I come?"

"I don't even know if I can go," I said. "I'm trying to figure out the rules and the closest I've gotten is that I think time travel is similar to transporting. But instead of focusing on a place, I need to focus on a place in time."

That part would be easy. I could imagine the bedroom I shared with my sister down to the last detail. I could picture the tree in the park down the street from our house where Glenn and I used to sit. I could go to Glenn's house or to my high school. So many options.

I slammed the compendium shut in frustration. I'd been scouring it for hours and hadn't found anything concrete. "The rule has to be in this book."

"Do you want me to help you look for it?" Dara asked.

She *was* bored. Looking for a specific rule in this book was like looking for a particular hippie at Woodstock. They were everywhere and all kind of looked the same.

Dara took the compendium from me and placed it in her lap. She flipped a page. Then another.

"There's nothing in here," she said.

"What do you mean? Of course there is."

"The pages are all blank." She held up the open book as proof.

"For your eyes only, Desiree." Indira said as she walked in. "Only she who is in charge can see the script."

"Can you see anything?" Dara asked, holding the open book to her.

"I could while I was filling in for Desiree but not anymore," Indira said. "And I can no longer remember what I saw when I could."

"And you're my second in command?" I asked.

"I know what I need to know in order to help you," Indira said calmly.

"Is that a Kaf rule or a universal one?" I rubbed my aching eyes. I was tired of rules. What was wrong with everyone having what they needed, when they needed it? Free exchange of knowledge. That should definitely be a rule.

"What are you trying to find?" Indira asked.

Suddenly, I felt embarrassed. "A way to get back to 1969."

"You're not happy here?" she asked, a taunting smile played at her mouth. She knew how uncomfortable I was being in charge.

"At one point," I said, "going back was an option for me. I'm trying to figure out if it's still possible."

"Kaf presented this option?" Indira asked.

I nodded.

"He didn't explain the consequences, did he?" she sat in the chair next to Dara's.

Consequences? My heart sank. Of course there were consequences.

"If you can figure out how to do this," Indira said, "it's a one-way trip."

"So I can't come back." I'd guessed that when he made the offer.

"It's not like a vacation," Indira said. "You can't go visit and be back in time for dinner. Kaf could have sent you, but my understanding is that it takes years of practice to even go back a few minutes in time."

And really, there was no guarantee that anything would be different if I did go. Maybe I'd get to live the life I'd always wanted. College, a career, and Glenn. I wasn't positive we could change our destinies. It was very possible that if I did go back I'd live my life the exact same way and end up right where I was now. That's part of the reason I wanted to go back, to see if that theory was true. If this was the life I was destined for, nothing I did would change the finish line.

Was that the truth for our charges, too? Did we grant a wish and really change a life? Or was the wish a detour on the journey and they'd ultimately end up where they'd already been headed? If the latter was true, what was the point of the wishes?

"I'm sorry," Indira said.

"You're only delivering the truth," I said. "Do you supposed Kaf would have explained that part to me if I'd chosen to go back?"

"The real question is," Indira said, "would you still have chosen the path you did once you knew?"

"Stop, please," I said and put my hands over my ears. "My head's going to implode."

So that was that. Running away, again, wasn't an option. Whatever bit was missing from my life I'd have to fill it in by going forward, not back.

"I'm leaving to attend to the requests I've received," Indira said. "I'm going to stay in my *vardo* so I won't be back for a few days."

A little twinge of jealousy ran through me, but had no idea why. I'd spent plenty of time alone in the past forty-five years so it wasn't that she was getting away. In fact, if I was being honest, I was starting to enjoy being around the Guides. Well, the ones that were okay with me being the boss. So what *was* I jealous of?

"Do good," I said. "Enjoy your solitude."

"Thank you," she said and gave me a respectful little bow. She tapped on her tablet and a moment later I received a message that 'Indira is unavailable until further notice.'

Adellika appeared at my doorway. She found someone

right away who wanted to trade rooms. Her feng shui was back in balance, and she was a happy Guide again.

"I am sorry to interrupt," she said with the same kind of respectful little bow Indira had given me. "I have a question."

I liked the bows. Maybe I'd implement bowing as a Desiree rule.

"Come on in, Adellika." She always insisted on standing on the front porch until I gave her permission. Even vampires only needed one invitation. "What's your question?"

"I do not understand." Adellika held up her tablet which she had covered in beautiful Oriental white silk with pink cherry blossoms all over it. "I have *played with it*, as you instructed, but I still do not understand how it works."

"I can help," Dara said, jumping to her feet.

"Hang on," I said. "Dara, we need a short conference."

"I will wait outside," Adellika said and bowed out the door.

"I wanted to check in with you about Robin," I said. "It looks like things have started out well with him."

"You've been watching?" Dara asked, offended.

"I have to. Especially with your first charge," I said. "He had a good day at school today."

"Did he?"

"See?" I said, stretching my neck side-to-side. "This is why I watch. You have to check in on him throughout the day."

"But you said the wish is supposed to follow its own path."

"It is. But you need to know what's happening."

"Why? It's not like I can do anything if there's a problem."

When Dara got pouty like this I was tempted to take over Robin's wish myself. There were a few wishes I wanted to take over, actually. They intrigued me and honestly, I missed guiding.

"Don't you care about him?" I asked. "If he summons

you, how can you advise him if you don't know what's been going on?"

"So I have to sit and watch him all day?" she asked.

"No, that's why I provided tablets. Just check in on him now and then. Guiding him is your job. This is one of the job's tasks."

She crossed her arms and slumped back in the chair. "Fine. But for the record, being a Guide isn't anywhere near as cool as I thought it would be."

Patience, grasshopper, I wanted to say. As her empathy grew, so would the cool factor.

"What's he doing right now?" I asked.

Dara tapped on her screen and brought up an image of Robin, sitting at his desk in his bedroom. "Homework."

"And now you know. See? That took about five seconds."

"Great. Can I go now?" Dara asked as though I'd been doling out a punishment instead of words of advice.

"Go," I said. "Help Adellika."

She sprang up and darted out the door before I'd finished talking.

I touched my finger and thumb together and my door closed with a soft *click*. The Guides knew, if my door was closed I was probably assigning wishes and they should only interrupt me if it was a true emergency.

More than a hundred wishes had come in since yesterday. Like a cowgirl corralling her herd, I directed the swirling, tie-dyed auroras surrounding me to the wall of windows. Each window was made up of small panes. Images of the wishers appeared on the panes as though they were televisions or computer monitors.

If only the universe would presort. Even though there was no way for me to make people fall in love, those wishes still came to me. Even though I couldn't make people become best friends, those wishes came to me, too.

I felt bad every time I had to deny someone. So I did

something special for him or her instead. Maybe that day they hit all the lights green. (Or red, if that was better.) Maybe they found a ten dollar bill on the street. Maybe the bakery was serving their favorite cupcake.

I tapped on the picture in the top left-hand pane and a woman appeared. Her father had died the night before and she desperately wanted him back. Her grief nearly tore my heart in two. Bringing him back was possible, but like time travel it had dire consequences. Once her father died, the bit that made him him—his soul or spirit, I guess—was gone. If I brought him back, he wouldn't be the dad she remembered. Maybe the spirit goes to an eternal place of rest. Maybe it goes to somewhere and waits to come back to live another life. I didn't know that answer. I wouldn't until I died. I just knew that while I could reanimate the body, the part of her dad that she longed for most wouldn't be there anymore.

What I could do for her was allow her to find a letter her dad had written her a few days before he went into the hospital. In it, he told her how much being her father had meant to him. How proud he had always been of her and how very much he loved her. He didn't realize the letter had slid off the kitchen counter and under the refrigerator.

I focused my thoughts on the refrigerator, the power cord in particular. I sent a surge of energy through the cord, causing the electricity to arc and the motor to burn out. The woman was putting his house up for sale and would be angry that, on top of everything else, she had to buy a new refrigerator. But when they moved the old one out, she'd find that letter and her heart would find a little peace.

I placed my hand on her picture and sent healing thoughts to her. Then I swiped the picture off of the pane and sent her wish back into the universe.

Chapter Ten

Robin

There was definite tension with the Lunch Bunch after Ivan's explosion. I felt like I'd been knocked back down a few rungs on the acceptance ladder. Not so much from Jeremiah and Emily, but the others were obviously giving me the cold shoulder. I followed Dara's 'be a friend to make a friend' advice and only talked about my game if someone asked. *Someone* almost always meant Jeremiah. I did my best to keep my answers short and then sit back and listen to the rest of the group. But Jeremiah kept asking questions.

"You should come over sometime," I said, uncomfortably aware of the lasers shooting out of Ivan's eyes at me. It would be awesome for Jeremiah to come over, but at that moment I was just trying to deflect attention away from me. "I can show you how the software works and you can give the game a try."

"Tonight?" Jeremiah asked, taking his phone out. "I'll send my mom a text and let her know to pick me up at your house."

It hit me then, Jeremiah might be about as desperate for a friend as I was.

"Me, too," Emily said. "I'd love to see your game."

"Okay. Sure," I said. "My mom works from home. We'll need to keep quiet so we don't bother her."

Ivan, Tabatha, and Pranav exchanged annoyed glances with each other and a rift forming in the group was undeniable. I was in danger of getting knocked down another rung.

"You all can come," I said, trying to smooth things over.

Pranav wanted nothing to do with it and said no practically before I'd finished asking.

"But you like tearing things apart," Tabatha reminded him.

He relented, but when Ivan said he wasn't coming because he had, "...more important things to do than play a video game," Tabatha's face fell.

"You mean like Computer Euphoria?" I asked him.

The lunch topic for the last couple of days had been about a new chatroom he found. He talked about it like it was the best place ever to find people who "know what the hell they're talking about." Ivan insisted every teacher in the school was an idiot—even Miss Clark, I kept my mouth shut—and that if we wanted to learn anything we needed to rely on sources other than high school.

"You check it out yet?" Ivan asked me.

"Nope," I said. "Haven't had the time. Too busy playing games."

Damn it. The words had left my mouth and there was no way to take them back. That was what happened when a social misfit tried to stand up for himself. He ended up sounding like an instigating smartass.

"This from the genius who didn't think to check his bit

rate." Ivan smiled. His tone was light and his words seemed to say, *look at us, playing with each other*. But his normally bright blue eyes had turned cold and icy.

Pranav and Tabatha laughed. Pranav even held out a fist for a bump, which Ivan ignored so he offered it to Tabatha. She ignored it, too. Jeremiah and Emily turned away, like they didn't want to get any of the aftermath on them.

Ivan leaned across the table and shoved my lunch tray toward me so far it almost tipped into my lap.

"For future reference, you shouldn't talk about something if you don't know anything about it," he said, defending his chatroom.

"Good advice for anyone. Even you," I said, not breaking eye contact with him.

What was wrong with me? What was I trying to prove with this act of bravery that I didn't remotely feel? I had no real issues with Ivan, but he was the leader of the Lunch Bunch. The position was self-appointed but still, if I wanted to stay in the group even I, moron that I clearly was, knew that meant I had to stay on his good side. And I really did want to stay.

"I'd like to get your input on the game so far," I said, offering a proverbial olive branch.

Slowly, Ivan's glare softened and he pulled the tray out of my chest. "Sorry. Got a little on you."

I looked down and saw a ketchup splotch, a perfect red circle about the size of a dime, in the middle of my chest.

"No worries. I hate this shirt anyway." I laughed. It came out sounding nervous and submissive.

Ivan leaned back in his chair. "Like I said, I got something goin' on tonight. Not Computer Euphoria." He looked at each member of the group in turn, holding their gaze before moving on to the next. "Thanks for the invite. You can all give me a report about Bird Man's game tomorrow."

Where Jeremiah's 'Bird Man' was fun, Ivan's held

muscle and malice. *Remember who you are*, it said.

Before leaving school I sent my mom a text: *Bringing some friends over.*

Mom: *I'm working.*

Me: *They just want to see my game. We won't bother you.*

Mom: *Thanks for the warning.*

I had no idea when I'd last brought a friend over. If I had to guess I'd say fifth grade. I thought maybe she'd recognize that.

That afternoon Jeremiah, Emily, Tabatha, and Pranav rode the bus with me. Funny, I assumed a group would be a better shield than tiny, old Mrs. Richards. When The Minions started talking about the pack of freaks, though, instead of banding together The Bunch divided. I recognized myself in their reactions. Pranav took out his phone and stared at the screen like the secrets of the universe were being revealed there. Tabatha leaned back, looking bored and picking at her already-chipped manicure. Emily dug around in her bag. Only Jeremiah sat with his head high. There were five of us and three of them. Why didn't we stand united?

We got to my house and went in the backdoor, straight into the kitchen, and found a spread of snacks laid out on the kitchen counter: crackers with meats and cheeses, fruits and veggies with dip, different drinks in a huge bowl of ice, and a plate of still-warm chocolate chip cookies.

"Wow," Emily said. "Housekeeper?"

Housekeeper? Was it standard around here for people to have housekeepers? Did my parents know that? If it was and they did, we'd have help soon.

"No," I said, "my mom likes to feed people."

It looked like a big deal, but we always had a stock of cut up stuff on hand. Mom ordered it from one of her customers. When clients came over, she wanted to be able to offer them something quickly. The cookie dough was frozen in little blobs so they baked while she put everything else on trays. Not as impressive as it appeared once you knew what went on behind the scenes.

We each filled a plate with food, grabbed a drink, and headed up to my room. I stopped them at the door because I knew there was a week's worth of underwear lying on the floor by my bed.

"Give me two seconds," I said.

While the Bunch stood outside harassing me to hurry up, I shoved all my dirty clothes into the closet and straightened the blankets on my bed. Good enough.

By the time I opened the door, Jeremiah had already cleaned his generously-filled plate. In the two short weeks that I'd been part of the group, I'd discovered that when Jeremiah was hungry, watching him eat was like watching an anaconda unhinge its jaw and swallow its prey whole. Not pretty, but so fascinating you couldn't look away.

"Are we locked and loaded?" Jeremiah asked and headed straight for my desk. He took over my chair and I'd be lying if I said I wasn't worried about it being able to support him. He wiggled my mouse and the screen saver dissolved to show the game indeed locked, loaded, and ready for analysis.

It felt strange for all of us to be together outside of school this way. There, even though there were times like today when things got tense between us, we existed in a bubble of commonality. Away from school, it was like we didn't *need* each other and became five individuals again.

We gathered around to watch while Jeremiah played. I took notes on the things he felt needed tweaking. Everyone else made comments on what they thought was cool and what wasn't. Well, Tabatha didn't point out anything cool, only things that were "lame-ass" or "in need of immediate axing." I was sure that every one of those *lame-ass* things would be in her report to Ivan tomorrow. They'd have a good laugh at my expense. I was sure that's why Tabatha and Pranav came. To run reconnaissance for Ivan.

They all stayed for a couple of hours, Jeremiah eventually let the rest of them have a try, and then parents started calling or texting that they were on the way for pick-ups.

"It doesn't completely suck," Pranav said.

High praise from the guy who had barely looked me in the eye since Ivan had blown up at me a few days earlier.

Emily didn't play games, but was into graphics big time and said, "Looks fine to me."

Tabatha reminded me what things did suck and needed fixing.

"Thanks for letting me check it out," Jeremiah said. "I think you could do good things with that game."

"Meaning..?" I asked, confused.

"Meaning it still needs work but after some tweaks you might be able to make a few dollars with it."

"God, don't say that too loud," I said. "My dad might hear."

After they left, Mom stopped working and came to my room. Normally she didn't emerge from her office until seven or eight o'clock.

"How'd it go?" she asked.

"Fine," I said.

"You said in your text these were friends? Not just classmates coming over to work on a project?" Like that would be the only reason a group of people would come home with me.

"Yep."

"You didn't tell me you made new friends."

Our fifteen minutes at breakfast every morning didn't leave a lot of time to catch her up on every aspect of my life.

"Yeah. I sat at their table one day at lunch. Turns out they're all geeks like me."

"You're not a geek."

"I am a geek, Mom. It's not a bad thing. It means we're smart and a little obsessed with computers and grades and stuff."

"A little obsessed?" She raised her eyebrows in question. "What did they think of your game?"

"They liked it." I gave her a few details then said, "Jeremiah thinks people might buy it."

"That's nice." She said, distracted by something on her phone.

"I've got homework to do now," I said, giving her an out.

She took it. "Oh. Okay. I should get back to my proposal."

☮ ☮ ☮

The lunch vibe was different. Not just because Ivan was, once again, dominating the conversation, but also the topic wasn't about anything remotely close to computers, science, math or anything else geeky.

"I can't believe we're talking about the homecoming dance," I said.

"I can't believe Ivan's playing matchmaker," Jeremiah said.

"Hey, I believe in love as much as the next guy," Ivan said. "Besides do you have any idea how much money there is to be made in romance?"

"Money?" I asked. "How?"

"He's setting up people who can't get date," Tabatha said.

"No, I'm pairing up people who don't have a date," Ivan said.

"Same difference," Tabatha said.

"It is not," Ivan said. "Can't get a date implies you're a loser. Don't have a date could mean you're just too shy to ask. It's all in the marketing and that's the genius of, well, me." Ivan did jazz hands by his face. Tabatha added her own jazz hands behind him. "I'm keeping track of who has a date, who they're going with, and who doesn't have a date yet. I've got a database."

He opened his laptop to show me a massive spreadsheet. One tab for each class. The basic info—name, address, email, phone number—he got from the school directory. Then he adds things like gender and interests. If someone already had a date he highlighted them in green.

"He started doing this two years ago," Emily said. "So he just has to add freshmen and new students each year."

"I also keep track of the dates and if they went well or not," Ivan said, clicking around the screen. "Don't want to set anyone up with an ex."

"So where does the money part come in?" I asked.

"I charge for my services," Ivan said. "For twenty-five dollars I'll provide the names of five people who appear to be a good match and don't already have a date. For fifty I'll actually contact the desired person to see if he or she is interested."

"And people really pay for this?" I asked.

He showed me another tab with the amount of money he brought in for this dance alone.

"You are a genius," I said, holding my fist out to him.

"Just this morning," he said, bumping my fist, "I connected Vince with Phillip and Stephanie with Eric. Our little lunch group hasn't enlisted my services yet."

"Not interested," Jeremiah said. "The last thing I care about is a school dance."

Ivan rolled his eyes. "I just haven't found you the right girl yet." He pointed at each of us in turn. "Tell me about your soulmates."

He positioned his hands on the keyboard, ready to add notes to his database.

Emily blushed from her forehead to her neck and took out study notes for her next class.

"I want someone who isn't interested in dances," Tabatha said and ran her hand seductively across Jeremiah's shoulder. Then she burst out laughing.

Jeremiah's expression didn't change. Not interested.

I, of course, knew who my soulmate was. Brianna had just walked past and stopped at a table three down from ours. I could see her, talking to someone. She pulled her hair around and over her shoulder then threw her head back and laughed.

I imagined her pulling her hair to the side that way and asking me to either clasp a necklace for her or help her with her zipper. Suddenly there was a hand in front of my face. I turned to see Emily grinning at me.

"I think I know who he wants to go with," Emily teased.

"I'm on it," Ivan said.

"Yeah right," I said. "The chances of you getting Brianna to agree to go to the dance with me are less than impossible."

"But you do want to go with her," Ivan said.

"I'd give my left nut to go anywhere with Brianna," I said.

Ivan snorted.

Pranav said, "Dude."

Emily and Tabatha looked at each other and burst into giggles.

"Oh man," Jeremiah said and shook his head.

That's when I realized that not only had I said it out loud, I'd said it loud enough for the table next to us to hear me. The table where Minions Thad and Ben were sitting.

Shit.

They started laughing and punching each other. I could only imagine the hell ride I was in for on the bus tonight. Maybe I'd walk home. It was only five miles. Maybe I could get Dara to transport me. For the rest of the school year.

"I'm on it," Ivan said again.

"No," I said. "Please, just leave it alone."

"You like her?" Jeremiah asked.

I looked Brianna's way again. She was walking our way

now and as she passed us, she gave me a little finger wave.

"He likes her," Jeremiah said. "Set the Bird Man up, Ivan."

☮ ☮ ☮

As I expected, The Minions started in right away on the ride home. If Ivan could pull it off, though, the humiliation would be worth it.

"What would you give up a nut for?" Ben asked.

"A date with Brianna Hauser?" Wayne said.

"I wouldn't even need a date with her," Thad said. "All she'd have to do is sit next to me and let me know that I wasn't the world's biggest loser, just an average loser. That would totally be worth giving up my leftie for."

Loudly, so the whole bus could hear, they kept listing all of the things they'd give up a nut for.

Finally one of the passengers said, "That's enough now."

"But you don't know the whole story," Wayne said.

By the time Thad had recounted every agonizing detail of me firmly inserting my foot into my mouth, the entire bus was laughing along with them.

Of course that's when I realized Brianna was on the bus that afternoon, too. I'd almost missed it so had to run to get on. I was a little flustered so hadn't seen her sitting there with another girl. While everyone else rejoiced in my stupidity, the two of them kept looking over at me, whispering behind their hands, and bursting out with laughter. Things were finally calming down when one of the Minions, called out, "Peanuts."

Another said, "Walnuts."

The last said, "Filberts" and the hilarity started up again.

This would be all over the school by tomorrow. Who was I kidding? Lunch was three hours ago. The whole school already knew what I'd said. The frantic way Thad was tapping on his phone told me he was spreading the word of the bus ride live as it was happening.

"Sorry, Robin," Mr. Lacey, the bus driver, said when I stood next to him, waiting to get off at my stop. "For whatever my opinion is worth, it's better to stand up for yourself. Staying silent is the same as condoning."

"For the record, I didn't mean to say what I said." I wanted one person to know I wasn't a complete moron. "The words sort of slipped out and everyone overheard."

"Some days the world pisses on you," Mr. Lacey said. "Tomorrow will be better."

I laughed. "No it won't. Tomorrow I'll have new humiliation to face."

"Well, if it helps at all," he said, pulling the bus to the curb, "you are far from the first guy to make an ass out of himself over a girl. And you won't be the last."

He opened the door and I stepped out. "See you tomorrow, Mr. Lacey."

Brianna and her friend sped off ahead of me, still laughing and looking back at me every now and then. The Minions followed me, making birdcalls and still talking about different kinds of nuts. I walked faster, trying to get away from them. They kept up with me though.

"Screw this," I mumbled and decided to follow Mr. Lacey's advice. I turned to defend myself and the second I did, a camera flashed in my face.

Within an hour my picture with the caption "He'd give his leftie for you" was posted on every social media site imaginable.

Chapter Eleven

Robin

It turned out that more than one picture of me had been taken. Someone had snapped one of me staring at Brianna during lunch and put the caption 'I Dream of Nuts.' Another picture showed me sitting at the lunch table with 'Missing My Nuts' written across it. There were others. Many others and I saw all of them. I couldn't stop myself from looking. If people were going to be talking about me, I figured I should know what they were saying.

Brianna would probably never speak to me again. One, stupid comment and my dream of going out with her was dead. On top of that, I'd probably ruined her reputation. I mean, how humiliated must she be to know someone as lame as me was drooling over her.

"We're leaving now," my dad said as he stuck his head into my room.

"What?" I asked, looking up from my perch on my bed and closing my laptop. If he came closer I didn't want him to see the pictures of me. "Oh. Right. Your dinner thing."

Mom's new client was having a sampler dinner of all the new dishes on her menu. Mom requested that her clients do these types of events so she could get firsthand knowledge of the food and find out what the other guests thought of it. Then she'd start putting together promo packages and advertising campaigns. For this dinner, spouses were welcome but children needed to stay away.

"Mom needs to consult with her customer afterward so we'll probably be late," Dad said. His voice had grown quieter as he spoke. "Everything okay?"

He could tell something was wrong. He never looked closely at me, neither of them did, and he chose tonight, the worst night I'd had since we moved here, to do so. Maybe I should take it as a sign from *the universe* and tell him... what? That I'd made a fool of myself and was getting picked on?

"I'm fine. Just a lot to do."

A total lie. For the first time in a long time, I had nothing to do tonight. I'd finished my math homework as soon as I got home. I had a sketch due for art on Monday. I could work on that. Mom insisted I take art so I could, "Use both your intellectual and creative sides. A happy brain is a balanced brain."

I wasn't very good with pencil and paper, computer graphics was more my style, but sketching was a good way to disappear.

"If you're sure," Dad said as he stood in my doorway, waiting for my response.

If I told him that no, everything was about as far from okay as it could get, would he stay home and try to help? Not that he could do anything. Only a miracle could fix my problems. What I needed was to summon Dara.

"I'm sure." I forced a smile. "Go. Have a good time."

A few minutes later Mom paused outside my door and said goodbye, too distracted to notice that I could use her attention as much as her client did. Once I heard the garage door shut and the car drive away, I went to my desk. As soon as I wiggled my mouse, my game came up on the screen. Funny, I hadn't opened it yet today. Maybe this was what Dara meant by responsive. I didn't even have to click on anything and my computer knew what I wanted.

Jeremiah had found a problem in Level 3.2, the mid-point option that meant you had chosen to search the jungle yourself to find the flower. The problem on this level was with the guns you needed to fight of the dangerous jungle animals, and, of course, the pharmaceutical guys who were hunting you. The bullets fired the opposite direction of the laser.

It took me a couple of hours but I finally had it working right. To be sure, I played the level a few times. First, I had to sneak around the scientists' camp and steal supplies. Finally, with only a headlamp lighting my way, I was ready to run through the jungle. Growling, breathing, and movement that didn't come from me indicated animals were surrounding me. I heard every one of my own footsteps crunching through the undergrowth. It was so creepy. The sound of big fern leaves rustling together told me something was hiding in the vegetation about ten feet away.

Slowly, this odd-looking creature emerged. It looked mostly like a panther, black as the night, but instead of being sleek, it had bulging muscles. And, I swear, beneath that black fur it had Zane's face and short, curly hair shaved almost smooth on the sides of its head.

It crouched and a rumbling growl sounded in its chest. I... well, my avatar drew his gun. Without warning the Zanther leaped and I... my avatar fired. The bullet went straight and true and hit the Zanther right between the eyes. Its head exploded, bits of brain and pieces of skull flew everywhere. When my avatar wiped his hand over his face, it came away red with the Zanther's blood.

I sat back then and pulled off my headphones. It took a few blinks before the jungle around me faded away completely. This game had become so real, like nothing I'd ever played before. What the hell had Dara done to my computer? I swear it was like I really was my avatar, like I was inside the game actually wandering through an animated jungle. I could feel the jungle floor beneath my feet. I could hear the noises of the creatures scurrying unseen around me as surely as if they were right here in my room with me. I heard the rumbling growl of the Zanther. I felt its hot breath on my face when it leapt at me. I felt the weight of the gun in my hand and the reverberation when I fired it. I felt the hot blood and brain matter splatter me.

My stomach lurched like I might puke as the fact that I'd killed a living being hit me. Yes, a fictional creature in a video game, but it was so real. It really did feel like I had just killed something that looked like Zane.

Even more curious, I felt no remorse about it.

Maybe it was time for me to step away from the game for a while. I couldn't even guess at how many hours I'd spent working on it lately. It was like I was starting to merge with it and the fantasy of it was starting to affect my reality.

"Work on your art sketch instead," I told myself.

We were working on shading and depth. The goal was a 3-D image that the teacher could practically pick off the page. I opened my sketch pad, sharpened my pencil, grabbed an eraser, and stared at the white page. What to draw?

On the monitor, the screen still showed the last thing I'd done in the game. My avatar's hand was holding out the blood-splattered gun. That ought to cause a little commotion at school.

As I started to sketch, the image of me firing that gun at the Zanther started replaying in my head. Was I capable of that? If I was about to be attacked, could I fire if it meant my life or the creature's? What if it was a human?

Despite Dad's numerous requests, I'd only been to the range with him once. It was just before we moved the first time. Cole and the kids were relentless. I was having bad headaches and stomachaches. Dad thought that, as it did for him, pumping some rounds into a bale of hay would release some of my stress. The opposite happened. All I could think was that the bullets I'd just fired could have killed someone.

That was so long ago I couldn't remember anymore what a real gun felt like or how heavy they were.

I frowned at my sketch. If this sketch was going to look real, I needed to look at the real thing.

Dad never locked his guns up. Irresponsible, my mom said when I was little. But I wasn't little anymore. Still, Mom insisted he kept them unloaded despite his argument that an unloaded gun was useless if someone broke in.

"What am I supposed to say?" he asked every time she brought it up. "Excuse me a moment while I load my gun so I can defend myself?"

"Keep them unloaded," she said, "or locked in the vault or it all goes."

He didn't want to take the chance that she was bluffing so they stayed unloaded *and* inside the gun vault, but he never locked the door unless he was leaving town. Guess Mom and I weren't allowed to defend ourselves.

I went the spare bedroom down the hall, Dad's den, and opened the vault door. His new gun, the one with the laser, sat at eye-level on the shelf. I set the case on the desk and sat down. The gun weighed about two pounds, maybe a little more. I was expecting something so lethal to be even heavier, to have more substance.

Dad wasn't a collector of old firearms. I could appreciate an Old West six-shooter. Some of those had intricately engraved barrels. Gleaming pearl, antler, or exotic wood grips. True pieces of art. This one was boxy and flat black. Purely utilitarian.

I held the gun, my arms out straight, and imagined I was

back in the jungle. Another Zanther had just crept out of the forest. I spun, both hands firmly around the weapon. A small red dot on the far wall of Dad's office caught my attention. I traced the trajectory from the spot on the wall back to the gun. The laser was on. According to the red dot, if the gun was loaded and I pulled the trigger, I'd blow a hole straight into the picture of the dogs playing poker. Right smack in the middle of the boxer's forehead.

An image of the boxer's head exploding the way the Zanther's did flashed in my brain. That's not what the bullets in this gun could do, I knew that, but my eyes started to burn with hot tears. My breathing became fast and shallow. This thing in my hand could take a life. I could take a life.

I lowered the gun and watched the red dot move across the floor, closer and closer to me until it was on my foot. I left it there for a few seconds then slowly drew an invisible red line up my leg until the dot held steady on my thigh. If the gun was loaded and I squeezed the trigger right now, I'd blow a hole into my leg. From this close, how big would the hole be? I lowered my free hand, placed it beneath the laser, and let the dot hover on my palm. If the gun was loaded and I squeezed the trigger right now, would it just make a hole or would it blow my hand off? Mesmerized, I watched the little dot as I dragged it from my palm, up my arm, and across my shoulder. I finally stopped it over my heart, my next target. If the gun was loaded and I squeezed the trigger...

I dropped the gun on Dad's desk and backed away.

What the hell was I doing? As far as I knew, the gun wasn't loaded. But I hadn't checked. Hell, I didn't even know how. Maybe it was. Mom was too busy with her business to make sure Dad was following the rules. I hadn't pulled the trigger, but I had aimed a gun at my own heart. My dad's number one rule about guns was, "Don't point a gun at something you're not willing to put a hole in."

With shaking hands, I put the gun away, exactly as I'd found it, grabbed my sketchbook, and ran back to my room.

The stone that Dara gave me wasn't on my desk where I thought I'd left it. I searched, picking up papers and books. Where was it? Mom hadn't been in here had she? No. The odds of her coming in to clean my room, for the first time in years, were astronomical. Unless she thought my new friends would be coming over more often.

That was the last time I'd seen it, when the Bunch was here. I remembered seeing it on my desk and thinking I should have put it somewhere else. If one of them picked it up and touched the circle, how would I explain the girl who suddenly appeared in my room?

Where was it? I held my hair back, hands clasped behind my head, and kept scanning. That's when I saw it, sitting on the corner of my dresser. I don't know how it got there and didn't really care. I lurched for it and placed my thumb on the circle as I picked it up. Within second my phone buzzed with a text.

Dara: *What's up?*

Me: *I'm not sure. Can you come?*

Dara: *Are you okay?*

Me: *I am now. Two minutes ago I was pointing a gun at my chest.*

Dara: *What? As in at your own heart?*

I could barely type my response: *Yes.*

Dara: *Why did you do that, Robin?*

Me: *I don't know.*

Dara: *Did you want to hurt yourself?*

Why didn't she just come? It would be a lot easier to have this conversation in real time than to type everything.

Me: *No, I don't think so. I don't know why I did it. I freaked myself out pretty bad.*

Dara: *Are you okay?*

Me: *I don't know. I think so. I'm not going to shoot myself if that's what you mean.*

Dara: *What can I do?*

You could come talk to me. I really wanted someone

there with me.

Me: *Can you come?*

There was a longer pause than there had been with her other responses.

Dara: *Is that really what you need?*

Guess not. Clearly she was too busy with something more important than to bother with me. Story of my life.

Me: *I'll be okay. I don't think this wish is going the way it should though.*

Another, longer, pause.

Dara: *Keep the faith. Remember, I told you things could go badly at times. It will all work out the way it's supposed to.*

Me: *How is it supposed to work out? I wished for everyone to leave me alone and the only one doing that is you. Do you know what happened to me at school today?*

Dara: *Yes. I'm sorry.*

Me: *And now they're putting pictures of me all over the internet.*

Dara: *Do you want me to take them down?*

That was an option?

Me: *Really? You can do that?*

Dara: *Yep.*

The damage was done. Everyone, including Brianna, had already seen them. There were tons of responses to the posts people had put up. The ones that hurt the worst were Brianna's. She didn't reply to all of them, but to the one of me looking across the lunchroom at her she said, *That is so creepy!* To the one of me turning to face The Minions after we got off the bus, *That bus ride was the worst!*

Me: *Yes. Please. Can you make everyone forget they saw them?*

Dara: *Sorry. That's beyond what I know how to do. Stand tall. You're not the one who did anything wrong.*

Dara: *You don't need to be embarrassed because you like a girl. Trust me, I know what it's like to feel like people won't approve of who you like.*

Dara: *That's all on them. You have the right to like who you like. Even if it turns out she doesn't like you back, you don't need to be embarrassed.*

She was right. I knew that. I also knew she couldn't understand what it was like to be bullied and publically humiliated. Dara was so pretty, I couldn't imagine that she'd ever been picked on in her life.

Dara: *Are you okay? I can come if you need me to.*

Too late. This was a test. It was only a test. If this had been an actual emergency, I'd already have shot myself.

Me: *No. Crisis averted. You'll take the pictures down for me?*

Pause.

Dara: *Done.*

Me: *Thanks. Sorry to bother you.*

Dara: *Robin, you didn't bother me. I'm here for you. You're good now, right?*

Me: *Hunky dory.*

I sat down at my desk and put on my headphones. The sounds of the jungle instantly filled my ears. I knew the gun would draw and fire as it was supposed to now so I didn't need to play that part of the game again. I was kind of afraid to anyway. I didn't want to have to shoot the Zanther again.

Instead I kept going from that spot. My headlamp guided me through the thick growth. At one point I brushed against a small spider web. I felt it on my arm, sticking to me. I imagined walking into a giant web, sticking to it, and a huge spider jumping on me. It would bite me and pump me with venom that would slowly start liquefying my insides as it methodically wrapped me with its silk.

I turned my head and the beam of light illuminated a giant web. How? It was a great addition, but I hadn't programmed giant spider webs.

As I continued along the path, getting closer and closer to the tree I'd need to start climbing, I heard another animal coming up on me. I couldn't do it again. I couldn't shoot another living being. I'd have to escape some other way this time.

I looked down at my belt to see what else I had available to use. A knife. It wasn't big enough to do more than cut the flowers I needed. Some flares. I couldn't get myself to fire even a flare gun at that moment.

There was a length of rope coiled and hanging off my hip. I could set a snare and trap the animal. Could I do it quickly enough to save myself though? The creature was coming for me.

I looked around and found a good spot to set up a snare. I fashioned it into a loop and tied it to one end of a sapling. When I held up the loop end so I could place it, it wasn't a snare loop anymore. It was a noose. I dropped it and backed away.

"It will still work," I told myself. "It will still capture the creature. Or, if you're quick about it, you can refashion it."

The noose knot would still slide but not efficiently. I'd have to refashion it. I bent to pick up the rope, but it wasn't on the ground where I'd left it. I spun, shining the light all around, but I couldn't find it anywhere. Frustrated, I stood and stretched my neck side-to-side. When I did, my headlamp shined on a tree a few yards away. There was a sign attached to the tree.

They're after you. There is no way out. Here is an escape if you choose to take charge.

I looked up and hanging from the lowest branch was the noose.

I ripped my headset off, threw them on my desk, and clicked off the monitor.

Chapter Twelve

Robin

I couldn't get out of bed the next morning. The game had freaked me out so much I had a really hard time falling asleep. When I finally did, I couldn't stay asleep. I had nightmares, or rather one nightmare that kept repeating. I was walking through the jungle and things were trying to ambush me. I had nothing to defend myself with except a gun and I couldn't make myself fire it. Then the gun spoke to me.

There's only one bullet. You're not a very good shot. You might not hit your attacker. But if you hold it to your head—

I woke up sweating and crying. When I fell back to sleep, the dream would start again. One time I woke up screaming into my pillow.

This game was messing with me. It was doing things I hadn't programmed it to do. I didn't program an animal that

130

resembled Zane. I didn't put that sign or that noose in that tree. At least I didn't remember doing it.

I tried to convince myself that all of it had been a dream, not just the talking gun.

"There is not a hanging tree in your game," I told myself.

To prove it, I turned on the monitor. When the image appeared, the first thing I saw was the last thing I'd seen before I turned it off. The noose.

I must have programmed it while in some sort of blackout fugue state. That happened to me sometimes. If I stayed up too late for too many days in a row, which I had been doing for a long time, I'd have an episode where I wandered through my normal routine on automatic pilot, and I wouldn't remember any of it. There was one time in seventh grade I stayed up late studying for a science test. I remembered sitting at my desk. I remembered the teacher handing out the test forms. The last thing I remembered was picking up my pencil and then the bell rang. I'd taken the test, even got a perfect score, but I had no memory of doing it.

That had to be what had happened with the game. I'd programmed during a blackout.

I turned off the monitor again and promised myself no more late nights. It would be lights out by eleven.

"Maybe if you do that, you won't say stupid things out loud about Brianna again either."

"Robin!" Mom screamed from downstairs. "You're going to miss your bus!"

I looked at my alarm clock. No time for even a bird bath today.

I grabbed the first piece of clothing my hand made contact with and shoved my arms into the sleeves. There was a ketchup stain on it. It was the shirt Ivan had shoved my lunch tray into. Not only was it dirty, the stain looked like a bullet wound right over my heart. I threw it across the room and grabbed another shirt. A wrinkled but unstained polo. I tugged it over my head and stepped into yesterday's khakis and socks. Good enough. It's not like anyone would notice.

When I got down to the kitchen, Mom was on the phone.

"Could you hold for one minute," she asked whomever she was talking to. She punched what I assumed was the mute button and spun on me. "If you miss the bus, you're waiting for the next one or walking to school. I have to take this call so you're going to have to get your own breakfast." She scowled at my clothes. "And put on a clean shirt."

I got the distinct feeling that not getting me my breakfast was the worst part for her. Mom ran her mornings with the discipline of a four-star general. She got up first and had one cup of tea before I got up. When I came downstairs she made my tea and toast. This had been the routine for years and had become like a necessary ritual. Any variation threw her whole day off.

It's not like I couldn't get my own breakfast. But the fact that I had to this morning bothered me. The last, what, eighteen hours had been bad enough and now, the one morning I needed her to ask how I was doing, she was too busy to put a piece of bread in the toaster for me.

I ate my breakfast and walked slowly to the bust stop, trying to time it so I'd get there just as the bus pulled up. The last thing I needed today was another incident with Zane and The Minions. Unfortunately my timing was off and when I got there, the bus was half a block away and picking up speed. The next one wouldn't come for thirty minutes.

Maybe Dara could do that transporting thing again.

Of course I hadn't brought the wish stone with me. I made a mental note to put it in my bag as I pulled out my phone. At least I had her phone number.

"Hey," she greeted. "Who's this?"

"It's Robin." Figures, my fairy god-teen didn't even remember me.

"Oh, hey, Robin," she said. "What's up?" Someone in

the background said something and she replied, "It's my charge. I have to talk to him… No, it'll just take a minute. Go make breakfast."

"Are you busy?" I asked.

"No. A little. What's up?"

"I just," I didn't even know what to say. "I had a really bad night and overslept and now I missed the bus."

God, could I possibly sound like a bigger loser?

"So what happened last night?"

She didn't remember? "We texted? The thing with the gun? Can you just come? The next bus won't get here for half an hour so I'm gonna be late for school. I was hoping you could do that thing where you magic me to school."

"No. Cinnamon-raisin, please."

"What?"

"Sorry," she said. "Bagel. So what about school?"

"Nothing. Forget it."

"No. Robin, I'm sorry. What do you need? I'll fix it again so they don't know you're late. Once you get there just walk in and head to your class. No one will see you."

"How's that any different from any other day?"

"What?"

Could she focus on me for like three seconds? "Never mind."

"You sound really down today," she said. "What's going on?"

"Gee, I don't know. Maybe it's the fact that I held a gun to my chest last night," I snapped. "And then while I was playing my game, trying to fight off this thing that was going to attack me, I turn around and there's a noose and a sign letting me know there's an alternate way of escape. I don't even remember putting it in."

"That's because you didn't," Dara said. "Not consciously, at least."

"What do you mean?"

"Remember I told you I fixed your game? I made it

intuitive? I linked your mouse and headset with the game. It measures your anxiety levels and presents options to situations based on your stress levels and perceived need."

I took a seat on the bench in the bus shelter. Fortunately no one else was there so I could talk about guns and nooses and no one would call the cops on me.

"So my game thinks I should kill myself? Awesome. I'm such a loser even my game wants me dead."

"No," she said. "Oh, thanks. That's perfect... Maybe some fruit? And cream cheese if you have any?"

"What?"

"Breakfast," she said. "And no. Your game does not want you to kill yourself. It's a game. It's simply creating alternatives for you."

"So what would happen if I... I mean my character used the noose?"

"Game over," Dara said with a laugh. "Winning the game means surviving all of the obstacles and getting the flower, so if your avatar kills himself, you lose the game. Of course it's a game, so you'd just start again. It's so cool that it's working. I wonder if there's any way to really make a computer do that? Without magic I mean."

So she'd magicked my game to read my mind through the headset and mouse. It was cool in theory, but in practice, I wasn't sure how I felt about my computer reading my mind, especially if it was going to keep suggesting suicide as an alternative to winning the game.

"What about last night?" I asked.

"What about last night?" She was chewing now. "This is so good. Thank you."

"I pointed a gun at my own chest." God, did every genie care this little about their charges? No, I'm sure it was just mine. This was how the world worked for Robin Westmore. The universe granted my wish but didn't bother giving me a genie that gave a damn what happened afterward. Screw it! I'd find my own way to deal with my crappy life.

"You didn't shoot yourself, Robin," she said in the same tone parents use on hysterical toddlers. "Do you feel like you want to do it again? Do you feel like you *want* to pull the trigger?" More from the voice in the background. "He's okay. He had a rough night."

"Who are you talking to?" I demanded.

"No one."

"Not no one. You're talking to someone about me and I have the right to know who."

She said nothing for a few seconds. "My boyfriend."

"That's why you can't come? Because you're with your boyfriend?"

"I haven't seen him in a week," she said. "A pipe broke at his school so he has a day off. Anyway, I'm talking to you."

"God, Dara," I said and ran a hand through my hair. I grabbed a fistful and pulled hard enough to make my eyes water. The pain actually felt good. "I want to talk face-to-face. Not on the phone. Not through texts. Face-to-face where you won't be distracted by boyfriends and bagels."

"I'll be right back," she said. A half-second later she was sitting next to me on the bus stop bench. She wrapped an arm around me and squeezed. "I'm sorry. What do you need?"

"I need to get to school," I said and shrugged her off. The last thing I wanted was her pity.

"What else?"

"Nothing. Can you just take me to school, please?"

She looked at me with a frown. "Sure."

She put her hand on my shoulder and it felt like I was being sucked through one of those tubes at the bank drive-up window. The feeling of being catapulted five miles across town only lasted for a second. The next thing I knew, I was standing by the front door of the school. Dara was gone. Back to bagels with the boyfriend, laughing about the joke of a charge she had to deal with.

The buses were still unloading so I hadn't missed

anything. What I wouldn't give for a pipe to burst in my school.

☮ ☮ ☮

"You look like hell," Tabatha told me when I dropped into my seat at the table.

"Rough night," I said.

"What happened? Is everything okay?" Emily asked, as compassionate as Tabatha was cold.

I didn't know where to begin, the incident with the gun, the way my video game wanted me to kill myself? What would they say if I told them? What could they say?

"Nothing," I said. "Up late. Couldn't sleep."

"Cheer up, my friend," Ivan said, slapping me on the back. Harder than necessary. "I've got news that's going to perk you right up." He laughed and gave me a wink. "In more ways than one, I think."

Pranav and Tabatha laughed, too. Emily rolled her eyes. Jeremiah stayed focused on *The Chocolate War* lying on the table in front of him.

"What's going on?" I was too exhausted to be suspicious.

"The homecoming dance—"

"Stop," I said and held up a hand. "That topic has brought more than enough public humiliation to my life."

"No, no, no," Ivan said. "It's all good. The only thing you did wrong was to say what every horny dude thinks at one time or another. I've taken care of the problem though. You already know about my matchmaking abilities."

"What did you do?" I cringed. There's no way this could end well.

"I talked to Brianna for you."

It felt like my insides had turned to cement. I couldn't react. I couldn't move. I could barely breathe.

"You did what?" The question came out as a whisper.

"Truth," Ivan said. "I asked her this morning if she was going to the dance and told her that you wanted to go with her."

She probably laughed in his face. After yesterday, the thought of her going anywhere with me had to sound like a colossal joke.

"He did," Tabatha said, slouched in her chair, popping grapes into her mouth. "I was like five feet away. He asked her. She said she wanted to go."

"With me?" I asked.

Tabatha put both hands in the air, palms up, and gave a shrug.

She said yes? Was the wish finally kicking in? I believed in the magic, but I'd given up on believing Dara could actually make my life better.

"Ask her yourself." Ivan stared at me, waiting to see if I would.

"So," Jeremiah said, clearly done with dance talk, "what's going on with your game."

"You'd never believe me if I told you," I mumbled.

He waited for me to continue then said, "Can't know if you don't tell me."

"I fixed the problem with the gun," I mumbled, still thinking about Brianna. "Now there's this creature that pops out of the woods. It's like half-panther half-Zane. I call it a Zanther."

Pranav shook his head. "Dude, you set yourself up to make the shit rain down on you sometimes, you know?"

The group had stopped shying away from the subject of me and Zane after the third day. Every one of us had been someone's target at some point. That's why even though Ivan was a year older, he hung out with us. He was wicked-smart, second highest GPA in the school, and practically everything he touched, like his matchmaking gig, worked for him. The problem was his arrogance had no off button.

Tabatha was the middle of something like eight siblings.

She got attention by using her mouth instead of her brains and turned people off. Pranav skipped two grades and was the youngest brainiac in the school, a combination that destined him for solitude. Emily, smart as she was, was so mild she just blended in to the background and was bullied via invisibility. Only Jeremiah was in the group because he chose this one over the others.

"That's just what I call it," I said of the Zanther. "It's not like I've labeled it that in the game."

"Passive retaliation," Pranav said with a nod. "That works. You're less likely to get pounded on that way."

They started discussing the concept of getting revenge without your opponent realizing you were doing so, but I'd already checked out of the conversation. Had Ivan really set up a date with Brianna for me? People praised the matchmaking thing he did. He had a pretty high success rate. Lots of second dates. A few long-term relationships. Could I dare to hope?

☮ ☮ ☮

I jumped onto the bus seconds before it was about to pull away. Good thing. I'd walk the five miles home before putting myself through Dara's indifference again.

I scanned the seats and found the only open spot. Next to Brianna.

It's now or never, I thought. If Ivan had set up a date for me, I needed to verify.

"Hey, Brianna," I said.

She looked up, looked back at The Minions, and at some of the other afternoon regulars. "Robin. Hi."

I pointed at the open seat next to her. "Is anyone sitting there? Well, obviously not. What I mean is, do you mind if I sit there? Or are you saving it for someone."

Shut the hell up and sit your ass down already.

She inched over and motioned toward the empty seat.

We sat in silence for a long time, she focused on her phone and I tried to work up the nerve to speak to her again. If I didn't say something soon, we'd get to our stop and I'd have to go through this again tomorrow. Not sure I could handle that much anticipation. I took a big breath and let it out in this rattling exhale that made me sound like an asthmatic with no inhaler.

"Ivan told me you want to go to the homecoming dance," I said.

She looked up from her phone and looked at me like she either forgot I was there or had no idea what I was talking about. If he set me up...

"Who?" She squinted. "Oh, *Ivan*. That's right, you eat lunch with him." She smiled—she was so unbelievably pretty when she smiled—then she shook her head and rolled her eyes. "Ivan the Matchmaker."

What was I supposed wear to a homecoming dance? A tux I suppose. I should go order one right away. And a corsage for her.

"Do you have your dress yet?"

"Funny you should ask," she said, sitting straighter. She swiped her phone's screen a few times then held it over to me. "I was just looking at dresses. I'm getting this one."

It was a short dress, strapless. The top was sparkly, made up of what looked like flower petals that went all the way around to the back. The bottom was a sheer blue material with shiny green material under it.

"Sequins on top," she said, pointing at the picture. "Teal blue tulle with a lime green lamé underskirt. Isn't it pretty?"

"You'll be beautiful," I said. "Well, you're always beautiful. You'll be breathtaking."

Her cheeks flushed pink and she looked down with a smile. "Thanks, Robin."

"I can hardly wait to see you in it."

Our stop was less than a block away.

"So, I'll see you there then," I said. Would Dad would

drive us?

"What?"

"At the dance. I'll see you at the dance. I'll see you before then. It's still a week away." *God, just stop.* "But I'll see you there. At the dance."

Where's Dad's gun when I needed it? I might as well shoot myself in the other foot, too.

"Right," Brianna said, her forehead wrinkling with confusion. It was so cute when she did that. "At the dance." The bus stopped and she stood. "Aren't you getting off?"

"Oh, no," I said and gestured down the street. "I've got to go do something."

"Okay. See you tomorrow then."

I closed my eyes and imagined that dress on Brianna. I could hardly wait.

I was pretty sure there was a tux rental place at the mall. I took the bus there, stopped at the store map thing at the entrance, and saw that yes, there was a tux place here. I walked in the store and immediately felt lost.

"What can I help you with?" The lady there asked.

"Um," I said, staring at the bazillion tuxes on the racks, "I need a tux."

"You're in the right place," she said. "What color? Black, gray, or white."

"I don't know. Does it matter?"

"Sure it does," she said, untangling two of the many necklaces she wore. "What's the occasion?"

"School dance." I mumbled.

"You're going with a date?"

I nodded. Yes, I had a date to the dance with Brianna, the girl I'd had a major crush on since she handed me her phone number on my first day at this stupid school. The girl who didn't care that I'd been publically humiliated more times than I could count.

"Then you'll want to coordinate. Do you know what your date is planning to wear?"

As I described Brianna's dress, my heartrate rose and the saleslady's eyebrows went up in approval.

"Sounds like you've got yourself a hot one," she said with a little wink. "I suggest white or silver-gray. She'll absolutely glow next to you."

I liked that idea. Brianna didn't need help being beautiful, but if I could help make her glow, I was all for it.

"Okay," I said with a shrug. "White, I guess. I don't know anything about this stuff. Whatever you think. Can I have tails, too?"

As she entered information into her computer, her bracelets jangled together. "This is for homecoming?"

"Yep."

"A tux and tails might be a bit formal for a homecoming dance," she said. "I've got them if you want them though."

"Brianna is worth it. She's going to look gorgeous. Figured I should look my best, too."

The saleslady stood there, analyzing me for a minute. Good luck with that. I'd been analyzed by many. Even I couldn't figure me out.

"Usually," she said, "moms come in to help."

Usual moms would.

"She's busy with work. I have a credit card. I can pay."

The lady gave me a pity smile and placed a hand on my arm. "I wasn't worried about that." She straightened her shoulders. "What color cummerbund and tie do you want?"

"What?"

"Cummerbund." Her smile returned. My ignorance amused her. "That thing that goes around your waist. Unless you don't want one. You don't have to wear one."

"Lime green," I said.

A laugh burst out of her. "Oh, honey, you're going to glow, too. I would love to see the two of you together."

As she measured me for the tux, a process that resulted in a bit of embarrassment on my part when she got to the inseam, she hummed softly. It sounded a little oriental, a

141

little Native American, a little Middle Eastern. It was such a soothing sound, I felt almost like she was putting me into a trance. She entered each number into the computer, then measured again to be sure. "Measure twice, cut once, as they say."

I gave her my credit card and she told me I could pick the tux up as early as two nights before or as late as noon on the day of the dance.

"It'll probably be the day of," I said. I didn't want to have a tux in the house for any longer than necessary. Explaining homecoming to my mom would start a whole gushing thing that I didn't want to be a part of. Maybe I'd change into it right here in the dressing room. "Do you know where I can get her a flower?"

The saleslady told me there was a place across the street and down two blocks from the mall. "It's a shame your mom isn't helping you. May I make one more suggestion?"

"Sure." I liked this lady. I'd take all the help from her I could get.

"Her dress sounds like it's quite involved with the colors and the intricate bodice. Keep the corsage simple. Get a wrist corsage." She was having fun with this. Her smile lit up her face. A lot like Brianna's did. "I suggest hot pink tea roses, a touch of baby's breath, and lime green ribbons." She handed me a fabric swatch of the lime green color I'd chosen for my cumber-thing. "They should be able to match the ribbon pretty well with this."

I'd totally lucked out finding this place. I could've gotten a crabby saleslady who would rather be home eating pizza, drinking beer, and crying over some stupid "pick-me" dating show.

"Thanks for all your help, ma'am. I really appreciate it."

"No need to be so formal," she said and tapped her nametag. "You can call me by my first name."

"Thanks, Indira."

142

Chapter Thirteen

Desiree

"Give me your phone," I said and held my hand out to Dara.

"Why?" she asked, hugging it to her chest like a mother protecting her child.

"You spend more time texting Wyatt than on your other responsibilities combined. You have to pay more attention to Robin."

"When we were in San Antonio you were cool. Now..." She rolled her eyes like here with me was the worst place she could be.

"You agreed to do this," I said. "You agreed to help people."

"Well maybe I'm not meant for this," she yelled. "Maybe making me a genie was a mistake and you should have just let me die."

It was like she'd punched me.

"You'd really rather be dead?"

"Since I don't have any other choice," she said, "yes, sometimes I think dead would be better. It's been super hard on Wyatt and my parents, too."

"That was the mistake," I said. "I was so concerned about you that I never stopped to think about your parents and Wyatt. Maybe it would be better if I wiped their memories."

"Kill me at the same time then." Dara's eyes stayed locked on me, challenging. "I can't be without them."

She was pushing me too far with this homesick, lovesick drama.

"Maybe you just need to suck it up," I challenged right back. "I never got to see any of my family. I'd been with my boyfriend a lot longer than you've been with Wyatt. I survived."

The look of pain on her face went right through me.

"I'm not as strong as you, Desiree."

I was trying to be understanding but this was the job she agreed to do. What was I supposed to do with her if she refused to do it?

"You are strong," I said. "I know how hard it can be at first, but it will get easier, I promise." She didn't argue. Was that a good sign? "Look, Robin is really hurting. He needs someone to be there for him. If you seriously can't do this, I'll assign a different Guide."

Dara said nothing for nearly a minute, then she let out a resigned sigh.

"That would be worse," she said. "He'll think I don't care and that's not true. I'll guide him. But don't take my phone. I told him he could text me if he wanted to. I need to be available for him, right?"

She seemed sincere. Should I trust her?

"All right," I said, "but you said it, he needs to know that you're there for him. You have to pay more attention to him.

I can't give you another chance."

That was four days ago. Apparently Dara didn't like ultimatums because she hadn't stopped by to see me since. She did focus on Robin and training the Guides on how to use their tablets was going well. A few refused to use them, preferring to message me via either carrier pigeon or coming out to the cabin to talk to me. While I didn't like that they were disregarding the new rule, I didn't mind them coming to the cabin. Since handing out the tablets, there were days now where I never saw anyone. When I was a Guide, even though I lived alone I saw at least one of my charges every day. Now all I did was assign wishes and answer emails.

I needed a companion. A pet to go on long, soul-searching hikes with. One that would be loyal to the death.

I touched my fingers together and a Hungarian Puli appeared in the aisle of my bus. He looked like a big mop of tangled dreadlocks. His white fur was stained almost gray and all I wanted to do was give him a bath.

"Let's have a little fun with you." I touched my fingers together again and his white-ish dreads turned a rainbow of yellow, green, and black. The colors of the Jamaican flag. I went over to him and placed my hand on his head. "I dub thee, Rasta Dog."

I look ridiculous, he thought at me. In a Jamaican accent.

"You look bitchin'," I said, loving him deeply already. I'd debated about giving him the ability to speak, but quickly decided on telepathy because everyone would be able to talk to him otherwise. The Guides could get their own pets. He was mine.

You cannot be serious, he thought.

"Don't you think the colors are fun?"

Not especially.

I stuck my lower lip out in a little pout.

Fine. But I have rules. We must walk every day. You need to groom my cords often to keep them looking gnarly.

"Not a problem. Let me finish sorting a few wishes and

then we'll go for a walk."

What did you do to my voice?

I shrugged. "I thought the whole Caribbean package would be fun. I'll change it if it bothers you."

After a minute he thought, *I'll give it a try.*

We went to the cabin where I manifested a big cushion for Rasta to nap on while I worked. He didn't nap though. He sniffed around the cabin, continuously investigating everything he could reach, which was everything that existed at about mid-thigh height on me. Worse, I heard every thought.

This smells good. This does not. When are we going for a walk? When are you going to feed me?

Finally I touched my fingers together and his thoughts turned off.

"I have to concentrate in here," I told him. "When we're outside the cabin I'll listen to your thoughts."

I manifested a big bowl of food, which he devoured, and then continued his investigation of the cabin. By the time I was done sorting wishes, Rasta was begging to get out.

"Let's go to the Lodge," I said pointing to the far side of the lake. "That'll be a good long walk for you and I should see what they're up to."

Half way there, I altered things again so I only heard his thoughts if they were directed at me. Who knew a dog thought about so much?

The Guides must have seen us coming because a couple dozen of them poured through the back doors. When they did, Rasta stood in front of me like a bodyguard.

Are they dangerous? I will protect you.

"Depends on your definition of dangerous," I said. "I have a feeling I'm not the one who needs protecting."

A chorus of squeals rang out from the Guides.

"Oh my goodness, he's so cute."

"What his name?"

"Is there a dog under there?"

146

Rasta looked over his shoulder at me. *Help me, Desiree.*

I held out my arms as a barrier to keep them from pouncing on him. "His name is Rasta."

You're sure they will not hurt you?

"I'm sure. Is it okay for them to pet you?"

He looked from me to them and back. *Not all at once.*

"One at a time," I told the Guides.

"He looks like a living yarn pile," Dara said standing next to me.

"Hey," I said, holding up a peace sign. "Haven't seen you in a while."

"You told me to do my jobs," she crossed her arms and turned partially away. "That's what I've been doing."

She was still mad. I could take it. Lots of people were mad at me lately.

"Things seem groovy for Robin," I said.

"You're still watching him?" She let out a sigh like I had totally invaded her privacy.

"That's my job."

"I thought his wish was my job."

"His wish, yes. But you, little sister, are mine." My turn to sigh. "We've already talked about this. He's your first."

"God. Gross." She made a face like I'd asked her to make out with him.

"Stop it. You know what I mean." That she was talking to me was a good sign. Still I asked, "How long are you going to be mad at me?"

She shrugged and stared at Rasta as he patiently tolerated pats and ear scratches. Although it was hard to determine exactly where his ears were. Every now and then he'd let out a high-pitched bark at someone or something he didn't like. The throng of Guides would back away and a few seconds later someone would be brave enough to try again.

"The dog is kinda cool," Dara said.

"Thanks. I needed some company."

"You know"—she finally turned to face me—"you

choose to live over there all by yourself. You and your insistence on being a lone wolf. Why don't you live here with the rest of us?"

Her voice was slowly rising and Rasta turned.

Are you in need of protection?

"No, everything's fine," I said.

"Who are you talking to?"

I nodded at Rasta. "I gave him telepathic abilities."

"See?" she said, throwing her arms in the air. "Even the dog has to be private."

"He is my dog. You can manifest your own pet if you want one."

"That's not my point."

"Dara, this is how I choose to live."

"Then don't complain about being lonely. You keep telling me to suck it up and deal with what I agreed to. You agreed to this, too."

My *you can do it and things will get easier* pep talk from a few days ago echoed in my head. I was such a hypocrite. This was the same thing I did at the commune. I went there voluntarily and then couldn't handle all that togetherness. Instead of just going for a hike or spending a few quiet minutes alone, I isolated myself. I became the outcast. Everyone else had bonded and acted like a family. I was the one always challenging the status quo, never happy to let someone else make the rules but not wanting to subject anyone to my rules either. Exactly like I was doing now.

"I'm not ready to live in the Lodge," I told Dara and touched my fingers together. The cabin appeared on the edge of the cliff, about fifty yards from the Lodge while Gypsy V remained on the other side of the lake. "I'll work here and sleep there." I looked down at Rasta, still surrounded by Guides. "That'll be better for him, too. They may pet him to death otherwise."

"It's a start," Dara said with a reluctant smile and then gestured at the Lodge. "You going to eat with us? Adellika is manifesting a killer Japanese dinner for everyone tonight. Tempura, sushi, sashimi, sticky rice, soba and udon noodles, a bunch of sauces…"

"Stop," I held up a hand. "You had me at sticky rice."

☮ ☮ ☮

During mealtimes, the commons area was filled with tables of varying shapes and sizes. Some of the Guides preferred being in bigger groups and the laughter, or arguing, got a little loud at times. Others wanted to eat alone or with only one or two others. Some liked restaurant-style booths. Some preferred to sit on floor cushions at short tables. None of them seemed quite sure what to make of me being there and for the first time in a very long time, I felt nervous. It had never bothered me if I didn't fit in with the crowd. I'd always been the different one with my independent attitude. Suddenly though, it mattered.

Instead of choosing a table, I sat at the enormous kitchen bar near Adellika. Dara sat next to me but wasn't ready to be chummy yet so she talked to the Guide next to her. I ate and watched as Adellika constantly refilled plates.

"This is excellent," I said as I popped another piece of batter-covered shrimp in my mouth. I closed my eyes to fully appreciate the flavor. "Far-out."

"Thank you," Adellika said in her clipped English. "This is my grandmother's recipe. She teach my mother. I watch lessons every day and then one day my mother teach me. I have no daughter to teach." For a second I thought she might cry. "I am happy to feed Guides, though."

Every time I saw her I got a déjà vu feeling. I couldn't say why.

"You want more?" She flicked her fingers at empty plates to fill them again and wiped down the bar with a white towel. When I told her I couldn't possible eat another bite she asked, "Everything okay, Desiree?"

I laughed. "You remind me of the bartenders in those old movies, wiping down the bar, cleaning glasses, and playing psychiatrist."

She frowned. "I do not have glasses to clean."

I laughed harder. "I didn't mean literally."

"Ah," she said and nodded but obviously didn't understand. "So everything is okay?"

"Could be better," I confessed. "I'm feeling a little lonely, I guess. I'll start coming here for dinner every night and hang out with everyone. Besides, if dinner is like this every night, I'm missing out."

"Best way to not be lonely is to not be alone," Adellika said.

I wasn't so sure about that. I was in a packed house and still felt isolated. I stood and took a deep breath. "Guess I'd better go mingle."

I wandered the commons, paused to listen to conversations that didn't seem private, and commented on simple things like tablet covers (they'd each created their own unique design) or jewelry or books being read. The longer I hung around, the more accepted I started to feel. One group asked me to sit with them by the fireplace. They were sharing stories of their favorite and least favorite charges.

"In some cases," I said, "favorite and least favorite can be the same charge."

Heads nodded as I told them about Mandy and Crissy. A few more Guides joined the group as word spread of what I was talking about. I'm not sure how, I don't question the power of the rumor mill in a group this large, but Mandy's and Crissy's wishes had become almost like folktales.

"Thanks for sharin'," said Anne, a 30-something Guide with curly red hair and a northern Maine accent. "We all heard about the charges that near tore apart the great Desiree."

The great Desiree? There didn't seem to be anything but sincerity in her words. Did they really think that way about me? Maybe some did, but definitely not everyone. Olanna stood close enough to hear our conversation but far enough away to not be part of the group. If her eyes could have shot lightning bolts, Anne would be fried right now.

"Some wishes," I said, "can be as hard on us as they are on our charges." Murmurs of agreement spread through the group. "Thank the cosmos everyone gets a satisfactory ending."

A few Guides groaned.

"It near drove me off my rocker when Kaf would say that," Anne said. "Satisfactory endings. Why can't we just let them have what they want? Why all the journeys and heartache?"

"Sometimes," I said, "what our charges want is very different from what will truly make their lives better. Our job is to make sure they're on the right path in the end."

The crowd went silent and I was sure I'd just blown any ground I'd managed to bridge with them.

"You oughtta know," Anne said. "There ain't never been a finer Guide than you."

A few of the others nodded. I placed my hands in Namaste and bowed my thanks. I'd taken a lot of pride in being a Guide. They couldn't have paid me a bigger compliment. Maybe I should have lived at the castle or at least hung out with them more.

The conversation turned from charges to some of the other Guides. I stayed with the group but only listened. Anything I said would come back to me. A nice comment would mean favoritism. Something negative might make the entire group turn on me.

Someone, I didn't see who, brought up Sarah. She still wanted to quit. It seemed nothing anyone said could convince her to finish her last two years.

"She only leaves her room at mealtimes. And she barely eats."

Casually, I opened my tablet and brought up her file. It

was empty. What happened to all her charges? There was only one person I could ask.

"Thanks for letting me join you," I said as I unfolded my legs and stood from the hearth.

"You're leaving?" someone asked.

I held up my tablet as though it was evidence in a trial. "Always on call. Maybe I'll join you again tomorrow night?"

"We'll hold your spot," Anne said, patting the hearth.

I scanned the room and found Indira sitting by the window wall, talking with a Guide.

"Can I speak with you for a minute?" I asked.

Indira followed me to a quiet corner. "Is there a problem?"

"There might be," I said. "Do you know what happened with all of Sarah's wishes?"

"She gave them to the other Guides," Indira said. "You told them they could trade as long as the wishes were properly guided."

The *I told you so* was loud and clear.

"All of them?" How did I not know this? How could I have been such a supposedly great Guide but such a pathetic leader?

"She hasn't guided anyone in over a week," Indira said.

"She has to," I said, panic rising in my chest. "She still has two more years of service."

"You told them the wishes needed to be guided. You never said every Guide had to guide a wish."

I couldn't argue with that. I had to get it together. I couldn't keep yelling at Dara and the rest of them about doing their jobs properly when I was performing the worst of everyone.

Indira looked at me with sympathy then. "What are you going to do about it?"

"I'm not sure yet."

"Let me know if I can help."

I said goodnight to everyone and found Rasta laying on

152

the back patio in the moonlight.

"Are you ready to go home?"

Ready. He looked exhausted as he slowly stood and followed me.

"Did you have a good night?"

Many people gave me attention.

"Is that a yes or a no? Do you like all that attention?"

Most of it. Some I don't care for.

We walked a few hundred yards in silence, listening to the water lapping on shore and the sound of the wind blowing through the pines.

You are sad about something?

"How'd you know?"

You are my mistress. I know.

That was comforting but a little odd, too. I wasn't used to anyone, not even a dog, being so devoted to me.

"One of the Guides has stopped guiding. I understand. I wanted to quit before Mandy's and Crissy's wishes, but hard as those wishes were, I'm grateful I was able to help them. Sarah still has two years left. Who knows what wishes might come in that she'd be perfect for?"

After a few more minutes of silence Rasta thought, *Are you sad for her or yourself?*

I blinked, my eyes suddenly hot with tears. What did he mean by that?

"Her, of course. Her contract states that if she doesn't fulfill her duties she will return to the state she was in just before she became a Guide. In Sarah's case, she will become engulfed in flames and burn to death."

Unpleasant. Does she know this?

My heart grew heavier by the moment. "She knows. What am I supposed to do?"

If a sheep were to stray from my flock, it would likely be eaten by a wolf. I would try to retrieve the lost one, but only if doing so did not put the rest of the flock at risk.

The good of the many. Life lessons from a dog.

Chapter Fourteen

Robin

The week of the dance had been relatively neutral. Brianna was a little quiet in chemistry, but I'd been too nervous to talk to her either. The lunchtime discussions were either normal computer-related stuff or the guys listening while Emily and Tabatha talked dresses and makeup. Ivan was consumed with last-minute matchmaking issues so ignored everyone.

Finally it was Friday, the day before the dance. Nothing was going to bother me today. Nothing negative would stick to me. That old kids' rhyme was my mantra: *I'm rubber and you're glue. Whatever you say bounces off of me and sticks to you.*

"Good morning." I entered the kitchen, not only on time but early, and placed a kiss on my mom's cheek.

Her hand went to her face and she actually blushed.

"You're in a good mood."

"Yep."

"Any reason in particular?"

"I decided."

"You decided to be in a good mood?"

"Yes I did. English Breakfast this morning, please. Do we have bagels?"

"Bagels?" she asked, placing a tea bag in my cup. "You've never asked for bagels before. Would you like some? I can have some delivered with the next grocery order."

"Let's go crazy," I said. "Blueberry bagels and some cream cheese. I'll take two pieces of toast this morning. And a banana."

Mom gave me a little salute and happily went about filling my order. A little spot of warmth sparked inside me. It was nice to have a positive impact on someone. That would be my goal for today. No matter what anyone said or did to me, I would come back with something positive.

Dad flew into the kitchen then. "I'm late."

"How can you be late?" I asked. "It's not even six-thirty."

"Conference call with Dubai. There's eleven hours difference. It's the end of their day..." He waved his hand, indicating I could fill in the rest. "I'll have to dial in and listen while I drive."

"Have a banana," I said, peeling mine. "It'll give you energy."

"No time," Dad said, tapping his fingers on the counter as though that would speed up his coffee's arrival.

"Did you know," I said, "if you peel a banana from the bottom instead of from the stem you won't get those little stringy things?"

Mom's eyebrows rose, analyzing the statement. Dad looked at me like I'd proclaimed Santa had just landed on our roof. I held up my string-free banana as evidence.

I nodded. "True story."

Mom placed Dad's mug into his outstretched hand. He held out his other hand. "Banana, please. I have to test this theory."

He shoved the banana in his suitcoat pocket and ruffled my hair as he walked past. "Have a great day, Robin."

He leaned across the counter to give Mom a kiss and left.

"Well I didn't get up early today," Mom said, adding more water to my tea cup. "I still need a quick shower before my first call." She waggled a finger at my breakfast. "You're good?"

I gave her a thumbs-up. Grinning, she ruffled my hair, too.

About a block from the bus, I heard the birdcalls followed by, "Hey, Tweety. How're the nuts hanging?"

I tensed and braced for the onslaught. Then I reminded myself I wasn't going to let anything bother me today. Still, I gripped my phone more tightly in case he decided to accidentally plow into me again. I glanced over my shoulder to see Zane with his hand between his legs. As if I didn't already know what he was talking about. The first thought that ran through my head was, *mine are good, are yours still there?* Instead, I turned toward him and walked backwards.

"Morning, Zane. Going to be a great day. Don't you think?"

Without taking my eyes off of him, I moved my thumb over to my camera button and took a quick shot of him. The look on his face was priceless. Confusion mixed with a bit of concern that maybe he'd slipped into a parallel universe where he had no influence. Not only would it be a place where he couldn't bully me, no one else would be impressed with him either. He'd be one of the numerous neutrals. So awesome.

I expected him to do something. One more birdcall. One more comment about a missing nut. The only thing he did was give me this smirk, like he knew something I didn't. For a second or two it shook me. Whatever secret Zane thought he was hiding from me, it couldn't be that big of a deal. Besides, I wasn't worrying about him today. I didn't even let the fact that he and Brianna sat next to each other at the back of the bus, for the fourth day in a row, bother me.

The first two periods of the day dragged. I couldn't wait to get to chemistry. I was going to ask Brianna if she wanted to meet for dinner or something before the dance. A little late, but I hadn't thought of it until last night.

"Um, Brianna?"

She looked up just as our teacher walked in.

"Never mind," I said.

I could pass her a note—*Do you want to go to dinner before the dance? Circle yes or no.*—but that seemed juvenile.

I was going to ask her after class, but the girls had been traveling in tighter packs than normal all day. I heard bits and pieces about dresses and hair and makeup. Asking her with all those girls around would've been painful so I just said, "See you at the dance tomorrow," as I walked by.

This resulted in a lot of giggling. I guessed she was as excited as I was.

In computer lab, Miss Clark gave me a list of computers throughout the school and the password for downloadable antivirus software.

It wasn't rocket science, but it was necessary especially considering the websites that had been popping up on the Visited Sites list. The school needed stronger protection. As I sat there, waiting for the software to install, I started feeling more and more like a jerk. Brianna was going to all this trouble to look gorgeous and I could even find the courage to ask her to dinner. I hadn't actually done any asking. Ivan did it all. It's not like I didn't have the chance. We rode the bus together. We walked home from the bus stop together sometimes. Normally it was easy for me to talk to her about stuff. Not the dance though.

Texting wasn't the same thing as talking, not even close, but if I didn't ask her right now, I never would. I'd had her phone number for five months and never used. Now was the time.

Me: *Hi Brianna. It's Robin. I was wondering if you wanted to go to dinner with me before the dance.*

Brianna: *Hi Robin! Sorry. I've already got dinner plans.*

My fault. Totally my fault. I waited too long.

Me: *That's cool. Just thought it might be fun. I'll see you there then.*

Brianna: *Okay.*

☮ ☮ ☮

"You ready for another test run?" Jeremiah asked at lunch.

"Almost." The only problem I found with the game was that I couldn't figure out how to get rid of that noose and warning sign. "You're still not going to the dance?"

"Told you. It goes against my principles," he said.

"What principles?" Pranav asked.

"The ones where I refuse to make a fool out of myself," Jeremiah said.

"I'll send you the game tomorrow," I said. "That way you'll have something to do while I'm with the beautiful Brianna."

"Sounds like you're ready," Ivan said. He claimed that once a date was arranged he was hands-off. Plans were up to those involved. But he kept asking people how things were going. Trying to insure a five-star rating, he said.

"I'm ready," I said as I poked at my burrito. All week I'd been back and forth between excitement and nerves. Right now, nerves were winning.

"You got a corsage?" Tabatha asked in her standard judgmental way.

"Of course," I said and shot her an *I'm not an idiot* look. "I pick it and my tux up tonight."

"You ordered a tux?" Emily asked.

"Well, yeah," I said. "You should see her dress. I figured I'd better go all out. I even got tails."

"Wow." Emily gave me one of those sappy looks girls give when they think something is romantic.

"Tails?" Pranav gave me one of those looks guys give when they just heard something moronic. "Did you get a top hat, too?"

"No," I said. "Never thought of that. Do you think I should?"

"No," Emily said immediately. "You've done enough."

Ivan and Tabatha looked at each other and burst out laughing.

"What's funny?" I asked. "Top hats are cool."

"No," Jeremiah said. "Fez's and bow ties are cool."

"What are you guys wearing?" I asked Ivan and Pranav.

"What are we?" Pranav asked. "Girls? You want to coordinate our outfits?"

"Shut up," I said and flipped my middle finger at him.

"Pants, shirt, tie," Ivan said. "Relax, dude. Plenty of guys get all done up in suits or whatever. There might even be a couple other tuxes."

Emily patted my hand on the table. "Wear that tux proudly. I can't wait to see it."

I rode the bus to the mall after school. The tux was ready and I had to admit, it looked really good. Indira wasn't there, but she had ordered just the right one.

"This is for homecoming?" the saleslady asked, double checking the pants and sleeve lengths.

"Yep."

"Good for you. Not the usual choice but I like to see a guy with style." She adjusted the cummerbund so all I had to do was put it on. "All right. You're good to go. Have a great time."

The corsage was really pretty. Indira had given good advice. Brianna was on the skinny side, like me. The little tea roses were the perfect choice. A bigger flower would've looked like she was wearing a shrub. The roses smelled really good, too.

"Put it in the fridge when you get home," the guy at the flower shop told me. "It'll stay fresh until tomorrow."

I put the corsage in the refrigerator in the garage where Mom and Dad weren't likely to look. Sneaking my tux up to my room without Mom seeing it was a cinch. She was in an animated conversation with someone about costs for a series of online ads.

Everything was set. In a little more than twenty-four hours, Brianna would be on my arm.

Chapter Fifteen

Robin

My luck couldn't get any better if Dara had magically arranged things for me. Then again, maybe she had.

"Your dad and I have two events tonight," Mom told me Saturday morning. She shook her head like she was tired. "What I wouldn't give for a night in front of the TV. I asked for this, though. I wanted my own business. Anyway, we have dinner with new clients of mine and then a party for your dad's company. One of the VPs is retiring and your dad thinks he may be in line for his position. It could be a late night." She frowned at me. "We haven't done anything as a family since the move."

"I understand, Mom." I did. Not that it made being second or third on the list any easier.

"You shouldn't have to." She smiled, a sad sort of smile. "You're a lot like us. Always putting homework first and getting such good grades. That work ethic will take you far."

"All I have to do is survive high school."

"What?" she asked.

"Nothing."

"No, what did you say? Is everything okay? You haven't said anything so I assumed things were fine."

If she had asked ten days or even a week ago I would have answered differently.

"Things are okay. You know how high school can be."

"It's hard, even for the popular kids," she said. "I remember."

The comment stopped me for a second. I had never considered things from their perspective. Mostly because that wasn't a category I ever needed to worry about getting into.

"You know about my new friends," I said. "Things are good."

"I can't tell you how happy that makes me," she said. "I need to go prepare some notes for tonight. And see if I can bump that dinner ahead an hour. Your dad wants as much face time at the party as possible."

I spent the next nine long hours doing homework and texting with Jeremiah. An hour after I sent him my game, he was sending me comments. Most of them were things like, *Great graphics. Love the sound bites. The top levels are way harder now. Excellent.*

He found a few things that needed tweaking and I took care of them right away. Before I knew it, it was five o'clock and Mom and Dad were ready to leave.

"Nice tux," I told my dad.

"Oh this old thing?" He brushed off non-existent fuzz as he looked down at himself. "Just something I found in the back of my closet and decided to throw on."

"He looks very handsome," Mom said. She had on her favorite red power-dress.

"You look nice, too," I said.

"I love this dress." She wore that dress a lot. I knew that

beneath the black business jacket was a party dress. "Just have to switch out my business heels for the trampy ones and add a little more bling."

I covered my eyes with my hand. "I don't want to think about my mom as trampy."

"She's a hot-looking tramp," Dad said.

I covered my ears. "I did not need to hear that. Go, before you traumatize me for life."

Mom gave me hug and reminded me that it would probably be a late night.

"Good. I'll be in bed by the time you get home so I won't have to witness any more of my parents' alter-egos."

As soon as I heard the garage door close and saw the car turn the corner, I hit the shower. I took a little effort with my hair and debated about shaving, but there wasn't enough fuzz on my chin to worry about. Besides, I didn't want to risk cutting myself. The last thing I needed was to bleed on a white tux.

Before I left the house, I sent Jeremiah a text.

Me: *Going to the dance now. Wish you were gonna be there, dude.*

It took a long time for him to answer. Probably too involved with my game.

Jeremiah: *Hope you have a good time.*

At the end of the driveway I realized I forgot the corsage and went back for it. Still fresh and beautiful. I couldn't wait to put it on Brianna's wrist.

Riding a public bus in a tux was a little embarrassing. I got a lot of stares as I walked to the stop and a few whistles. Once the bus got there and I saw that Mr. Lacey was driving, I relaxed.

"Since when do you work the weekend shift?" I asked.

"Since I took my wife to Hawaii and she blew the budget." He laughed. "Worth every penny." He nodded at me. "You're looking mighty dapper. What's going on?"

I sat in the front row and told him about the dance and

how I was meeting Brianna there.

"*Our* Brianna," Mr. Lacey said. "That cute little girl who gets on and off at your stop?"

"Yes, sir."

"Very nice." Mr. Lacey nodded his approval.

"Not sure how I got lucky enough to get her for a date," I said.

"Because you're a nice guy," Mr. Lacey said. "Nice guys rule the world."

In no time the bus was pulling to a stop across the street from the school. There were kids everywhere, like ants around their hill. I did spot one guy in what looked like a tux and relaxed a little.

"Have a great time tonight, Robin," Mr. Laccy said. "I'm done in an hour so I won't be here for your ride home. I can't wait to hear all about it Monday morning." Then he gave me a wink. "That is if you can pull yourself away from Miss Brianna long enough to talk to me. I expect you'll have a permanent seatmate after tonight."

I stepped off the bus and crossed the street. The line waiting to get into the school was really long. They'd warned us that they'd be checking purses and pockets for alcohol and other illegals even more closely than on a regular school day. Finally, I made it in the doors, down the hallway, and into the gym.

"Robin!"

I turned and there was the Lunch Bunch, waiting for me right inside the door like we'd agreed.

When I got to them, Emily and Tabatha started circling me, checking out the tux. Tabatha picked up one of the tails and let it drop.

Emily straightened my bow tie and said, "Look at how nice he cleans up."

"You two are like vultures. Leave me alone." I couldn't help smiling though. "You look good, too, ladies."

Tabatha had on a short dress that was sparkly electric

blue on top and blue, pink, yellow, orange, and turquoise stripes on the bottom. Emily's dress was also short with a poofy skirt. It was all white with black flowers that ran up the side, over one shoulder, and down the back.

"Look at us in our matching whites," Emily said, standing next to me. "We could be the bride and groom on top of a cake."

She took out her phone, leaned her head on my shoulder, and took a selfie of us. That started a round of selfies. I even took a few and, as a rule, I didn't like pictures being taken of me. Even before the nut stuff, they almost always came back to haunt me.

"Have any of you seen Brianna yet?" I asked.

"I have," Tabatha said. "She looks hot. Just wait."

"Where is she?" I'd been waiting for this night for ten days. Well, really I'd been waiting five months. I liked her the first day I met her. I was crushing big time on her a week later.

"Easy, big guy," Ivan said. "She's here somewhere."

"Let's go get something to drink," Tabatha said. "Then I want to dance."

Our geek pack wandered to the far side of the gym like a school of fish. Punch and pretzels—regular and gluten free—and other snacks were set out. Tabatha offered me a cup of punch and I took two steps away.

"Not a chance," I said. "I'm wearing all white. No way I'm touching red punch. Or being anywhere near you while you're drinking it."

Emily handed me some white grape juice and told me to relax.

"Maybe we should spike it so he calms down," Pranav said dryly.

As I lifted the cup to my mouth, I saw her. If it wasn't for the dress, I almost wouldn't have recognized her. Usually she wore her dark blonde hair straight, sometimes twisted in a knot on top of her head. Tonight it floated over her shoulders in wave after wave of soft curls. That shiny lime green fabric under the blue glowed like neon. She was the brightest, most beautiful girl in the gym.

Ivan snapped a picture of me. "Calling this one 'Awestruck.'"

Someone else, probably Emily, gave me a gentle push and whispered, "Go get her, tiger."

Everyone and everything else blurred out of existence. All I saw was Brianna. She was smiling and laughing, covering her mouth as she did.

"Hi, Brianna," I said when I finally made it to her side.

She looked up at me, her hazel eyes sparkling. "Robin. Hi."

"You look"—I held my hand out to her and her dress— "amazing."

She grabbed a bit of the dress and held it out as she did a little curtsy. "Thanks. I love this dress. I'll never find a better one." She indicated my tux. "You're looking mighty fine yourself."

"Thanks." That's when I remembered that I was holding the corsage. I held the box out. "I got this for you."

Her smile faded a little. "For me?"

"Yeah. The lady at the store thought hot pink would be nice with your dress. I described it to her." I took the corsage out of the box and held it up to her dress. It looked great.

She looked from the corsage to the group of girls around us and then to me. "Robin—"

"She said a wrist corsage was a better choice than a pin-on one. I agree." I motioned to her dress. "There isn't a good place to pin one anyway. Besides, it would get crushed when we dance."

She leaned in and quietly asked, "Robin, what's going on?"

The girls surrounding us all stared at me. A couple, naturally, took pictures of me as I stood there holding the corsage out to Emily. Others were laughing and talking to each other behind their hands.

"What do you mean?" The room suddenly felt like it was closing in on me.

Brianna took a step away and started looking around. The more she looked anywhere but at me, the more obvious it was that something was very wrong. That's when I realized she already had a corsage on her right wrist.

"There you are." From nowhere, Zane appeared. "Lost you in the crowd for a minute. Oh, hey, look at Tweety all dressed in white." His gaze dropped to the corsage. "Holding a flower out to my date."

He put his arm around Brianna and pulled her close to him.

"Your, um, date?" I wanted to die. I wanted the floor to open up and swallow me. I wanted something to fall from the ceiling and slice me in two.

"Yeah, my date," he said like I was too dense to comprehend the concept. "I suggest you get away from her before I make you."

"But I thought," I said and leaned in to Brianna. "I thought we were meeting each other here."

Her friends started laughing. More pictures were taken. The worst thing was the look of confusion on Brianna's face. The more everyone laughed, the more she searched around for an escape.

"Meeting here?" she asked. Not mean. Still confused. Still searching. "Why did you think I was meeting you here?"

Then her search stopped and she focused on something behind me. I turned to see Ivan standing there with his phone pointed at me, the flash blinking like a strobe light as he took picture after picture.

Zane put a hand on my shoulder and pushed me. "You need to get away from *my* date. Don't know what made you think you and Bri were a possibility, but no way *loser*."

Brianna stepped between us then, "Zane…"

The crowd had grown bigger. They were all laughing or

making disgusted faces like they couldn't agree with him more.

"Brianna and Tweety?"

"In what twisted universe would that happen?"

"You mean in what level of hell would that happen?"

My eyes locked on Brianna's. This couldn't be right. She said she'd go with me. Ivan said... Ivan. Everything inside me turned to water.

"Robin," she said, her eyes glistening, "I—"

I couldn't hear what she said next. Humiliation clogged my ears as much as the jeering going on around me. I turned to walk away, but the crowd had closed the circle around us. People were laughing and pointing at me, some with fingers, others with their cell phones.

"Excuse me," I mumbled, my gaze cast down. I stood there, numb, waiting for them to decide to part and let me pass.

"Robin, wait." I felt a hand on my shoulder. It might have been Brianna's. It might have been someone else playing Paparazzi, wanting another picture. I didn't turn to find out.

When I finally made my way through the crowd, I saw the Lunch Bunch and it was like time had stopped. In what couldn't have been more than a second or two, I took in the entire scene.

Ivan still had his phone pointed at me. Tabatha, on his right, bent forward with her hands resting on her knees she was laughing so hard. Pranav, on his left, was shaking his head like *holy shit I can't believe what an idiot he is*. Emily stood off to the side behind them with her hand over her mouth and tears forming mascara-black streaks beneath her eyes.

"What's going on?" I saw that I was still holding the corsage, but I'd gone so numb I couldn't feel it.

Emily ran past me. "I'm so sorry, Robin."

"I can't believe this worked," Tabatha said, high-fiving

168

Pranav.

Ivan, still taking pictures of me, nodded. Then he dropped his arms to his side and gave me a dad look. The kind that said *son, we need to have a talk.*

"I can't believe you believed Brianna would go to the dance with you," he said. "God, this was so much easier than I thought it would be. I knew it was gonna be good when you told us about the tux. You should have seen yourself, trying to give her that corsage." He flipped through some screens on his phone. "Here, wanna see? I got a great shot of you holding it up to her dress. The look of horror on her face is golden."

"What?" I said, still not understanding.

"Ivan set you up, dude," Tabatha blurted like she'd been holding in a secret. Which, I guess, she had.

All I could do was stare at Ivan.

"You want to know why, don't you?" Ivan asked, suddenly cold and serious. He moved in closer until we were inches apart. His voice low and threatening. "You come in and try to take over *my* group? You talk about your stupid game and invite everyone over to your house. You think I don't know what you're doing? You think I'm just gonna to sit by and let that happen?" He jabbed me hard in the shoulder with his finger.

I reached up, absently, and put my hand over the spot. "All you had to do—"

"All I had to do was exactly what I did," he said. "You think I'm going to grovel to you? Bullshit." Another jab. "I told you once to shut up with the constant yammering about your stupid game. You swayed Jeremiah. I wasn't about to sit back and watch the rest of my group fall apart. I decided to show them just how much of a loser you are." He started laughing then. Loudly so everyone around could hear him. "You really thought Brianna would say yes to a date with you?"

What hurt even worse than realizing they were never my

friends, was knowing that Ivan was right. I was an idiot to think that Brianna would ever want to go out with a loser like me.

I looked back. Brianna stood there, staring at me with her arms hanging limply at her sides, as her whole group buzzed around her. A lot of them were on their phones, surely plastering my face all over the internet. Again. A few high-fived Zane.

Zane. Of all the guys she could be here with. Did she really like him or was this all Ivan's doing? Did it matter?

You've done enough damage. Just go. Everything you touch turns to shit.

In a daze, I started for the gym doors. Some kids stepped aside and made a pathway for me. Some made me wait until they decided to move. The taunts of "Fly away, Tweety" and "God, can you imagine Brianna with him?" flew around the gym, echoing in my head.

Just outside the gym door sat a large garbage can. I tossed Brianna's corsage in as I passed by.

Chapter Sixteen

Desiree

I didn't know how to be a leader. I didn't know how to the fix problems in a group and keep everyone happy at the same time. I had no idea what to do about Sarah. I couldn't force her to guide and I couldn't let it go unpunished if she continued to refuse. I spent two days wandering the forest with Rasta, an exercise that always centered me and allowed me to find the answers I needed. This time, I came home just as clueless and even more restless than I had been before I left.

I opened Gypsy V's door and mounted the first step when Olanna appeared. She'd visited me here exactly never. This couldn't be good.

"Where have you been?" she demanded.

"On walkabout." Flippant, yes, but my business wasn't any of hers.

She was practically vibrating with fury. "Desiree, we've been summoning you for two days."

"Indira's in charge when I'm not here."

"The wellbeing of this community is your responsibility, not Indira's."

I dropped my head back and exhaled. "A fact I'm well aware of." I pinched the bridge of my nose, the little stress I'd walked off already returning. "If you have something to say, Olanna, just say it."

"You cannot simply disappear that way," she said, eagerly taking the opportunity to speak freely. "While you were *walking about*, things have turned to absolute chaos here. In a few short weeks you have destroyed what it took Kaf two hundred years to establish."

"I'm trying to create an atmosphere of trust and responsibility," I said. "I trusted that everyone was responsible enough to honor their agreements. Guess I was wrong."

"Perhaps leading by example would be the better way to achieve that goal."

Cosmos help me, sometimes she sounded just like Kaf.

"You have no idea what's going on around here, do you?" Olanna asked.

"Sure I do," I said. "I've been eating dinner in the Lodge every night."

"So you know that the wishes are being treated like the cards in a game of Go Fish?"

"That's a little dramatic, isn't it?"

"Desiree," Olanna said in a tone that reminded me of my second grade teacher when she caught someone eating paste. "A group gathered yesterday to trade wishes based on things like eye or hair color, age, or where the charge lived."

"Why would they do that?"

"Because after years of structure," Indira said, suddenly appearing next to Olanna, "you've set them free with no boundaries or guidelines."

"You tossed Kaf's rules aside like they had no meaning," Olanna said, recharged by Indira's presence.

"What, now you're tag-teaming me?" I asked.

"If that's what we have to do," Olanna said. "I cannot believe Kaf chose someone so inept—"

"We're not tag-teaming you," Indira said, putting a hand on Olanna's shoulder to calm her. "We need you to understand what's going on."

"Exactly." Olanna's cocoa-brown cheeks flamed red. "It is not our responsibility to—"

Indira interrupted her again. "Let me talk to her. You go gather everyone in the commons. We'll be right there."

After taking another moment to glare at me, Olanna disappeared.

"Desiree," Indira said, "I know you're overwhelmed and hurting."

"I don't know what you're talking about," I said, holding my hand out for Rasta.

"He left you." She paused as those three simple words sliced through me like the Grim Reaper's scythe. "You love him and he left you. You've been changing everything in an attempt to erase him and his memory from everyone's minds. Your own included."

"Again, I don't know what you're talking about."

"You moved us to the opposite side of the world," Indira said as though I hadn't spoken, "You're running as far away from his memory as you can. What you don't see is that the further you run, the more attention you're drawing to his absence."

I couldn't argue with that. It's like trying not to think of purple butterflies. Suddenly your mind is filled with nothing but purple butterflies.

"Kaf was a tyrant," I said.

"He was tough but fair," Indira said. "You're angry and hurt. Why don't you admit it? Release that frustration."

Because if I released it I'd fall apart and the Guides

would circle me like hungry sharks.

"The problem," I said," is that he left without giving me direction. I don't know what I'm supposed to do."

"I cautioned you about changing so much so quickly," Indira said. "You need to wait until you know what works and what doesn't."

"So I should reinstate his rules?" I asked.

"Be prepared that more change, even a return to what they're used to, may result in backlash."

"They want Kaf. I can't bring him back." My voice caught. "They prefer his ways. If I restore his rules then at least the wishes will get properly guided again. That's why we became Guides after all, to make the lives of those whose wishes are deemed grantable happy or at least satisfying."

"That is our mission statement," Indira said and smiled. "Keep in mind that some of the Guides simply wanted out of a bad life. They don't have quite the compassion for the charges that you, I, and some others do."

"Maybe those whose hearts aren't in it shouldn't be here anymore," I said, pushing my shoulders back. "Maybe it's time to thin the herd."

Dara was right. I agreed to this position. It was mine until I found a replacement. I didn't like being the leader, but I did care about the charges. Indira was right, too. We needed to go back to what had been working until a better way presented itself.

"Backlash be damned," I said and held out my hand, manifesting my granny glasses. "Let's go be Kaf. Come on, Rasta."

Indira went ahead to make sure everyone was gathered. I told her I would walk with Rasta because he really hated transporting.

You are angry, he thought at me in his gentle Caribbean accent. *What is making your blood boil so?*

"Kaf left me." Tears started as I dropped to my hands and knees. Sobs wracked my body, draining me until I collapsed all the way to the ground.

Rasta lay down next to me, his face inches away from mine.

Slowly my tears turned to gasping breaths.

"They already think I'm weak." Gasp. "I can't let them see me like this."

The Guides are your friends, aren't they? Don't friends understand?

Mandy would. Crissy, too. The Guides? Probably not.

"Maybe eating dinner with them and trying to be one of them, was a mistake. I think that's why Kaf lived in seclusion. It's too hard to be both a boss and a friend." I sat up and forced my tears to stop. "I'm the Wish Mistress. I have to do what is right for our charges and the good of our community. I have to protect the flock." I pushed Rasta's cords away from his eyes. "This is why I brought you into my world. I can tell you everything, and I'm not really alone."

This Kaf, he should have a Rasta dog.

I hugged him close then scratched the spot on his neck that he loved so much.

When we walked into the commons, I immediately climbed on top of the kitchen bar and touched my fingers together. The gong, signaling that I wanted to speak, rang out. They all ignored it. I looked down at Indira and she gave me a look that said *you brought this on yourself.* I touched my fingers together again and the gong rang out louder than it ever had. This time half of them grew silent. The other half looked at me like I was interrupting their party.

When my brother, sister, and I used to get loud, my mom would get quiet. She'd turn off the lights and stand in front of us, not saying a word, until we were so creeped out that we huddled together like a pack of gazelles protecting each other from the angry lioness.

When I turned out the lights in the commons, the majority of the still-chattering Guides quieted. The longer I stood there, waiting on those still talking, the others started to shush them. Once the room was totally silent, I turned some of the lights back on. Indira and Olanna were in the front row. Adellika and Sarah behind them. I didn't see Dara anywhere. Maybe she was with her charge. That was an acceptable absence. I'd fill her in later.

"Thanks for your attention." My pulse was throbbing. This felt like the last chance for me. I needed to be Kaf, tough but fair. "We need to rap about some rather un-groovy things going down around here. I'm sure it's clear as crystal to everyone in this room that things are out of control. I understand wishes are either getting passed around like trading cards or ignored altogether."

"You told us we could trade," someone called out.

A murmuring of agreement echoed.

I sounded the gong again.

"Let me speak, please," I said, looking over my glasses at the crowd. I manifested a Kaf-like cloud, eased onto it and pulled my legs into full lotus. "I am not certain why the universe granted us the powers that we have. I am not certain why Kaf had the powers he did or why he decided to bestow them onto me."

A few voices called out "Me either" and "What a mistake."

"Whether you or even the universe itself likes it," I said, "Kaf's power *is* mine. I forgot a very valuable lesson I learned while living on the commune: when no one is in charge, chaos steps in as leader. I take full responsibility for letting chaos in. Now I'm kicking it out."

I took out my tablet and tapped out a message while the wary Guides looked on. Half a second after I closed the cover, a chorus of alert tones rang out through the commons.

"I have just repealed my previous offer of freedom to trade. I trusted you all to do the right thing, to do your jobs and look after our charges, and you took advantage of my trust." Murmurs started again, but this time when I held up my hand to sound the gong, they silenced immediately. "As explained in the message you all just received, I will assign wishes. You will not trade. You will use the tablets because I do not care for pigeons. If you need help with your tablet, Dara will teach you." I waited while a few read the message. "I assume you all remember the bi-weekly meetings we had with Kaf."

Heads nodded. Yeses were called out.

Mine were every other Wednesday at ten in the morning. At first I thought they were annoying, an intrusion on my week. All of my wishes ran smoothly after all. I didn't appreciate him nosing in on my territory.

Then I started looking forward to those twenty or thirty minutes. The meeting forced me to actually think about my charges, how their journeys were progressing, and what, if anything, I could do to help. I looked forward to seeing Kaf, too. If there wasn't much wish-related business to talk about, we'd spend those minutes annoying each other. That time morphed from an unwelcome interruption to what I secretly considered to be a bi-weekly date. What I wouldn't give to be able to annoy him again.

"I will send out a schedule," I said. "We will meet every two weeks so you can give me an update on your charges. As many of you admitted, I do know how to guide a wish and can help make sure you are guiding yours properly."

That had to be why Kaf put me in charge. Because I had been the best Guide, as he must have been at one time.

The Guides gazed around at each other, but no one spoke.

"Any questions?" I asked.

"What if we choose not to?" Sarah stepped out of the crowd.

I swiped away the cloud and lowered myself to stand on the bar again. I didn't have to ask. We all knew exactly what she meant. My heart had already begun to race and my palms to sweat. I didn't want to do this.

"I told you a couple of weeks ago," Sarah said, "I won't do this anymore. I'm an old woman. I can make my own decisions." She stood tall and proud. "I've done my time. I've helped many, many people find happiness. My children are fine and my husband is dead. I'm ready to join him again."

She stood with her arms at her sides, palms open to me as if ready to receive whatever I cared to dish out.

"Every one of you agreed to a contract with Kaf," I said. "The specifics for each of you are slightly different, but they all state that if you do not fulfil the terms of your contract, you will return to the state you were in when Kaf came to you." I looked down at Sarah, like an executioner. "Do you understand what this means?"

"We were traveling down the interstate," Sarah said, a shadow darkening her face, "when an accident occurred a few cars ahead of us. My husband couldn't stop in time and we rear-ended a truck transporting propane canisters. One of the tanks ignited and the flame was heating the tanks around it. An explosion was imminent." Tears filled her eyes but did not fall. "Other travelers were able to pull my husband and children from the car. The passenger's side, where I was, had wedged beneath the truck. I was pinned."

She paused and the only sound, ironically, was the crackling of the fire in the fireplace.

"They couldn't get me out," Sarah said. "That's when Kaf appeared."

"What happened," I asked, even though I already knew.

"He told me he could let me live if I wanted to." She blinked back her tears. "I agreed to his fifty year term as long as I could watch my children grow and ensure that they and my husband had happy lives."

"You only have two years to go and you're free," I said, silently pleading with the cosmos to make her stick it out.

"I won't do anymore," Sarah said without emotion, her head held high. "I understand the conditions. Do what you must."

"Sarah, don't," one of the Guides called out.

"Desiree, you can't be that cruel," another said.

"What would Kaf have done?" I asked, my voice loud, my heart breaking. "If he was standing here instead of me and Sarah refused to complete the terms of her indenture, what would he do?"

Horrified silence filled the room. They all knew. They'd seen him make good on his threats. Only twice in the forty-five years I was with them. Still, he'd done it.

"You all want me to walk in his footsteps until it means something you don't like." I had to swallow a huge lump in my throat before I could ask Sarah, "Are you sure? What about the fact that all of your charges would be guided by someone else?"

"That's a condition Kaf implemented, isn't it? Whose path are you following?"

I looked to Indira, who had gone pale, and Olanna whose jaw was working so hard the muscles in her neck stood out like Rasta's cords. I looked out at the Guides. This is what they'd asked of me. This was what I had agreed to when I agreed to take over for Kaf.

"Very well," I said to Sarah. "Thank you for your service."

I touched my fingers together and she disappeared.

Chapter Seventeen

Robin

I was two blocks away from the school before I realized that I'd gone right past the bus stop. Whatever. I just kept walking. Five miles. I'd be home in an hour and a half. Well before Mom and Dad were supposed to be back.

How had I let this happen? How had I let my guard so far down that I didn't see what was coming? And Brianna was part of it? No, I never expected she'd want to be my girlfriend. But she was always so nice to me. She'd said she was going to the dance with me, hadn't she? I tried to remember exactly what she'd said that day on the bus.

I pulled out my phone and sent a message to Jeremiah.

Me: *Did you know?*

I'd gone three blocks before he finally responded: *They're putting pictures up everywhere.*

Me: *Answer my question. Did. You. Know?*

Half a block later: *I knew they were up to something. I didn't know the details and I didn't take part in it, I swear.*

Me: *You also didn't have the balls to tell me.*

Jeremiah: *Ivan threatened I'd be next if I did.*

Me: *You sold me out.*

Jeremiah: *What did you expect me to do, man?*

Nothing. I had learned over the last three and a half years to not expect anything from anyone. Not even my parents. They were too involved with their careers to deal with me. They swore I wasn't an accident. That they'd always planned to have kids. They stopped after me though and never, ever said anything about brothers or sisters. If they'd never had me, their lives would be so much easier. They'd have the money they wanted without the expense of me. They wouldn't have to deal with me and my stupid problems. They wouldn't have to worry about whether the kid they ended up with would be a source of pride or of embarrassment. They'd be so much better off.

Jeremiah sent a couple more texts. *Where are you? Are you okay? Can I do anything?*

I didn't respond to any of them. He'd done enough. Besides, anything I did or put in writing would get captured in a picture or screen grab and used against me. Nothing I did was ever right. Except my game. That was right. But only because of magical intervention. If not for Dara, it would be as big a piece of crap as I was.

I reached into my pocked for the wish stone. Not there. I'd gotten too confident, sure I wouldn't need my genie anymore. I'd given up hope that this so-called wish could end well. I would like an explanation though. I pulled out my phone and texted for her to come. Four blocks later my phone buzzed.

What's up?

Me: *I need you.*

Dara: *Aw, that's sweet.*

Me: *I'm serious. Everything is falling apart.*

Dara: *What happened?*

Me: *The dance was a disaster.*

Dara: *What? What dance?*

That's right. I hadn't talked to her since before the whole "date" had been set up.

Me: *I thought you were supposed to keep track of my wish.*

Dara: *Sorry. What happened?*

Me: *Can't you just come?*

Why did I ask? Whatever she was doing was more important than me.

Me: *Never mind. Just be with your boyfriend.*

Dara: *I'm not with my boyfriend. I'm with my parents. I never see them and I was able to get together with them for dinner. We're almost done. I can come in a little while.*

Me: *Whatever.*

Dara: *Robin, tell me what happened.*

So I spent the next mile texting her the details. I almost got hit by cars twice. Too bad. That they missed I mean. Would have solved all my problems. Then again, with my luck I'd probably end up paralyzed instead of dead.

Dara: *I'm so sorry, Robin. Really.*

Me: *Well, be sure to tune in later. The worst is yet to come.*

Dara: *What does that mean? Seriously. You're kind of freaking me out.*

Me: *Nothing. Everything's fine.*

The damage was done. Even if she took down their posts, everyone knew what had happened. They'd just keep putting up more. There was no way this would die down by Monday. No way I'd be able to go to school.

Me: *Enjoy dinner with your parents. I'll be fine.*

Dara: *You're sure?*

Me: *Promise.*

Dara: *Okay. You're home?*

Me: *Almost.*

Still had a mile and a half. What did it matter? It's not like she'd come.

Dara: *I'm going to check in with you later.*

Me: *Whatever.*

I turned my phone off then. There was no one else I wanted to communicate with. Whatever texts might come in would be hate-mail. Picture after picture and links to posts that would show what a loser I was.

I just wanted to be home.

I wanted to disappear into my game where none of them could bother me. Forty-five minutes later that's exactly what I did.

The house was empty, as I expected. Mom and Dad wouldn't be home for at least three hours. If only I could literally disappear into my game. I knew that world. I knew where to get what I needed when I was in trouble. I was the master of my domain. Anything I didn't have, the game provided for me.

I took off my tux, hung it neatly on my closet door, ready to be returned. It rained for the last six blocks so the whole thing was wet and the pant cuffs were practically black with dirt. There would be a big cleaning charge.

The game must have been sensing my stress levels. It only let me play in nighttime mode where I could fully hide. No moon. No stars. Cracks of lightening and rolls of thunder vibrated my headset. I'd almost made it to the tree where I could finally start climbing to harvest the flower.

I was just starting to relax, to feel like I had control when the game began to throw creatures at me. More Zanthers than I could count. Then new creatures, bird-like beasts that dove at me and pecked at my head. Every time I looked up or reached for a weapon, a bird would swoop in and peck at me. They tore pieces of flesh from my arms. Ripped chunks of hair from my head. I looked up and they went for my eyes. That's when I realized, as much as the Zanthers looked like Zane, the bird creatures looked like me.

I ran through the jungle, hiding behind trees, in bushes, under large roots.

I stayed put until I was sure the creatures had left, then crawled out and ran for that tree again. The bird creatures returned with even more of their kind to attack me. I drew my gun and fired until all the ammo was used up, then I reloaded and fired again. Nothing was working. I couldn't stop the attack and I couldn't take them down.

They circled me, moving in closer and closer. My gun and clips were empty. I had dropped my machete ten minutes earlier. I had nothing to defend myself with.

That's when I looked up and saw the noose.

They're after you. There is no way out. Here is an escape if you choose to take charge.

The game had added boards, like rungs of a ladder, to the tree trunk. I scurried up them, thinking if I could just get into the tree I'd be out of the creatures' reach. But, of course, panthers can climb trees and birds can fly. There was no way out.

I took the noose and slipped it over my head.

Game over.

Chapter Eighteen

Desiree

The moon was full and glaring like a spotlight off the lake as Rasta and I left Mystic Lodge to go back to Gypsy V. I kept telling myself I didn't have a choice, I had to be tough with the Guides. My peace, love, and granola attitude, as Mandy would have called it, wasn't working.

Desiree, Rasta thought at me when we were about halfway there.

"Yes?" I took yet another deep breath. I couldn't seem to get enough of the clear, crisp air into my lungs.

What happened to Sarah? You didn't burn her, did you?

"Not in the way you mean," I told him. "I sent her to a sunny mountain meadow filled with wildflowers. There she fell asleep and dreamt about her life and all of the happy times with her husband and children. While she slept, I let her heart stop." I wiped away a tear that was leaving a cold trail down my cheek. "There was no pain. Her husband was cremated so that's what I did for Sarah. Her ashes are with his now."

Rasta trotted along in silence then thought, *I'm glad you didn't explode her in a car.*

I nodded. "I don't care what Kaf would have done. I have to live with myself and my choices."

That was the one thing I had figured out on my two-day walkabout.

At that moment, an alarm blared throughout the valley. It took half a second for me to recognize it. That alarm had gone off a handful of times while I was a Guide. It was a warning that something really bad was about to happen to one of the charges. The last time it went off Brad had beaten Crissy and was tracking her through the yards of her neighborhood with murder lust raging through him.

What is that noise? Rasta asked.

"Something's going wrong with a wish. Do you want to transport with me or meet me at the cabin?"

Transport.

I picked up my dog and a second later we were in the little cabin next to the Lodge. Indira appeared a blink later.

"What's going on?" she asked.

"I don't know yet."

I tapped the corner of the largest window in the cabin and an image of Robin instantly appeared. He was in his garage, fashioning a noose from a thin rope which he'd hung from a rafter.

"It's Robin," I said.

"What's happening?" Indira asked. She couldn't see his image. Only the assigned Guide and I were allowed to see what happen with a charge.

"I don't know. He's not—?" I started to ask just as he stepped up on a chair and slipped the noose over his head.

What was going on that he had gotten to this point? Why wasn't Dara with him?

"Where's Dara?" I asked.

"I don't know," Indira said.

I couldn't wait for her. Robin couldn't wait for her.

"Find her," I said. "Bring her here to the cabin. Don't let her leave. I'll be back as soon as I can."

In an instant I was at Robin's side. But for what felt like eternity, I froze. All I could do was stare. The folding chair he'd climbed on lay flat on the ground beneath him. He was clawing at his neck, his feet searching, searching, searching for that chair. Then he went limp and hung perfectly still.

The act of him no longer moving is what finally made me jump to action. I released him from the rope, a faint purple V-shaped bruise already forming on his neck. I placed my mouth on his and blew breath into him until his lungs started to work on their own again. Then I manifested a phone and called for an ambulance.

"I was walking past the garage," I told the officer who got there before the ambulance, "and I heard a sound. It must have been the chair falling." I pointed to the side garage door. "It was unlocked so I came in. He was hanging here. That's all I know."

"Good to know there are people like you in the world," the officer said. "He's a very fortunate kid."

Was he? Was he fortunate that I assigned a Guide that was too self-obsessed to realize the pain her charge was in? And I'd known he was struggling but had no idea of the depth of that pain.

I waited until the doctors had moved Robin from the ER to a private room and then I went to him. His parents were on the way so I didn't have a lot of time with him. He was sleeping. The rise and fall of his thin chest assured me that he was still alive. They had tied his wrists and ankles with restraints, he was on suicide watch.

As I watched him, my heart ached. How did a person get to the point where doing what he did—jumping from the bridge, pulling the trigger, swallowing the pills—was better?

Then I thought of Marsha. Did she know the drugs were killing her? Was she trying to die? I had loved her like a sister. Did she know that? Wasn't that enough to at least make her want to try to get past her demons? I would have done anything for her. All she had to do was ask.

All I had to do was see.

Robin started to move like he was waking up. He swallowed and grimaced. His throat would surely be sore for a while. Slowly, he opened his eyes.

"Where am I?" he asked, his voice gruff and scratchy.

"Hospital," I said.

"Who are you?"

"Desiree. I'm Dara's boss."

"Where's Dara?"

I shifted in my chair. I couldn't remember a Guide ever being dismissed from a wish. Plenty had asked and Kaf always refused, claiming he chose carefully. So had I. But mistakes happen.

"You won't be seeing Dara anymore."

He tried to lift his hands and frowned when he saw that he'd been restrained.

"Why am I tied to the bed?"

"Do you remember what you tried to do?"

He stared at the ceiling as he thought.

"I was playing my game. It got really weird and super intense." His eyes narrowed. "I was trying to get away from these creatures. I used all my ammo and had no other weapons. The only way to save myself from being torn apart, was the noose." He swallowed again and turned to me with blank eyes that chilled me straight through. "Seemed like a good plan. I'm not dead though am I? Looks like I couldn't even do that right."

"I found you in your garage," I told him. "You were hanging from a rafter, clawing at the rope around your neck." My voice broke. "Your feet were trying to reach the chair you had kicked over."

He didn't react. Nothing. Not even a blink.

When Crissy had made her wish, she was desperate to get away from Brad and ready for a new future. As bad as things were, she had hope. Robin had no hope. I'd never seen a person so empty, so ready to cash in.

"It would help a lot," I said, "if you could tell me what's been going on. Dara hasn't communicated very well with me so I don't really know what's happening with your wish."

He laughed and then grimaced again. "My wish? What a fucking joke. I thought wishes made life better."

"They do, if that's what you wish for," I said. "You wished to make it all stop. Right?"

"Isn't that the same thing?"

"It could be." I pulled my legs up onto the chair. "Your wish came from your soul." I tapped my chest. "From the very depths of what makes you, you. So it depends on what your soul wants."

He shut down then. Like so many charges, he didn't want to talk about what was in his soul.

"Tell me," I said, "do you think you're worthy of happiness?"

I could almost feel the light starting to fill the room. He would see that what he'd tried tonight wasn't going to fix anything. He'd reached his rock bottom. Now he could start the climb back up.

"I don't know," he said. Tears burst free from his eyes with his next blink.

I sat straight up as if my spine had just received a jolt of electricity. "Really?"

Rock bottom for this boy was further down than I'd guessed.

"There have to be those," he said, "destined for crappy lives. I'm one of them. What other reason can there be for me being a constant target?"

All those wishes that got rejected filled my head. Some of them surely believed that if they wished hard enough their wishes would be granted. Were they still holding out hope or had they given up like Robin had?

"That has to be it," Robin said in his scratchy voice. "If the world was a perfect place for everyone there would be no need for psychiatrists. No need for doctors. No need for firefighters or police officers... none of those jobs or things that have to do with fixing the broken, bad, or negative. If nothing needed fixing, what purpose would those people have? They'd all be unfulfilled. The world would be unbalanced. I don't think the world can exist without chaos."

The concept of yin and yang. Was he right? If he was, what did that mean? When we granted happiness to one, were we stealing it from another?

"The world does balance itself," I said. "Where there are floods in one area, there are droughts in another. Where there is wealth and overabundance for some, there is dire poverty for others."

My brain was screaming at me to keep exploring this. The answer would tell me if I'd really been making a difference for the last forty-five years, or if I'd merely been moving pebbles from one pile to another. The universe did indeed have a strange sense of humor, but I couldn't accept that I'd been given these powers simply for the amusement of some higher power.

"Consider this," I said, feeling a little like I was coming out of a haze. "You're right. Those who have a calling to help those in need would be left unfulfilled if there wasn't anyone in need. There would be an imbalance. The self-correcting universe would need to provide someone or something to fill the need and restore balance." I smiled, pleased that I'd just saved myself from an existential crisis. "So, hypothesis proven. The world can't exist without chaos."

"You also just proved my point," Robin said, shaking his head. "Some people are destined for an unhappy life."

"Or maybe the balance shifts around." I leaned forward

in the chair, resting my elbows on my knees, chin in my hand. "Are you really telling me that you believe you destined for eternal unhappiness?"

He paused and raised the mattress so he could sit up then leaned forward, mirroring me. "What if I am? I didn't wish to be happy. I wished for it to all stop."

My mind spun, rewinding my memory to when his wish came in. What exactly had he said? I closed my eyes and envisioned his file. When I opened my eyes, he was staring desperately at me.

"Your exact wish was 'I wish I could make it all stop and just be myself'," I said. "That doesn't sound like someone ready to check out."

He shrugged. "Things have happened since then."

"I want you to listen to me," I said, "and for a few minutes I want you to pretend I'm right. Can you do that?"

Another shrug, but the kind that said he was listening.

"The universe saw fit to send me your wish. That means something." I paused so that could sink in a little. "No one has a perfect life. But I believe, whether you do or not, that everyone has the right to be happy. The concept of yin and yang is about balance and harmony. We've established that the world self corrects, but the concept applies to the individual level, too. Where there is bad in someone's life there will be good to restore harmony. What if you've had your bad and now the universe has decided it's time for the good?"

He looked at me in that sideways way Dara did when she didn't want to admit she liked what I was saying.

"If you really want to end your life," I said, "eventually I won't be able to stop you. But if you want to fully accept the chance you've been given to make your life better, I need you to meet me partway."

Chapter Nineteen

Robin

R obin! Oh my god."
My mom burst through the hospital door. Dad followed. She was still wearing the red power dress, he was still in his tux.

"What happened?" She asked like it had to be some kind of an accident.

Yeah, that's it. I remember it clearly now. I accidentally went to the garage. I accidentally found a rope and accidentally turned it into a noose. I accidentally climbed onto a chair and the noose accidentally fell over my head. Then I accidentally kicked the chair over.

"What do you think happened?" Dad looked anywhere but at me, disgust thick in his voice. "Our son tried to kill himself."

The second they entered the room Desiree moved, like a

ghost, to the farthest corner from us. With her eyes locked firmly on mine, she pointed at herself then at me then she nodded. *I'll be back* is what I understood it to mean. As I watched, she disappeared. Literally. She was there and then she wasn't. Like a light going out. Or a life ending.

"Why, Robin? What's going on?" Mom asked. "You said things were better."

"Better?" Dad asked. "What was wrong?"

Of course he didn't know. The two of them spent about as much time alone together as the three of us did. Sure, they went to their dinner parties, but that was business. Family stuff didn't get talked about then.

Dad let his head drop back and he groaned. For the first time, he looked at me. His eyes went first to my neck—I could feel the bruising—and then to my face.

"Is this about getting picked on? I thought we resolved this. You're still letting that stuff get to you?"

Picked on. Right. That's what it was.

I was just trying to exist but no matter where I went, I was either the center of everyone's attention, not in a good way, or the invisible boy. The so-called experts looking out for my well-being—my last principal, my teachers, my parents—told me to just ignore it. Deal with it by pretending it wasn't happening. Eventually the bullies would get bored and move on to something, or rather, someone else. That's what we Westmores were really good at. Pretending bad stuff didn't happen.

A woman in a simple black skirt and light-orange sweater walked in the room. She held her hand out to first mom, then dad, and introduced herself as Dr. Rice.

"He'll be fine," Dr. Rice said. "Physically that is. He was lucky that girl found him."

"What girl?" Mom asked and looked around the room. "The one sitting here when we walked in?"

"He has some bruising, obviously," Dr. Rice continued, "and his voice will be scratchy for a few days, but physically he will be fine. He's fortunate. I've seen attempted hangings that resulted in things like brain damage or paralysis. His emotional state, however, is something we need to discuss."

For the next fifteen minutes they talked about me like I wasn't there or like I was too incompetent to be involved with a discussion about myself. Invisible again. The doctor did most of the talking. My mom asked a few questions. My dad stood there with his arms crossed and didn't say a word.

"I've prescribed a pain medication and something to help him sleep," Dr. Rice said. "I'll make sure he has a prescription for both before we send him home. If he's like most teenagers, he's not getting enough sleep. He needs time to rest and heal. Also, someone from psychiatry will be right in to talk with you."

Dad looked at his watch. "Does this have to happen now? It's late. We've all had a long night."

For the first time Dr. Rice fixed her gaze on me.

Sadness. Pity.

Yep, I wanted to say, this is how it is. It's not breakfast time. That's our scheduled 'talk about important stuff for five minutes' time. Come back in a few hours.

"I think now is best," Dr. Rice said. "We need to understand what's going on with Robin. We don't want this to happen again."

"Oh, don't worry," Dad said. "It won't."

He wouldn't stand for it.

Mom placed a hand on Dad's arm. The signal for him to return to his mute-in-the-background position.

"We'll wait right here," Mom said.

The doctor shook their hands again and then came over to my bedside. She gripped the bedrails as she said, "We're here to help you, Robin. Whatever the problem, all you have to do is talk to us."

As soon as the doctor left, Mom was at my side, tears flooding her eyes.

"Why didn't you talk to me, Robin," she said. "We fixed

this before, we certainly can again. It didn't need to come to this."

"If we fixed it before," I asked in my raspy voice, "why did it happen again?"

She stood straight, like I'd just insulted her. I suppose I did.

"Let's see what this psychiatrist has to say." She stood, impossibly, even straighter. "Whatever help you need, we'll get it for you." She put her hands over her heart. "Sweetie, it hurts me to know that you're hurting this much. What happened?"

"Perfect timing." A man, probably in his thirties, with moppy hair sort of like mine walked in. "That's what I'd like to know, too. I'm Dr. Stewart Bell." He held out his hand to me first, but the restraints kept me from shaking his hand. "I don't think you need those right now." He unlatched my wrists. "I will have to put them back on when I leave. Just so you know."

"You're from psychiatry?" Mom asked.

"I am." He shook her hand then Dad's. "Let's find out what's going on?"

"Can I have some water first?" I asked.

Mom leaped to her feet, practically knocking Dr. Bell out of the way, and grabbed the Styrofoam cup of water they'd left on my bedside table.

It hurt to swallow, but the water felt good at the same time. I took a long drink and then words spewed from my mouth like vomit. I left out Brianna's name because I didn't want anything coming back on her.

As I'd talked, my parents said nothing. The only reaction from either of them was Mom getting paler and paler.

When I was done she mumbled, "I'll make sure the tux gets back tomorrow."

Really? That was her concern.

"So what made you decide suicide was the way to deal with this?" Dr. Bell asked.

Mom gasped, presumably at the word suicide. I liked Dr. Bell. He was direct.

"I don't know." I stared out the window. The looks of *what the hell's the matter with you, boy* from my father were too much. "I'm just so tired of it. I thought things would be different here. But it's all the same."

Dad looked away. Mom's tears finally spilled.

"You're right," Dr. Bell said. "It is the same. There will always be bullies. Nothing to be done about that. What can be different is the way you deal with them. We'll work on that over the next couple of days."

"Couple of days?" I asked.

"Standard procedure with a suicide attempt. You'll stay here and see a lot of me in that time. For now, it's late. I'll come back in the morning and we'll talk more."

But I didn't want him to leave.

"Do we need to be here for that?" Dad asked.

"Not necessarily," Dr. Bell said. "If you sign a form giving me permission to see him without you, Robin and I are good chatting alone. That would actually be best. We can have family discussions later. In the meantime, here's my card." He handed a card to each of my parents and set one on my bedside tray. Then he stood at the end of the bed and put a hand on my ankle. "Call me, night or day, if you need to talk."

He stared me in the eye until I nodded.

A nurse came in after Dr. Bell left. As she gently reattached my wrist restraints she said, "You can stay if you'd like, but Robin could use some sleep."

"We'll go," Dad said and was already out the door.

"Don't let him upset you," Mom told me. "He has a hard time dealing with things like this."

"Things like this?" I asked. "You mean the inconvenience of his son trying to kill himself?"

"Robin," she said, a little anger blending with her tears, "do you have any idea how much we love you? Do you have any idea how devastated we would be right now if you had… succeeded?"

My already aching throat closed up. I couldn't respond.

"I am horrified that I didn't know what was going on," she said. "I wish you would have said something to me. You said these kids were your friends. I thought things were looking up for you."

"Yeah," I said, "me too. Guess the world doesn't need any more happy people right now."

She frowned. "What do you mean by that?"

I just shook my head.

She leaned down and placed a kiss on my forehead. "I realize it may not seem like it, but I am always here for you. Don't you worry, we are going to fix this."

Chapter Twenty

Desiree

Could a wish end badly? Was that even possible in this realm of satisfactory endings? If Robin had actually ended his life, effectively stopping the bullying and his unfathomable pain, would that mean he had or had not gotten his heart's desire?

What he had said, about certain people being undeserving of a happy life had shaken my foundation. Was he right? I fully believed he was right about the world existing on a balanced scale. When something happened on the Yin side, something equal and opposite needed to happen on the Yang side to restore equilibrium. What if my fear was valid and that by granting the wishes of some we were taking away the happiness of another?

"Desiree." Indira was coming toward me as I walked toward the cabin.

I still had to deal with Dara, but after leaving Robin I needed to get all these thoughts and questions racing through my brain to be still. A few minutes sitting by the lake, meditating on its shimmering surface had helped.

"What happened?" Indira asked. "Is Robin okay?"

"Physically, yes. Emotionally, this poor kid is a mess. He tried to hang himself."

"He what? I just saw him the other day. He looked so happy. So excited about the dance and that girl."

As we walked to the cabin I told her what had happened. How he'd been setup. How half the kids at the dance harassed and bullied him and made everything worse by papering social media with pictures of him.

"He couldn't take it anymore," I said. "He thought things were getting better and they only got worse."

"Was Dara aware of any of this?"

"I don't think so. That's my fault. I trusted her just like I did the Guides. She took advantage."

"He's still alive," Indira said, placing a hand on my arm. "It's not too late to help him."

Olanna and at least a hundred Guides had gathered around my cabin. As always, word had spread like wildfire in a windstorm.

I was about to tell them all to leave, to go back inside the Lodge and attend to their own business. Then I realized I could use this as another 'teaching moment' as my mom would have called it. They needed to understand that just because a wish had been granted, a satisfactory ending wasn't guaranteed, that was where they came in. Their job was to guide the wish and the charge to that satisfactory ending.

Inside the cabin, Dara was sitting near the fireplace and jumped to her feet when I walked in.

"Is he okay? Why did you make me stay here? I should have gone to him."

"You should have gone to him a week ago," I said.

Not only did I have the aurora lights hovering around me, I had a tie-dyed swirl of emotions going on inside me, too. Red hot fury. Moody blue sadness. Pea green nausea. A white void of not knowing how to handle this. A black hole of knowing I had to be hard on her now.

"He told me all you've done is text him when he summons."

"What?" Indira demanded. "How could you be so irresponsible?"

"Indira—" I started.

"If I had known," Indira said, "that you'd been ignoring him I would have stepped in to help."

"I haven't been ignoring him," Dara said. "I've gone to him."

"Indira," I said placing my hands on her shoulders. "You are welcome to stay but you have to let me handle this."

"Because you've done such a great job so far?" she asked.

Her words made me flinch. I don't think I'd ever seen Indira angry. Irritated sure, but even then she handled situations with poise and fairness. Her anger now only emphasized how screwed up Robin's situation was.

"You're right," I told her. "Please, stay and make sure I do this right. But let me do it. Okay?"

"You're as lost as Dara is, aren't you?" Indira asked.

The question caught me completely off guard.

"I was, but I think I found the path again. There are some things we can't know until we've walked that long and winding road in someone else's moccasins."

Slowly, her hard expression started to soften and she pointed across the room. "I'll go stand over there and keep my mouth shut." Her bracelets jangled as she mimicked locking her mouth.

I turned to Dara and indicated the big leather chairs. "Sit. Please."

"Desiree, I didn't know."

"That's exactly the problem," I said while settling into my own chair. "It was your job to know. How many times did I ask you to check on him? How many times did he ask you to come and you didn't?"

"I talked to him."

"He asked to talk to you face-to-face. You texted him. It's not the same thing. Not even close." I opened my tablet, clicked on her file and then Robin's. "Let me refresh your memory on how one *conversation* went: Robin texts, 'Can you come?' You respond, 'Is that really what you need?' Robin texts, 'I'll be okay. I don't think this wish is going the way it should though.' You respond, 'Keep the faith. Remember, I told you things could go badly at times. It will all work out the way it's supposed to.' Robin says, 'How is it supposed to work out? I wished for everyone to leave me alone and the only one doing that is you.'"

I paused to look at Dara to see if she was getting it yet. By the way she was avoiding eye contact, I guessed she was.

"Robin continued, 'Do you know what happened to me at school today?' You said, 'Yes. I'm sorry.' He said, 'And now they're putting pictures of me all over the internet.' You asked, 'Do you want me to take them down?'"

The more I read, the more Dara squirmed.

"Do you remember that conversation?" I asked like a prosecuting attorney. "That was the night he pointed his dad's gun at his own chest."

In the corner, Indira gasped.

"I remember," Dara said. "He said he was fine."

"He asked you to come," I said. "Your solution was to take down images from social media."

Dara frowned, but didn't say anything more.

"Last night," I said, opening another file, "while walking home five miles from the dance he sent you a text and asked you to come. Instead of going to him, you texted with him again. He said, 'I need you.' You said, 'Aw, that's sweet.' He said,"—I paused to make sure she was listening—"'I'm serious. Everything is falling apart.' You asked, 'What happened?' He said, 'The dance was a disaster.' You responded with, 'What? What dance?'"

Indira lurched forward like she was going to attack Dara. I held up a hand, stopping her.

I went on quoting the texts. "He said, 'I thought you were supposed to keep track of my wish.' You said, 'Sorry. What happened?' Again he asked, 'Can't you just come?'"

Dara was crying softly now.

"Why didn't you know about the dance? I thought you were checking on him." I asked, pacing now, too upset to sit any longer. I had to keep reminding myself that Robin wasn't my responsibility. That's why there were Guides. I couldn't possibly keep track of all the wishes. Why did I feel so guilty then?

"I was checking on him," she insisted. "Every hour or so I looked to see what he was doing."

I remembered the first time she checked on him. She opened a picture, saw him sitting at his desk, and closed the file again. The entire process took about five seconds.

"Did you just look," I asked, already knowing the answer, "or did you take the time to find out what was going on with him?"

Dara responded by staring silently at her hands.

"What were you doing that was more important than your charge's pleas for help?" I asked, even though I already knew that, too.

Dara sniffed and ran her sleeve across her nose. "I was having dinner with my parents."

"And that first time he asked you to come?"

"I was with Wyatt," she said, picking at her bracelets. "But I did go that time."

I checked the file. "And what did you do when you went to him?"

She glared at me this time and jutted her chin at the file. "Apparently you know all. You tell me."

"I'm asking you," I said.

She threw her right leg over her left and kicked her foot. "I transported him to school because he missed his bus."

"And then you left."

Another glare. "You'd make a really good detective. You've got the bad cop thing down perfectly." She jerked a thumb over her shoulder at Indira. "The gypsy queen over there can be the good cop."

"I know you're embarrassed," I said.

"Why should I be embarrassed?" Dara asked, slamming her hands on the arms of the chair as she jumped to her feet. "I was only doing what you gave me permission to do. You said I could spend time with Wyatt and my parents. You also said I wasn't supposed to interfere with Robin's wish. Just be there to guide."

"I told you that your charge came first," I said.

She threw her hands in the air and turned away.

This was the part where the path got foggy. Kaf would have been unforgiving if a Guide had neglected a charge. But he also would never have allowed a Guide the kind of freedom I had given Dara.

The Guides had completely converged on the cabin by this point. They had filled every available inch of the porch and pressed up against the windows. Olanna was most likely projecting the conversation on a screen for everyone outside the cabin.

"You're right, I did say you could see them." Scale tip to one side. "That was my mistake. I didn't realize how big of a distraction they'd be. So I'm going to have to revoke the privilege." Tip back to even.

"You can't do that," Dara said, panicked. "I'll do better."

"Dara, a boy nearly killed himself. I can't take the chance that something like this will happen again."

"You can set the rules." Dara stood in front of me with her hands folded together. I'd never seen her so desperate. "You can set times for when I can text with Wyatt. You can make it so I can't go see him or my parents unless you specifically okay it."

"That's not good enough," I said, the black hole inside me growing bigger and colder. "See, I've been letting you do things that the others cannot. It's not fair."

"No," Dara said simply and with finality.

"What?"

"You can't. That was part of my agreement. Either I got to see Wyatt and my parents or Kaf could let me die."

"Are you seriously telling me," I said slowly, not believing the turn this was taking, "that you would choose death?"

"Are you telling me that you'll let me?" She startled at the unintelligible rumble that rose from the crowd then turned on me with a glare. "This is okay with you? Public shaming? How is this any different from what Robin's so-called friends did to him?"

I'd given her too much leeway. I couldn't let her disrespect me this way in front of the Guides. Time to pull back.

I held out my hand. "You can give me your phone or I can make it inoperable. You can go once more to say goodbye, but then you won't be able to see them anymore."

Would that make it easier? I would have given anything to let my parents know what had happened to me. They suffered so much. But how do you look a person in the eye and say goodbye knowing you'll never see them again?

"No," Dara said again. "That isn't what we agreed to."

I had only known Dara for about three months. In that short time I had learned that she had a stubborn side that was impenetrable. She wouldn't back down. Either she'd get her way or she'd die for what she felt was right. The hippie in me respected that.

I looked at Rasta, lying like a pile of yarn next to Indira. When I did, he sat up. He knew I needed help.

Sarah did not burn.

God, I loved that dog.

"I guess we're at an impasse," I said. "What happened with Robin is a huge problem. I can't let it happen again. There's only one solution."

Dara's eyes went wide. When Kaf saved her, she'd been lying in a pool of blood, literally moments from dying.

"You have to go," I said.

Indira, who had been leaning against the wall, stood upright.

"You're going to let me die?" Dara asked. "You would really do that?"

"You can't have special privileges." I wasn't even talking to Dara anymore. I was saying these words for the Guides' benefit. "If I allowed everyone to come and go as they pleased and be distracted from the needs of their charges... No, that can't happen."

"What are you saying?" Dara asked, her voice rising with hysteria.

Dara ended up volunteering at Rita's soup kitchen because I dragged her there. Kaf used her to make me take this position. He knew how important she was to me. How I would have done anything to keep her alive.

"Go back to your family and Wyatt," I said, envy flooding my body. "You never should have come here."

Dara's expression shifted between joy and sorrow. "You're making me leave? You won't compromise with me?"

"That's not what you want," I said. "You don't want to be here."

The momentary silence was interminable.

"Will I ever see you again?" she asked.

I had to get my emotions under control before answering that. I didn't trust my voice.

"No. You truly have become like a little sister to me, but I have to do what's best for the group. I'm disappointed that you can't put others' needs above your own desires and I hope someday you can. It really is much more gratifying to do for others than to take for yourself."

My heart was splitting in two. I had agreed to her conditions and the scales tipped to the side of good. I had to be as cold and nasty as I had ever been to tip them back and restore balance to the throng listening outside.

I touched my fingers together and the same glow that had surrounded her when Kaf infused her with magic returned. This time instead of growing strong and bright, the glow faded until it went out like a candle extinguishing.

"Where would you like to go?" I asked. "Home or to Wyatt."

"Desiree—"

"Stop," I said with a shake of my head. "You made your choice. This is the last thing I will do for you so choose well. Where do you want to go?"

"I'll miss you so much," she said, her voice barely a whisper. "Thank you for saving me."

She had to leave. I couldn't do this for one more second. "Where, Dara?"

"Send me home, please."

☮ ☮ ☮

When I got back to my bus, numb after everything that had happened, I found Adellika waiting for me.

"What's going on?" I asked. "If it's not an emergency, I'd prefer to wait until morning. Come find me at the cabin in the morning."

Gypsy V was, as it had always been, my happy place, my sanctuary. My rule was very clear, no negative vibes in my home.

"You need help," Adellika said.

"Oh, I'm fine," I lied. "This was a rough day, but everything will work out."

She shook her head. "There is no harmony. You need

help."

I was about to protest again, repeat that everything was fine, but she had already vanished.

I'd taken charge tonight and I was actually quite proud of the way I'd handled Dara. Suddenly, however, I felt completely out of control. Adellika had been quietly on my side from the start. If she thought I needed help, maybe things were worse than I realized.

Chapter Twenty-One

Robin

Dr. Bell came to my room every day for three days and we talked for at least an hour each time.

"Let's review the strategy we talked about," he said on my last day. "First, clean up your social media. Unfriend or block everyone who's harassing you now or has in the past. Delete their posts. Don't even read them. Don't give them power over your feelings or your life."

"Like any of that is going to stop them," I said. "The posts will still go up."

"That doesn't mean they have to affect you. You can't control what others think or do but you can control how you respond to it. We talked about this, remember?"

"I remember."

"How often do they bother you in school?"

"Every day."

"Do you stand up for yourself?"

I laughed.

"What's funny?" Dr. Bell asked.

"The bus driver says that staying silent is the same thing as condoning."

Dr. Bell jumped to his feet and clapped his hands. "Yes! That! I couldn't say it any better. Why are you squirming?"

"Because everyone has always told me to ignore the bullies. That eventually they'll get bored and leave me alone."

"And? How's that been working for you?"

I bit back a smile. "They don't seem bored yet."

"Have you reported the instances?"

"To who? No one even knows I exist," I reminded him. Okay, that wasn't true. Mr. Emerson and Ms. Rolfing knew me now. Miss Clark, too. "Even if I did say something, the school won't do anything. They claim zero tolerance, but unless you have witnesses and irrefutable proof, it's just your word against the other guy's. Zane has his minions to back him up. Who do I have?"

"You'll need to build your case," Dr. Bell said. "Don't confuse asking for help with whining or tattling. You have the right to defend yourself. You need to make them do something about it. There's no one who's witnessed any of the harassment who could back up your claims?"

I stood from the uncomfortable vinyl-cushioned chair to wander the room. None of the teachers. Zane and The Minions always did their tormenting out of adult view. Then I thought of Mr. Lacey. "The bus driver, maybe."

Dr. Bell jotted his name in his notebook. "People don't like to get involved in situations like this, but you never know. Maybe he'll talk to your principal or write a letter. Have your parents contacted the school yet?"

"They didn't know there was a problem until two days ago."

This earned me a sad smile.

"That's almost always the case," Steward said. "Parents don't know until something big happens. We'll all come together for some family counseling sessions. We'll make sure they understand exactly what's going on with you, and what they can do to support you." The alarm on Dr. Bell's phone went off then. "Our time is almost up but there's one last thing I want you to think about."

"Sounds like homework," I said and sat cross-legged on my bed.

"Yeah, but you like homework," Dr. Bell said with a wink. "I want you to consider what might be going on in Zane's and Ivan's lives. There's usually a reason someone becomes a bully. Maybe they're getting bullied themselves. Maybe there's a problem with one of their family members and they take their frustrations out on others."

I thought of Cole back in Wisconsin and how his brother beat on him.

"I have to go see my next patient," Dr. Bell said. "You have my card, right?"

"Yep."

"I'm here. Any time, any reason. We're going to fix this. I need you to hang in there with me. Okay?"

"Yep."

"Your three days are up," he said. "You've got some coping skills now."

I nodded.

"Okay. You can go home in the morning and I'll be in touch with your mom to set up regular appointments."

He stood there, waiting for me to respond.

"Yeah. Thanks."

As sick as I was of the hard hospital bed, uncomfortable chairs, and bad food, I didn't want to go home. Here the nurses came in every couple of hours to check on me and see if I needed anything. Dr. Bell came in to talk to me. I knew that was their job, but they paid attention to me. I didn't feel invisible. Even though I didn't like talking about my *issues*, I liked that they asked.

I woke up early the next morning, ready to go. Mom said she'd be there at nine. At nine-fifteen I figured traffic must be heavy.

By nine-thirty I was worried. I hoped she hadn't gotten in an accident or something. Worry quickly turned to anger. What were the chances she'd been in an accident? Remote. Why was it always okay to put me on the back burner?

At nine-forty-five I realized the truth was, she didn't care. I was right before. They would have been better off without me. I was obviously an inconvenience.

She finally walked into my room at seven minutes after ten. More than an hour later than she said. No phone call to let me know she was running late. I didn't even warrant a five-second text.

"Sorry," she said as she entered my room. "I had to take care of a phone call. Let's get you home. I've got all your favorite foods waiting for you."

Nothing had changed. Her clients would always come first. Food would always be the salve for what ailed me.

She signed the discharge papers after Dr. Bell and a doctor talked to her about my aftercare. As if I'd been admitted for surgery instead of for trying to off myself. Of course they'd messed with my brain and my feelings enough that it felt like they'd been digging around inside me. Emotional surgery.

Mom and I didn't talk on the way home, she had a business call she *had to take*. It was all I could do to stop myself from ripping her phone out of her hand and hurling it out the damn window. I was right, nothing had changed. Don't know why I'd bothered to hope for anything different.

Once home, she said I could skip one more day of school. Good, I had tons of homework to catch up on.

She took a few minutes to make me some tea and toast a bagel.

"See, I remembered," she said of the bagel. Proof that

she had been listening. Gold star for Mom. She stood there watching me eat for a long, uncomfortable minute. "I'm sorry, Robin. I wish you would have come to me."

"You were busy," I said, not bothering to hide the anger in my voice.

Her cheeks flushed. "Yes, but I will always make time for you. You can always tell me when something is going on. So tell me, how can I help?"

That was how she answered her phone. *Marjorie Westmore Marketing, how can I help you today?*

"How can you help?" I asked. "For starters you could have been on time today."

"Robin, I had—"

"I know, you had to take that phone call." Why couldn't I have been wrong about this? "One day, *one hour* away from your precious clients. That's all it would have been. You couldn't have rescheduled your morning calls just this once? When your phone rang when we were in the car why couldn't you have said 'I've got something important I need to take care of, can I call you back?' It would *help* if you'd stop telling me that you'll make time for me and just do it."

I was yelling at my mother. It should have felt good to get this off my chest. Instead I only felt sadder and more pissed off that after everything that had happened, I still had to ask for her attention.

She came around the breakfast bar and spun my barstool so I was facing her. Then she put her fingers under my chin and lifted my face.

"I'm sorry. I'm really truly sorry." Her eyes were full of tears but her voice stayed strong. "I will show you. I'll prove to you how important you are to me. Tell me what you need."

"You don't know?" How could she not know?

"I need you to help me help you. I don't want to guess at what you need." A bit of frustration broke through her composure. Good. "We're out of practice at being a family. We need to figure this out again."

Dr. Bell and I had talked about this, ways to make things better at home. Mom's thing was food. She was happy when she was feeding people.

"Maybe we could have dinner as a family more often." My voice was flat, robotic. The anger was still raging inside me. I shouldn't have to ask.

She smiled and held her arms out. "Can I hug you?"

My throat tightened so I could only respond with a nod. My body relaxed, like it was releasing a long-held sigh, as she held me close. I couldn't remember the last time anyone had hugged me.

"I like the idea of dinner together," she said. "I really do."

But she didn't commit to it. Which told me if I wanted dinner with my parents, I'd have to make dinner and then sit in the kitchen until they came in to eat. The chances of them coming in at the same time were slim to none.

"I know that look," she said. "You think I'm humoring you." She picked up her phone and tapped the screen a few times. "What day?"

"What day what?"

"What day should we go out for dinner? If we put it on the schedule we'll do it. So, what day?"

Out for dinner? A little thrill of hope skittered through me. "Friday. I'll only have two days of school this week, but they might be kinda weird. It would help to know I'll be able to talk to you about them."

She nodded as she tapped. "Done." Then she stood there, fidgeting and glancing at the clock on the microwave.

"Go to work," I said. "I'm fine."

"Okay," she nodded tentatively. "You're sure?"

I answered her with a blank stare. She answered me with another hug.

☮ ☮ ☮

When I opened my laptop, I found ten emails from the Lunch Bunch—seven from Jeremiah, two from Emily, one from Pranav. Emily went on and on in both emails saying how sorry she was and how it was just supposed to be a joke and she didn't know it would get so out of control and how she'd been praying I was okay. She begged me to forgive her, which didn't surprise me. Emily was emotional that way. What did surprise me was her insistence that Brianna didn't know.

"She's so nice," Emily said. "A genuinely, really nice person. Ivan used her as much as he did you. Don't be mad at her."

God, please let that be true.

Pranav's email simply said, "Sorry, man."

His sincerity was completely underwhelming.

Jeremiah was frantic. Each message got longer and more involved with how Ivan had planned the whole thing with Zane and how Ivan threatened them all with retaliation if they said anything to anyone. He asked me to *please* email or text or call to let him know how I was. He also claimed Brianna didn't know and my hope grew a little bigger.

In Jeremiah's sixth email, he said he realized they probably wouldn't let me have a laptop or phone in the hospital—they didn't—so whenever I could contact him was cool. In the seventh, he talked about my game and how fun it was and how he thought I'd really be able to do something with it. Sucking up, basically.

I'd never had anyone suck up to me before. It was kind of nice, but it made me mad at the same time. If he would've stood up to Ivan, or said just one damn word to me, none of this would have happened.

Dr. Bell told me to stay away from social media, but I needed to delete and unfriend or block people. It would be a little hard to do that without seeing what they'd said.

"One last time," I told myself. "I'll never look again."

I meant it.

Of course I was everywhere. For someone who was so invisible and such a loser, it was unbelievable how much attention they gave me. There were dozens of pictures from the dance. There were pictures of me standing next to Brianna holding out the corsage that had been turned into oh-so witty memes.

I'm a loser, but I got you this pretty flower. Please like me.

I don't always make a fool out of myself. But when I do, I give my left nut.

I know it's social suicide, but would you dance with me?

Next came awful pictures of hanging corpses. Zane posted all of those and, of course, he got tons of praise for them.

Tweety tried. Tweety failed.

Can't even do this right.

Better luck next time.

The one that upset me the most was a picture Zane had posted to Ivan's page of two hands high-fiving. Beneath it: *Mission accomplished.*

That proved it. They'd been in on the whole homecoming dance setup together.

I debated sending the posts to my principal. Dr. Bell suggested that I get screen grabs of them so I could establish a "pattern of abuse" if it came to that. A little contradictory to the 'stay off social media' advice but I got his point. That way maybe the posts would get taken down. Even though the damage would have already been done and nothing is ever gone from the internet. They'd probably organize an assembly to talk about cyberbullying. The kids in my school were stupid, but they weren't dumb. They'd claim freedom of speech or some other right. The principal would back down because the kids' parents paid big tuition to this school and if the school wasn't happy with their money they could easily take it elsewhere. I'd heard it all before.

I blocked everyone I could and then tried to do

homework. I was too pissed off at Zane to concentrate though. I'd do it later. Instead I turned on my game and disappeared into the world of *Pharm Runner*.

I still needed my headlamp, but it wasn't pitch black in the jungle. The sky was starting to lighten. As I got closer to the harvesting tree, the Zanthers and bird-creatures crept out of the jungle. There were hundreds of them.

I ran and this time when I got to the hanging tree, there was no noose. The sign was still there but now it said, *Look in the roots.*

The tree had a massive bird's nest of roots, tangled and intertwined. I hesitated, sure if I stuck my hand in there something would grab me and pull me in. The creatures were getting closer, I had no choice if I wanted to live. I reached into the roots and felt something cool and metallic despite the heat and humidity of the jungle. I pulled out a machine gun. Immediately, I turned and sprayed round after round into the Zanthers and bird creatures. I rejoiced as the creatures cried out in pain, until I realized that their cries weren't animal, they were human.

I jerked off my headphones and pushed away from my desk. This was not what *Pharm Runner* was supposed to be. It was just a simple, fun, dorky game about harvesting flowers. There weren't supposed to be this many creatures. There certainly shouldn't be enough that the only way to escape was via machine gun.

I didn't want to play anymore, not until whatever Dara had done to my computer was removed. Instead I laid on my bed and listened to music.

Mom popped her head in my room at one point. "There's a pot of chicken stew on the stove and some biscuits you can zap in the microwave. Okay?"

Even tonight she couldn't take ten minutes to eat with me? Of course not. Stupid me. Dinner wasn't on the schedule until Friday.

"Sure," I said, "thanks."

216

"You're doing all right?"

"I'm fine, Mom." She kept looking at me like I was someone she didn't know, a stranger in her house. Or like I might self-combust at any moment. "Just chilling."

Later I was lying there, watching TV and waiting for the sleeping pill the doctor gave me to kick in. I thought of the Zanthers and the bird creatures and how they kept multiplying and relentlessly coming at me. There had to be a way to fight them off other than blasting them with a machine gun. Maybe there was another option that I hadn't found yet. A cheat to the top of the tree or something.

I was just dozing off, wondering if there was a cheat for doing away with Zane without getting caught, when I heard Dad get home. He had to know I got out of the hospital today, but he didn't stop by my room. I think he paused outside my door, but then moved on. No time to bother with his inconvenient son.

So if we were going to see each other today, I was going to have to go to him? I would have to volunteer how I was doing in a way that would make him believe I was not only mentally fine but remorseful as well. Then, maybe, he'd talk to me again.

It was all on me. Stay off of social media because the jerkoffs of the world were mean there. Don't dare like a popular girl because everyone will let you know what an idiot you are for even thinking about her. If you're having problems tell your parents, but don't expect that they'll do anything about it.

Make your dad give a damn that you're still alive.

All on me.

Another hour later, I was still wide awake, thinking about Dad and Ivan and Zane. Mostly Zane. He'd started all this.

Why the hell wasn't the sleeping pill working? Maybe I'd gotten too much rest in the hospital. Was that possible? I was used to staying awake late into the night and surviving

on little sleep. I read the pill bottle: *take 1 or 2 as needed.*
The only thing I wanted to do was sleep so I could stop
thinking about stuff.

I popped another one.

After another hour without even a yawn and that high-
five on Ivan's page flashing again and again in my brain, I
went downstairs to get a glass of milk.

Dad's gun case was sitting on the counter. What was
going on there? I couldn't remember a time he had ever left a
gun out. In his den or bedroom sure—that's what made Mom
implement the vault rule—but never, ever in a common area
of the house.

Dad's words from a few days ago whispered to my
overloaded brain. *If I was a betting man I'd guess that I'm
going to want to blow off a little steam.*

It always seemed to work for him. The pressure in my
head was reaching critical mass. Couldn't hurt.

☮ ☮ ☮

I knew Zane's house because of the mountain lion.
"Can't miss my house," he told everyone one day. "Mom put
a freakin' lion in the front yard." Plus, Zane was right there,
standing with his back to his bedroom window, lifting
weights. At one in the morning, Zane was lifting weights.
Then he stopped and did jumping jacks. Then picked up the
weights again.

I squinted and centered the red dot on Zane's white tank
top, right between his shoulder blades. The pressure in my
head started to ease as I slowly applied pressure to the
trigger. I imagined the dot becoming a seeping spot of blood.
Zane would drop the weights, then he'd drop to the floor.

Fifty feet away, Zane kept pumping weights and doing
jumping jacks, no clue that a gun was aimed at his back.

Just as I was about to pull all the way, Zane's bedroom
door flew open, startling me and making the laser bounce all

around. A man, his dad I guessed, came in. He'd see the laser. I jerked the gun so it was pointing straight up into the sky. Now I'd have to start all over again.

The man said something. Zane didn't respond. The man yelled something and Zane silently absorbed the words. He shoved a piece of paper in Zane's face, his free hand flailing angrily. Then he left, slamming the door shut as he did. After a few seconds of standing there with his hands on his hips and his head hanging, Zane went back to lifting.

What was that all about? Guess maybe Zane's perfect life wasn't so perfect.

I want you to consider what might be going on in Zane's and Ivan's lives, Dr. Bell had said. Maybe they're getting bullied themselves. Maybe there's a problem with one of their family members and they take their frustrations out on others.

Shit.

I couldn't do it. I wanted to. Every atom in my body screamed at me to just pull the damn trigger. Show them that they couldn't continue to fuck with me and get away with it.

But I wasn't my avatar. I wasn't a killer. If I wanted to blow off steam using a gun, I'd have to do it from inside my game.

I tucked Dad's gun into the inside pocket of my jacket and ran the eight blocks home.

Chapter Twenty-Two

Robin

If his dad hadn't shown up when he had, would I really have shot Zane? The question kept playing over and over in my mind. Was I capable of killing someone? I'd almost killed myself. Were those things different sides of the same coin or not even remotely related?

The anger I'd felt after coming home from the hospital yesterday felt like it was still bubbling just under my skin. I needed to diffuse it, but going to my tormentor's house with a gun in the middle of the night wasn't the answer.

I wasn't a violent person, I knew that. I was a smart person. Smart people don't react emotionally. They sit back, analyze, and carefully figure out their response. Last night had been an emotional reaction. So how would a smart, non-violent person respond to a situation like mine?

I was still trying to figure out the answer to that question as Mom chattered at me all through breakfast.

"Is something wrong with your hand?" she asked.

I blinked a few times. "What?"

"Your right hand."

She pointed and I looked down. I was opening and closing it. Stretching it.

"Didn't realize I was doing that."

"Is something wrong with it?" she repeated.

"It's just kind of achy. Don't know what's wrong."

"Maybe it's a result…"

She let the thought die. Message received though. There were a lot of nerves in the neck. The rope might have done some damage.

"If it doesn't get better, we'll have the doctor look at it." She gathered up her phone and her tea. "Have a good day, sweetheart. If things are too hard today, call me."

"Great. Will do." Yeah, great. They'd all be looking at me like I was a time bomb, ready to go off and slice my wrists with a pair of scissors right there in class.

Four blocks from the bus stop I heard someone running up behind me.

"Robin." Brianna jumped in front of me, forcing me to stop walking, and stared up at me. Her round, hazel eyes were full of compassion and her chin quivered. After a second, she threw her arms around me. "I'm so sorry. I didn't know, I swear. Thank god you're okay."

Right. I'm so okay I almost blew a hole in your boyfriend's back last night.

"You are, aren't you?" She was pleading more than asking. "Okay, I mean. I broke things off with Zane. It was our first and last date. I swear I had no idea."

Everyone was proclaiming innocence. Emily swore she thought it was just a joke. Jeremiah claimed he had knowledge but wasn't involved.

"So they used you," I said, hoping I didn't sound as robotic as I felt.

"They did," Brianna said, slumping with relief that I believed her. "I never would have gone along with this. You *know* that."

She was laying it on too heavy. Did I dare trust any of them anymore? For all I knew I was getting set up for another round.

"Right," I said and started walking again. "I know that."

Zane and his minions were already at the bus stop when we got there.

"Ignore them," Brianna said.

"What do I need to ignore?" I asked. "It almost sounds like you know they're going to do something."

"Of course they will. They're jerks." She cocked her head to the side. "You don't believe me, do you?"

I said nothing, just stared at the spot on Zane's back where the laser dot had been a few hours earlier. How very different this morning would be if I had pulled the trigger. How long it would have taken them to trace the shooting to me?

"It's okay. I understand," Brianna said, nodding as if giving convincing herself. "You'll see, I'm on your side."

Thad pointed at us and Zane turned. When he saw Brianna, standing next to me, the cocky smirk on his face faded. Maybe she really did mean everything she'd said. If that was the case, Brianna should be careful. She could be Zane's next victim.

"So Tweety flies again," Zane said.

"Shut up, Zane," Brianna snapped at him.

"No, I'm impressed," Zane said. "I thought only cats had multiple lives. You should run an experiment, Tweety. See how many tries it takes to kill a bird. Let me know if you need help tying knots."

He went on and on, his minions laughing and encouraging him. Brianna stayed by my side and told Zane what a jerk he was. Dr. Bell's words about standing up for myself kept sounding in my ears, but if I said anything they'd just laugh and intensify the torment. Then again, defending myself didn't have to be verbal.

I took out my phone and started taking pictures of all of them. Phase one, under way. They were so involved with their own congratulatory high-fives, they didn't even notice.

But Brianna did.

"What are you doing?" she asked.

I shrugged and mumbled, "Eye for an eye."

It took about two seconds for her to understand. She stepped in front of me and gently lowered my hand holding my phone. "An eye for an eye is not the way to deal with them. You'll just make it worse."

"What am I supposed to do?" Stand up for yourself but don't antagonize. How the hell was I supposed to do that? "If you have an idea, I'd love to hear it. Preferably one that will have a real impact."

The bus pulled up and Brianna got on first. She patted the seat next to her when I got close. I was going to pass her by. There were other seats available. I could take one of those and disappear into my own thoughts for five miles. If I sat next to her, it would probably be five miles of her telling me how sorry she was and what a jerk Zane was. But sitting next to her would bother Zane and I liked that idea. Be a thorn in his side. I sat next to her but told her I didn't want to talk.

They kept provoking me with taunts and birdcalls. Finally, more for the sanity of the other passengers than myself, I stood up.

"Robin," Brianna pleaded, her hand on my arm, "just let it go."

I pulled away and went to the back of the bus. That silenced them immediately. The same *shit, he's a live grenade* looks I'd been getting from my parents. Excellent. I pushed my shoulders back and held my head high, making sure they could clearly see the purple-blue line around my neck.

"Say what you want to, jerkoffs. I already proved I can survive you and I'll do it again."

Thad opened his mouth but no words came out. Ben looked down at his phone. Wayne turned to Zane. Zane narrowed his eyes at me. Contemplating retaliation? Bring it, baby.

In school, things were no different than they'd ever been. Well, there were more silent stares as eyes locked on the bruising between my chin and Adam's apple. There were the usual whispers, but instead of bumping into me, the crowd parted as I walked down the hall. Like I had a disease and they didn't want to catch it.

Or maybe like a messiah, back from the dead with a message to deliver.

I got to first period history, took my seat, and about fifteen seconds into class, a call came for me to report to the guidance office.

"He needs it," someone said.

"Not like they can do anything for him," someone else added.

"That's enough," the teacher said in her stern teacher's voice.

I stood and walked to the front of the class. Again, pushing my shoulders back and holding my head high.

"Let me make it easier for you." I turned slowly from the left side of the classroom to the right, making sure those brave enough to look could see. "Are you going to keep being cattle? Or do any of you have the courage to stand up and be a leader?"

The teacher held a hall pass out to me but didn't let go right away when I took it. She wanted me to see her sad smile.

See, I'm on your side, the smile said.

Where the hell were you before? I wanted to ask.

I pulled harder on the pass and left without giving her the satisfaction of acknowledgement. At the guidance office, the secretary sent me straight in to my counselor.

"Oh, Robin, have a seat." Ms. Sutherland took off her glasses and held a hand out to the two hard-plastic chairs in front of her desk. "I wanted to chat with you about what happened this weekend."

"I've already *chatted* with about a dozen people," I said. "I don't have anything else to chat about."

"Dr. Bell from the hospital shared your details with me."

"Isn't that privileged?"

"Your mother gave him permission," Ms. Sutherland said. "She wanted to be sure we knew so we could help."

How caring of Mom. Would've been nice if she'd asked me for permission first, it was my life everyone was messing around in after all.

"I'm fine," I said and stared at the college posters taped all over the walls of Ms. Sutherland's closet-sized office.

"You tried to hang yourself."

I winced. "Yeah, I was there."

"Robin—"

"Ms. Sutherland, do I have to talk to you about this? I've got Dr. Bell and he's cool. I don't really want to talk about it with you. Nothing personal."

After a long pause she said, "Okay. Will you promise me something though?"

"Can I go back to class if I do?"

She smiled then. Ms. Sutherland was pretty. A few years out of college, I guessed, with blonde hair pulled back into a ponytail and shining blue eyes. If I did have to talk to someone at this school, it would be okay if it was her.

"I know you'll be meeting with Dr. Bell and that's great. But if things go dark on you again and you can't get with him right away, will you come and talk to me?" She took out a business card and scribbled something on the back before handing it to me. "You're only supposed to talk to me here, but if things get bad, my cell is on the back. I give you permission to call me anytime."

I stared at the card and thought stupidly, *Wow, a girl gave me her number.*

Who knew attempted suicide could work as a pickup line? Ivan better watch it. I might be on to something that could offer a little competition to The Matchmaker. The Terminator? No, that's been used. The Executioner?

Then Mom's voice entered my head, too. *Robin Alexander Westmore! That's not at all funny.*

Oh come on, Mom. It's a little funny.

"Tell me one thing," I said to Ms. Sutherland.

"Sure." She sat forward in her chair, elbows on her desk, hands clasped, face beaming with eagerness.

"What can you do about the stuff they put on social media about me?"

She squirmed, the eagerness dimmed. "I haven't personally seen the social media posts you're referring to. I will certainly look into your complaint. We take this kind of thing very seriously."

Your standard, non-committal answer. I just blinked at her, causing her to squirm more. Was she uncomfortable? Did she want someone to come to her assistance? Yeah, been there.

"We always encourage compassion between our students," she said.

"Does that mean you can do something or not?" I asked.

"If you provide me with a list of the students you feel have bullied you, I'll arrange a meeting and we'll have a discussion."

"You'd better reserve the gym," I said.

"What?"

"The whole damn school has been bullying me, Ms. Sutherland." The look she gave me said I was exaggerating. "Don't tell me you don't know what happened at the dance."

"I do. I'm sorry that happened to you, Robin."

"Never mind." This was such crap. If I wanted things to change, I was going to have to take control. Stand up for myself like Dr. Bell and Mr. Lacey said. "Will you sign my hall pass, please?"

I sat in a daze through second period English. I kept my back to Brianna through third period chemistry. When I got to the computer lab for fourth period, Miss Clark seemed genuinely happy to see me.

"I'm so glad you're back, Robin." She gave me a sympathetic arm rub. "I was so scared for you when I heard about what happened. High school can be so hard. I hope you're okay."

"I'm fine," I said automatically and gave her the answer my dad told me to say. "It was a dumb thing to do. I should have gone to an adult with my problems."

Miss Clark narrowed her eyes at me then nodded. "I hope you do. You can come to me if you want. I'll listen."

Everyone was suddenly so eager to listen to me. Where had they all been before?

"Thanks. What do you need me to do?"

"I'm absolutely swamped with requests today and we're having problems with the video feed for the morning announcements. I'm hoping you can figure it out."

"I'll take a look," I said, happy for a challenge. "I'll need your sign-on to get to that part of the network."

She debated this for a second, she could just log me on, but she told me her password instead.

"Don't tell anyone I gave it to you," she said and wiggled her fingers in front of my face as if hypnotizing me. "Forget it as soon as you've used it."

I laughed at that. An actual genuine laugh. My first in nearly a week. It felt good.

It took me half an hour, but I got the video problem sorted out.

"Principal Service will be thrilled," Miss Clark said. "He likes everyone to see his face first thing in the morning."

Like standing by the front door everyday wasn't enough.

Fixing the video feed only took me twenty minutes. That

left me with almost half an hour left and nothing to do.

Not only hadn't I forgotten Miss Clark's password, I'd burned it into my memory. After verifying that she was still absorbed in whatever she was working on, I brought up my student file. They had me flagged as a code D for dangerous student. That meant I had potential to be either a danger to another student or myself. Glad to know I had potential. There was a write up explaining my attempted hanging. I wanted to correct their write up. I actually did hang myself, I just hadn't died.

The hair demerit was in there, too. I highlighted it and hit delete. Easy-peasy. If they ran a report to show changes to students' files, Miss Clark's name would come up as the initiator, not mine. Hopefully she wouldn't get in trouble for tampering with student records.

I opened Zane's file next. His grades sucked. In fact he was about two-tenths of a point away from academic probation. Maybe that was the paper his dad had been waving in his face at one in the morning. Maybe that's why he pushed himself so much athletically.

Ivan was next. His grades were stellar, a solid 4.0, but he'd been flagged as being disruptive in class. Not surprising. He never let anyone in the Bunch have an opinion on anything. Why would he accept a teacher's word as gospel?

I almost added a note to their files about them being bullies, detailing what they'd done to me, but I didn't want that coming back on Miss Clark, too.

I still had time so peeked in a few other files. Tabatha had issues in English and history. Emily did well in every class but math. Pranav also had a 4.0. Jeremiah had great grades and a note excusing him from gym. Brianna wouldn't have a hard time getting into the college of her choice.

Next came lunch. I filled my tray, everyone watching and whispering as I went through the line. My old seat, the one closest to the doors, was empty. It was the perfect spot. I could see everyone from there. As I scanned the room, I paused occasionally on someone who had made a comment about me or gave Zane a high-five for one of his hilarious posts. While I knew who these people were, I didn't *know* them. Other than their names and grades, I couldn't give one detail about anyone in my school except for Brianna and the Bunch.

They didn't know me either. But that didn't stop them from posting whatever they felt like all over the web.

I took out my phone and started snapping pictures. I got them as they entered and left the cafeteria. I got them as they sat with their friends, bitching about something or professing ultimate knowledge of some topic. Same thing I'd done with the Lunch Bunch. Professing my knowledge of computers and game design, bitching about my parents and homework. Laughing at funny stuff. See? We were all alike.

Why, then, was I to be poked, prodded, and made fun of? Because Zane decided five months earlier that I was less than? Why was he the ruler supreme? Because his parents had money and he could throw a baseball? Because Zane *told* everyone he was the best? Was that all it took?

I pushed away from the table and wandered around the cafeteria, taking pictures. When they looked up and started the eye-rolling and pointing, I stopped and took extra pictures. If someone in a group was obviously professing to his or her followers, I stopped and took extra pictures. When the Lunch Bunch tried to summon me, I flipped them off and stopped to take extra pictures. Their expressions were priceless. When I stopped to take pictures of Zane's minions, they tried to fight back.

"What the hell are you doing, Tweety?"

"Why do you have to be such a freak?"

Thad came up to me. I scanned the room, locating the closest teacher. It wasn't likely Thad was stupid enough to lay a hand on me in front of the entire school, but it was possible that I was underestimating him.

"Put the phone away, Tweety," he said, throwing his

shoulders back to make himself look big and impressive, like a peacock flaring its tail.

I took his picture because the thing was, peacocks did that to attract a mate. A meme with Thad as a peacock flashed in my head and I laughed out loud. An unfortunate thing to do at that moment.

"Delete it," Thad said, breathing his hot pizza-breath all over me.

"Delete what?"

He snatched my phone out of my hand and tried to access my pictures. The screen had already locked so he couldn't get at them. He decided instead that simply destroying my phone was the best alternative. He threw it on the floor and it bounced back up at him, hitting him squarely in the nuts. When he picked it up and tried to bend it and break it into a million pieces, he couldn't do it. So he set it on the floor and stomped on it. Nothing. Thank you, Dara, for the magic genie glass.

I started laughing again, as did a few other kids. Thad grabbed me by the shirtfront with both hands.

"Both of you," one of the lunchroom monitors said, charging over, "to the office now."

"Me?" I asked, picking up my phone. "I'm the victim here. He attacked me."

"Zero tolerance. You were involved," the monitor said. "Get to the office."

Thad was suspended for two days. I got a one-day.

"You're kidding me, right?" I asked Mr. Service. "You're seriously going to suspend me for getting bullied?"

"Mr. Westmore," he said, "an altercation in the lunchroom is hardly bullying."

"What about all the other incidents?" I asked. "The tripping and harassing in the hallways. Physically assaulting me in the bathroom."

"None of that," Mr. Service said, "can be substantiated. Not one other person has ever corroborated your stories.

You've never given us proof."

"What about the social media stuff? You do know what they did to me at the dance."

A shadow passed over his face then. For the first time, Mr. Service showed me a little compassion.

"I know what they did, Robin. I am sorry about that." But...

"But according to school policy—"

"Never mind," I said. "Ms. Sutherland already quoted this to me earlier. She's arranging a meeting."

"I know you're frustrated," Mr. Service said, cutting me off, "but there's only so much I can do about things students do away from the school."

"Only so much you can do or only so much you will do?"

I already knew the truth, but any lingering hope I'd had that things might get better died right there in my principal's office.

"According to the lunchroom monitor," Mr. Service said, "you were involved in an altercation with another student."

"I didn't do anything."

"I understand you were taking pictures."

"Everyone takes pictures. Are you going to suspend the entire school?"

Mr. Service held up a hand to silence me. "The definition of an altercation is an angry or heated discussion or argument. You were involved with such an event and therefore the rules state that you are to be suspended for two days."

"For doing nothing," I said with as much disgust as I could manage. I was pushing my luck and I didn't care in the least.

"In light of recent circumstances," Mr. Service said, clearing his throat as he glanced at mine, "I am only going to send you home for the remainder of the day. I won't list this as a suspension. Your record will state you weren't feeling well. You can come back tomorrow and your punishment will be considered complete."

He picked up the phone and simultaneously clicked around on his computer screen. I realized too late he was looking for my home phone number.

"Mrs. Westmore, this is Mr. Service from Robin's school... Well, we have a bit of an issue. Robin was involved in an altercation with another student... No, Robin's fine. This was not a physical confrontation."

"Yes it was," I said loudly. "He put his hands on me."

Mr. Service again held up a silencing hand. "An argument really. At any rate, I'm sending Robin home for the rest of the day as punishment. I'll need you to come pick him up."

He listened and I could tell by the way his expression went blank and he kept looking at me that she was refusing that order.

"School policy states... Yes, all right." He hung up and turned to me.

"Let me guess, she said I'm supposed to take the bus." It wasn't a question.

"Robin," Mr. Service said, "is everything okay at home?"

"Yeah. Sure, I guess. Why do you ask?"

"Your mother's reaction is unusual. She didn't ask many questions about the altercation and her refusal to come and get you..."

He didn't finish the thought, just let it kind of hang out there for me to do something with.

"My mom opened her own business when we moved here. She's really intent right now on making sure it's a success."

I could read his expression. It said that she should be more concerned with me and *my* success. That would be nice, but those weren't the parents I got.

"Should I try your dad?" Mr. Service asked.

Now he was pitying me.

"I wouldn't suggest it. I'll be fine. I take the bus all by myself every morning and in the afternoon, too."

Mr. Service took his glasses off and pressed his fingers over his eyes. "I know you haven't been in this school very long, Mr. Westmore, but believe it or not I do care about your wellbeing."

I placed my hand over my heart. "And I've felt that from you every single day."

Chapter Twenty-Three

Robin

Mom was waiting for me in the kitchen when I got home. She held up a finger and then pointed at a stool, indicating I should sit and wait.

"This is going to be a fabulous campaign. Can I ask a favor? I need about fifteen minutes to take care of something. Would it be all right if I called you back…? Great. Thanks."

She set her phone on the kitchen bar and poured hot water from the kettle waiting on the stove into two cups waiting on the counter. She set one cup in front of me as she sat on the stool next to me.

"What happened?" she finally asked.

I filled her in on everything from the bus stop that morning through the discussion of the *altercation* in Mr. Service's office.

"What did you do to upset this boy at lunch?" she asked.

"Why do you assume I did something?"

"Because your attitude is very high and mighty right now and you're looking kind of smug. What did you do?"

Huh. She knew me better than I thought.

"I took a few pictures. Guess they didn't like being on the receiving end of it."

She tilted her head side-to-side, a loud *pop* released from her neck. "Why did you take their pictures?"

"I don't know."

"Robin?"

"It was just a spontaneous thing." Preparing to give them a little taste of their own medicine. Not that she needed to know that. "It's not going to be an issue anyway. Mr. Service said my record will only show that I wasn't feeling well and went home."

"What's the real reason?" she asked. "A violation of their zero tolerance policy, I assume?"

"Yep."

"You did antagonize."

"How is that different from what they do to me every day?"

She tapped her fingernail on the teacup. "It isn't. Were you hurt?"

"No."

"You're rubbing your hand again."

I looked down. So I was. Hadn't even noticed.

"I'll make an appointment to get it looked at." She said nothing for a minute then let out a heavy sigh. "I don't agree with that policy, but you did break a school rule. Since it's not going to show up on your records, I'm not going to push it with them."

"But they—"

"I know," she said, stopping my objections. "I'm proud of you for defending yourself." She checked the time on the microwave. "I have to get back to work. Is everything else okay?"

"Spiffy. Had that nice little chat with my guidance counselor. Thanks for sharing all my personal stuff with her."

"You're at school all day, not here where I know what you're up to. I felt that someone there needed to be aware."

Like she ever had clue what I was up to. Sure, she could say she was a stay-at-home mom, but the last time she stayed at home for my benefit was when I was four.

She went back to her office. Conference over. I put my teacup in the dishwasher and went up to my room. Time for phase two.

For the next ten hours I converted all of the pictures I'd taken into stupid gifs and memes. One of Zane and Thad that looked like they were holding hands at the bus stop, the caption *You're my best friend* in a thought bubble coming out of Thad's head and *I love you* coming out of Zane's. A gif of Brianna making a disgusted face at Zane with the caption *I smell something. Oh, it's you, Zane.* Some were pictures of people caught at the exact wrong time, for them at least, so their faces were twisted into grotesque expressions. It went on and on.

I tagged everyone I knew and then scheduled the releases. One post every ninety seconds. I'd made enough that the releases would go on for more than three hours. Satisfied that I'd caused enough chaos for one night, I went to bed. Tomorrow was the final phase. It was going to be a big day and I wanted to be well-rested.

☮ ☮ ☮

I woke early, full of energy, eager to get on with phase three.

Mom was already in the kitchen despite the early hour.

"You're up early," she said with a smile.

"You are, too." I checked out her suit and heels. "And you're dressed. In business clothes."

"I'm meeting with a new client in Fort Collins this

morning. I want to get on the road early and beat as much traffic as I can." She got out a teacup for me and held up a clear plastic bag. "Bagel?"

"Yes, please. And Irish Breakfast."

"Irish?" She looked both pleased and surprised.

"You always drink it. Figured I'd give it a try."

"Add some milk," she said while putting my bagel in the toaster oven, "I think you'll like it."

A few minutes later I said, "You're right, it is good this way."

She set the bagel on a plate in front of me along with cream cheese and a knife.

"Mom?" A sour lump formed in the back of my throat. I had to wait for it to go away before I could continue. "Have I ever thanked you for making me breakfast every morning?"

She froze with her teacup raised halfway to her mouth. "Robin, is everything okay?"

"Of course. Can't I thank you without getting a lecture?"

"It's just—"

"Dr. Bell told you to watch for change in behavior."

She looked me square in the eye. "Yes."

"Can't a change in behavior be genuine? Isn't it possible that I'm realizing the mistake I made?"

She didn't answer at first then nodded. "Yes, I suppose that is possible. And no, I don't think you ever have thanked me."

"I apologize for that," I said and clinked my cup against hers. "Thank you."

Her cheeks flushed and she nodded.

"That's your thing, isn't it?" I asked. "Feeding people."

Mom sat next to me and spun my stool until I was facing her. "I know how hard things have been lately. The move was hard enough, that's stressful for anyone. But to come to this new place, have your mom basically disappear on you, and then be treated the way you have been by your classmates." She shook her head and blinked. "It would be too much for anyone. Always remember I am here for you and I love you more than you know. Try to stay strong and come to me if you need me. If I'm not giving you the attention you need"—she laughed through pooling tears—"then sit on my desk and demand it. Things will get better. I promise."

I couldn't even respond. My throat was clogged with emotion so I just nodded.

"It's Friday," she said emphatically. "We're going to dinner. I should be back from Fort Collins by four. I put Antonelli's on your dad's calendar for six-thirty."

I nodded and my voice came out in a harsh croak. "Sounds great, Mom."

She glanced at the clock on the microwave. "I better get on the road. You'll be okay?"

"I'll be fine."

"If you need me today, call me. It'll take a while to get back from Fort Collins, but I'll come as fast as I can."

She kissed my cheek, grabbed her travel mug of tea and her bag, and left.

A few minutes later, Dad came into the kitchen and set his gun and briefcase next to the door.

"Your hand still bothering you?" he asked.

I was opening it wide and closing it tight, trying to stretch out the pain.

"It's cramping. Mom said she'd make an appointment for me."

He plugged a pod into the machine and set his mug underneath.

"Good," he said. "Your mom told me what happened yesterday." He had this cautious way of talking to me since the attempt. Like if he spoke too loud or said anything remotely upsetting I'd go running back out to the garage again. "Everything okay?"

I thought of the pictures, gifs, and memes that had been posting throughout the night and couldn't help smiling.

"Yeah. Everything's fine."

"Good." He nodded as if verifying his feelings on it. "That's good."

"Mom wants us to have dinner together tonight," I said. "She put it on your calendar."

"Dinner," he took out his phone and flipped to his calendar. "That works."

Neither of us said anything more while he plugged in the second pod. Once it was ready he screwed on the cover and grabbed his briefcase. "Would you do a favor for me? Put this back in the vault."

He set his gun case on the counter next to me.

"No range today?" I asked.

"Nope. I've got dinner plans." He gave me a wink. "See you later."

I waited until his car pulled out of the drive and went up to my room.

☮ ☮ ☮

The first class of the school day started at seven-forty-five. Mr. Service did the morning announcements at precisely seven-forty-six. I waited until seven-forty-seven and hacked his feed. Well, I didn't technically hack it. I had Ms. Clark's password after all.

"Good morning, Woodland Academy," I said. "A lot of you know me. Some of you don't. If you're not sure, I'm Robin Westmore, the kid who tried to hang himself. You may be wondering why I'd do that. That's what I'm here to explain.

"My personal hell started before lunch on my first day here about five months ago. Not because I'm so different from any of you. Or maybe I am, but you couldn't possibly have known that at the time. I hadn't even spoken to anyone yet. So what horrible crime did I commit? I stood in the wrong place at the wrong time. Something embarrassing had happened to Zane Zimmerman, you all know him, and he decided to take it out on me. Seriously, wrong place, wrong time. That's it."

I had to pause. I was getting emotional. My voice was going to crack. I had to keep it together if I wanted to make a real impact.

"So I have to ask, why do you all stand by while Zane, Thad, Wayne, and Ben treat me the way they do? Not one of you ever came to my defense. Wait, that's a lie. Brianna, you did."

I blew a kiss into the camera for her.

"I hoped for better from the student body of Woodland Academy. We're supposed to be among the best and brightest, aren't we? I figured that meant at least one of you was a leader." I paused and frowned. "Turns out you're all followers. Not one of you is brave enough to stand up and do the right thing."

I held a piece of paper up to the camera. "I made this list of all the people I wanted to be sure got credit for my torture."

I cleared my throat.

"Ivan, you think you're a leader, but really you're a coward. You welcomed me into the group and then, instead of telling me when I did something that upset you, you decide to publically humiliate me? Only someone insecure and weak would do what you did. I don't know what made you this way, but you should get some help.

"Tabatha, why do you need to make yourself feel better by tearing others down? A little self-reflection and counseling might be in order for you, too.

"Pranav, what a complete wimp you are. Do yourself a favor, find a backbone and a set of balls.

"Emily. What a sweet and unbelievably weak person you are. Not only did you stab me in the back, you let your *friends* take the fall for the betrayal you helped set up.

"Jeremiah. Man, you hurt me the worst." I blinked, tears

wanted to fall. "You had me convinced that I'd finally found a real friend. But you didn't have the courage to send me even an anonymous tip to let me know what they were planning. What kind of friend does that make you?"

The front office had to be in chaos right now. Trying to figure out how I was doing this and how to stop me. Ms. Clark would likely figure it out soon so I needed to hurry. Unless she was going to be a leader and let me have my moment.

"To the staff of Woodland Academy, I was all but crucified by the students of this fine establishment. Have a meeting, reevaluate the school's priorities. To the rest of the students, I know I'm not the only one. I know others of you are being treated the way I have been. Join together. Stand up for yourselves. Say it loud and say it proud, you deserve better. You are worthy of happiness."

As the words Desiree told me came out of my mouth, I started crying. I didn't care. Let them see the real me. God knows they hadn't yet. I stared straight into the camera, desperate for my message to reach even one of them.

"Zane, I don't know what kind of pressure your dad is putting on you, but you need to stand up for yourself too, man. I'm sorry you're hurting."

I wiped my hands over my face. Time was almost up and this was the hardest part.

"Mom and Dad, I know you did the best you could. I know you love me. I love you, too." I couldn't hold it together anymore so I choked out the rest. "This hurts too much. Nothing is changing no matter what we try. I can't do this anymore."

I picked up Dad's gun which had been sitting in my lap, waiting for this moment. I held it in front of the camera and could almost hear the collective gasp at the school.

"I pray for those of you like me, hurting and not knowing where to turn. I hope my words can make a difference in your life. Reach out, before it's too late. Take a chance, trust someone. To all you bystanders, next time someone says they're a target, I beg you to take it seriously. We're in so fucking much pain. We need help. All that stuff you say to and about us, it isn't a joke. Your words hurt and they cut deep. For ten seconds, imagine those words are being directed at you. Now imagine it happening all day, every single day. How does it feel?"

With a shaking hand, I released the gun's safety and held it to my temple.

"Robin."

A gentle voice. A hand resting on my shoulder. Trying to stop me. I wanted her to. At the same time, I couldn't take it anymore. I couldn't keep living with the pain.

"Robin, look at me."

I turned. Desiree was right beside me.

"What are you doing here?" I asked.

"Let go of your mouse," she said. "You're stuck in your game. Let me help you out."

What was she talking about? Stuck in my game?

She placed her hand on top of mine and slowly peeled it from around the mouse. My hand screamed out with pain.

"You've been playing your game since you got back from Zane's house."

What was she talking about? I blinked at her, slowly starting to come out of the deep zone I'd been in. "I went there with a gun."

"You did."

Stuck in my game? What was real and what wasn't? "I didn't shoot him, did I?"

"No, you didn't shoot him."

Thank god. "How long?"

"In your game? More than a day."

"I've been sitting her for more than twenty-four hours?" She nodded again. "No one checked on me?"

"Your mom did," Desiree assured. "You convinced her that you needed one more day away from school."

"I don't remember that."

I couldn't get out of my chair on my own so Desiree helped me stand, walked me over to my bed, and helped me lay down. She pulled my chair over and sat next to me. "What's going on, brother?"

I had no idea. What *was* going on?

"You said I was inside my game," I said. "But that wasn't my game. It was my life."

"Dara enhanced your system, remember? Apparently it took over."

As the fog cleared from my brain, details came to me. "Do you know what happened to me in there?"

"I do," she said. "I've been watching you very closely."

"You're *sure* it was my game? It was so real." Except the real me didn't have the courage to stand up that way. I only had that kind of confidence while playing my game. "Why did it make me do all those things?"

"When you play," Desiree said, "the game responds to what you need. It must have sensed that you needed to confront your tormentors. I think it was letting you play out what your subconscious wants."

I raised my aching arm—my shoulder screamed, my elbow wouldn't bend—and let it fall over my eyes. It was so real. I swear, I really did all those things.

"I had a gun to my head, Desiree. Are you saying that subconsciously I want to shoot myself?"

She looked so sad suddenly. "I don't know. You tell me. Is that what you want?"

She wasn't judging, just wanting to understand. Everyone else kept telling me *You don't want to die, Robin. You have so much to live for, Robin.* No one had given me permission to say that's what I was truly feeling. Not even Dr. Bell.

"If I say yes," I moved my arm so I could see her, "would you'll let me?"

"Well," she said, "I won't hand you the gun. I told you

before, if you really want to die I won't be able to stop you."

When I got back from the hospital, before I got stuck in the game, I read the emails from Emily and Jeremiah. They were real. They were sorry for what they'd done. They cared that I was still alive. Maybe they were telling me the truth about Brianna, she really wasn't in on Ivan's plot.

"I don't want to die." A sob burst out of me. "But I can't keep living like this. Something has to change."

"For the past few weeks," Desiree said, "I've been going through something similar to what you have. I wasn't tormented like you have been, but on a much smaller scale I was bullied. The Guides have been trying to turn me into the kind of leader they wanted rather than letting me figure it out for myself. I finally realized, *they've* been running the place, not me."

"Not good," I said.

"Not good at all," she said. "I had to stand up and take back my power. It's not possible to make everyone happy, so I had to decide what's most important. That means putting the needs of our charges first and staying true to myself, too."

"Staying true to yourself," I repeated, remembering the red dot on Zane's back. "That's important."

She studied me for a minute. "Your experience in the game was pretty powerful. Is there anything you did in there that you'd really want to do?"

I thought about it and told her, "There are a few things."

"Like what?"

I smiled. "I liked telling everyone what I thought of how they've treated me. I liked how Mom took the time to talk to me when Mr. Service sent me home. That's just how I'd want her to react." I thought about the end, just before putting the gun to my head. "If I had the chance to talk to the bystanders and the other bullied kids, I'd say *exactly* what I said to them in the game."

She leaned her head against the back of the chair and closed her eyes. The peace emanating from her was calming me, too. "Robin? What if you were just given a gift?"

"A gift?" How was knowing that subconsciously I wanted to die a gift?

"There are countless people living with the kind of pain you have been. Do you suppose they all want to die?" She peeked at me then closed her eye again. "Or do you think that if they *knew* things could get better they'd choose a different option?"

The question annoyed me. "I'm sure they'd choose a different option. All I've wanted all along is for things to get better. I told you, I don't want to die."

She nodded. "Forget for a minute what the bullies say about you. Are you proud of the person you are?"

I'd never thought about it, but there was no reason I shouldn't be. "I guess."

"What if all of your pain has been for a reason?" She lifted her head and looked straight at me. "What if you're meant to do something with your experience?"

A jolt of pain shot through my cramped hand as the feeling started to return. In the game, while making that video suicide note, I kept thinking that if my message could help one of the other bullied kids that would be a win.

"If what I went through could somehow help make someone else's life better, that would be a good thing."

"Welcome to martyrdom," Desiree said, raising an invisible toast to me. "You have people to help you, you know. You just have to ask."

"I know." I believed that now.

"Dr. Bell wasn't supposed to be working that night I brought you to the hospital. The woman who was scheduled to be there,"—Desiree shook her head—"she wasn't the right one. She ended up with two flat tires and had to take a personal day."

"Two flat tires?"

She gave me a mischievous smile and wink.

Ah, genie intervention. How cool would it be to have

even a little of that magic?

"I chose Dr. Bell for you," she said, serious again. "He will do everything and anything he can for you. I promise. Your parents love you more than you know. But you have to talk to them. If you say nothing they'll assume everything's groovy. Lean on them. Ask them to help you, and then make room to let them in."

"Okay," I said, but the word barely came out.

She started singing this song about life having pain and sorrow, leaning on a friend when you needed to, and letting that friend lean on you, too.

"I don't feel like I'm at a hundred percent yet," I admitted. "Will it keep getting better?"

"It can," she said, still in her eyes-closed peace-and-serenity bubble. "That's not something I can do for you with magic though. You have to do the work and learn the skills to keep the idiots of the world from tearing you down again. Because there will always be idiots." She opened her eyes. "Happiness needs balance after all."

I lay there, wiggling more feeling into my stiff fingers, wrists, and arms.

"Don't be afraid to walk your own path, Robin. It's those who are fearless and blaze a trail who make a difference in this world. You're different. You're a little weird. You don't quite fit in. Do you realize the potential that means you have?"

I couldn't help but laugh. "Potential? You really think so?"

"My brother, I know so." We sat quietly for a minute then she said, "You look like you could use some sleep. Don't use those sleeping pills. Pharmaceuticals are bad." She held out her hand and a cup appeared in it. "Drink this instead."

"What is it?" I sat up, with a wince, and took the cup from her.

"Chamomile and vanilla tea. Best thing ever to help you

sleep."

I took a sip. It relaxed me immediately. Truth was, I was so exhausted all she probably needed to do was shut off my light and I'd be out.

"Do you still have the stone Dara gave you?"

I patted my pocket. "Right here. Do you want it back?"

"Oh, no. You're not done with me yet." She pointed as if into the distance. "We can see the start of your path, my friend, but we have not yet reached it. I will be here for you until I know you're on it and ready for me to split."

My heart sank a little. "That's what Dara said. That she'd be here for me."

Desiree dropped down on her knees next to my bed. "Have I given you a reason not to trust me?"

"No."

"Then unless that time comes, I'm asking you to put your faith in me. Like Dr. Bell and your parents, I am here for you. There are others, too."

"Who?"

She winked. "You know."

I handed her the mug, lay back down, and pulled my covers up. It might have been the pure exhaustion from not having slept in something like forty-eight hours, but my body instantly relaxed. For the first time in a long time, I didn't feel afraid. In fact, I almost felt hopeful. Mostly, I felt tired.

"Desiree? Would you turn the lights out, please?"

I heard a soft chime and the room went dark.

Chapter Twenty-Four

Desiree

The San Antonio night air was chilly enough that I needed to manifest my poncho. I went to the balcony's glass wall and looked down at the Riverwalk. I wanted to absorb the enchantment of the sub-street level world, instead I kept staring at the spot where Dara had lay dying and Kaf had appeared to save her.

I'd thought a million times since that night that I shouldn't have agreed to his bribe. My life would be so much happier if I had stayed with Rita—the woman who had become a surrogate mom to me—gone to school, and started life as a normal college kid. No real worries other than making it to class on time and maintaining a GPA I could be proud of.

But here, at the scene of the crime so to speak, reality hit me again. I had no other choice. I don't know if Kaf would have let Dara die, but at the time I believed he would. There was no way I could have lived with that. Just like I couldn't let her die when I sent her away a few days ago. Or Sarah nearly two weeks ago.

"Desiree?"

I turned to see Elena, Dara's family's butler, standing by the door that led into the penthouse. Elena, her husband Andres, and Dara's parents all knew about the magic. I'd seriously considered wiping their memories, Dara's too, after I sent her away. Who would they tell though? And I liked knowing there were a few non-magical people in the world who knew the truth about me.

"Hi, Elena."

"What's wrong?"

"What makes you think something's wrong?" I tried to laugh off her accusation, but it came out forced.

"You're crying."

I touched my hand to my cheek and found tears there. How was I supposed to be the Wish Mistress if I couldn't stay in control of myself?

"Is Dara here?" I sniffed.

"She is. I'll go get her." Elena paused and asked again, with more emphasis, "Are you okay?"

I shook my head. "Not really. I'll figure it out though."

A minute later, I saw Dara running through the penthouse toward the balcony. She burst through the door and stopped in her tracks.

"What are you doing here?" Her face looked hopeful, but her tightly crossed arms said she was as conflicted about what to think as I was. "You said I'd never see you again. Do you have any idea how awful it was to hear you say that?"

"Probably about as awful as it was to say."

She took a few more cautious steps toward me and stopped, still a good ten feet away. "What's going on?"

"I just left Robin."

She inhaled. "And?"

"And I think he's going to be okay. The game took over and let him play out his revenge fantasy in a virtual world."

Dara exhaled and the corner of her mouth twitched a tiny bit. "It worked. That's great."

She led me over to a tall table and stools next to the balcony and turned on the heater standing there. It seemed like only days ago that we sat here eating and talking and looking down on the twinkling lights of the Riverwalk. Everything had seemed so perfect then. Or at least everything had the potential for perfection.

But I knew, perfection was an illusion. A person could drive herself crazy trying to achieve it.

"Is that what you thought would happen all along?" I asked. "That a virtual world would save him?" I didn't know what response I was hoping for. If she hadn't, it was a happy accident. If she had, it meant she'd known what she was doing all along.

"We can only give them the tools to get to a satisfying conclusion. Right?"

"But you knew the game could do something like this?"

"You know," she said, "it was pretty damn awesome for me to realize I could combine my already impressive computer skills with magic. I don't know if you realized how perfect a Guide I was for Robin or not"—she paused and smirked at me—"but it looks like my plan worked."

She could be such a brat sometimes. "Perfectly. You still should have paid more attention to him."

"I should have," she agreed. "Is that what you came here to tell me?"

"No. I came here to apologize. I didn't trust you and I should have. I should have trusted myself and my instincts. The Guides were giving me such a hard time. The atmosphere around there was so negative and nothing I did seemed to make anyone happy."

"You gave in to peer pressure."

I nodded. "I let you take the fall. I'm sorry."

"Humpty was pushed." She pointed an accusing finger at me and added a laugh to let me know she wasn't mad. "So? What are you going to do about it? Call in all the king's men and put it back together?"

That she had forgiven me was such a rush. "No. But maybe I'll call in the queen's women."

She stood there, blinking at me, then said, "That was really lame."

"Well there aren't any men in my queendom."

"Stop, I can't take the hilarity." She rolled her eyes and pointed at a spot next to me. "Your swirl is getting bigger, you know."

"They're summoning me," I said. "They have been for a few hours."

"And you yelled at me for—"

"I know," I said, halting the accusation. "I needed to tend to Robin and tell you I was sorry first."

Now that I had, I needed to talk about something other than magic and wishes and the chaos of my world for a few minutes.

"How is everything now that you're back? I can smooth things out if necessary."

"You know," Dara said, nodding, "it's all good. My parents couldn't get themselves to tell the school I was 'dead' so said I was sick. They were working up the nerve to tell them I'd taken a turn for the worse when you sent me home. I'm going to take a few weeks and travel with my mom and then go back at the start of the next quarter."

"The school didn't want details or doctors' notes or anything?"

"It's funny how a donation to the new computer lab can silence questions." Dara blushed fiercely, as she always did when she talked about her parents' money. "Are you good now? Ready to go back."

"Yes. No. Better, but not good yet."

"Remember who you are," Dara said. "What happened

to my favorite take-no-crap hippie?"

"She's still here," I said and forced a smile. "She just has to dig out from beneath all that peer pressure."

A roar of laughter drifted up to us from the Riverwalk below. Normal people, having fun together. Would I ever have that again? Kaf had sentenced me to this position until I found a replacement. How long would that take? For how many decades would I have to be nineteen before I got to turn twenty and give normalcy a try for a third time? Then again, who got to decide what was normal? Did we get to choose that for ourselves or was it up to a higher power?

"Stalling won't make it easier," Dara said. "It'll probably make it worse."

A few months ago she was a spoiled rich-girl begging on the Riverwalk because she was lonely and bored and wanted something to do. Now here she was giving me advice. Good, grown-up advice at that.

"You're right. I should go."

She popped out of her chair and stood next to me, arms wide, fingers wiggling, waiting for a hug. I stood and let her wrap me up. I was the 'big sister' and here she was making me feel like a little kid.

"Will I ever see you again?" she asked with a teasing, dramatic sob in her voice. So much nicer than the heart-wrenching first time.

"Yes," I said. "If I have to suffer through this job for the next however many years, I'm not doing it alone."

She pulled back. "Wait. I am getting older, right? Hang on. You're not going to turn me back into a Guide are you?"

Now she was the little kid again.

"No," I said, laughing at her. "You never should have become a Guide. If Kaf wanted me to take over, he should have asked me like a decent person. Not bullied me and used you."

She gave a little shrug. "I did help save Robin so, you know, there's that."

252

"You totally saved Robin." I pulled her into a hug this time. "I mean it when I say you're like a little sister to me. No way will I be able to stay away from you."

"God, stalker much? Who do I talk to in the genie world to get a restraining order?"

"Shut up. I need to go."

"Yes, you do. See you soon."

☮ ☮ ☮

I could sense the chaos the second I appeared at the little cabin next to Mystic Lodge. The entire valley seemed to be vibrating with it. What the hell had happened? Why couldn't I go away for a few hours without the world coming to an end?

I sat in my chair and picked up my tablet. There were over a hundred messages for me. The vast majority were Guides complaining about wishes they didn't want. At least they hadn't traded.

Indira appeared in the doorway then.

"We need to come up with a system of rewards," I said as soon as I saw her. "Maybe a week off after every twenty successful wishes."

"Desiree—"

"I know, it goes against the way things used to be, but I have a different leadership style."

"Desiree—"

"I know. I'm sorry. You've been summoning and summoning. I had to take care of some important things."

"Desiree, he's back," she blurted.

And time stood still. The breath froze in my lungs. My focus tapered down to Indira and the words coming from her mouth.

"Say that again?" I was terrified she'd repeat what I thought she said. I prayed she'd repeat what I thought she said. My stupid, traitorous heart leapt.

"Kaf is back." She said softly, compassionately, and with a hint of warning.

How? Why? Where had he been? What right did he have to come back now? Just when I felt confident to truly take the reins, he was back to once again put me under his thumb?

Remember who you are. I heard Dara's words like a delayed echo.

No. He gave me this power. I was not relinquishing it.

"You told me," I said as calmly as I was able, "that you didn't know where he was."

"I didn't," Indira said.

"Then how—?"

"I tell you," Adellika said, appearing from behind Indira, "you need help."

"I don't need help," I said, rising to my feet. "Where is he? Send him away. This in my world now. I don't want him here."

Inside though, I had crashed to the floor and lay shattered in a million pieces. He was here, somewhere in the valley, *my* valley. My heart, my betraying bitch of a heart, was pleading to be near him. To feel the warmth of him radiating around me. To maybe, possibly, be in his arms again.

"Send him away." My voice broke as it came out in a whisper so soft they couldn't possibly have heard me.

They stood there, staring at me. Indira with a look of such compassion and understanding it ground me from a million pieces into a fine powder. Adellika with a look of absolute loyalty. But not for me. Then I saw it.

"You knew where he was," I said. "How?"

"He went home," Adellika said in the same broken English Kaf used.

"You know where his home is?"

"Yes."

"How?" Again, I held my breath as I waited for the answer.

254

"It was once my home, too."

"Your home? You're—"

"Adellika is my sister."

And there he was. I couldn't move. All I could do was stare.

He looked different. He looked familiar. How could he look so different? As always, he took up the entirety of my doorway. Adellika was less than half his size.

"Let me guess," I said hysterically. "Twins?"

Indira place a hand on Adellika's back and led her out of the cabin, closing the door as they left.

Kaf and I stood there, a mere ten feet apart from each other. Ten feet that felt like ten miles. Even from that distance I could feel his heat. It wasn't the comforting kind though. It was angry.

"Adellika has been keeping me informed," he said. "Telling me all that has happened since you"—he paused, dramatic as always—"took over."

"You told her to spy on me?"

"Not at all. She was one of the first to join me in the magical realm. She cares about this world almost as much as I do."

"Did," I said. "It's not yours anymore."

"Do," he repeated gently, locking eyes with me. "You do not stop caring about something because you have been away from it."

My heart sank. It wasn't me he cared about. Only *his* world.

"You never cease to amaze me, Desiree."

"I do my best," I said, trying for coy and confident. Succeeding only in sounding pathetic and insecure.

Damn it, girl, I scolded myself, *get a grip. Have a little self-respect. He left you. He set you up and abandoned you. Remember who you are!*

"I have been gone less than two months," he said, his chest heaving with anger, "and you have nearly destroyed what it took me two hundred years to build."

"New management," I said with a shrug, "go figure."

"You have not taken this seriously. I expected more out of you."

"And I expected a little direction," I said, calling him out. He actually deflated a little, reminding me that I had the magic now. He had given it to me. There was no need for me to resort to the relationship we had before. I could send him away again with the tap of a finger.

I needed his help, though. I had all along. The Guides responded to and respected him. Partly because he was so damn hot. Partly because he was an effective leader. One thing I had learned was that the successful people in the world didn't necessarily know everything. But they were intelligent enough to surround themselves with those who knew what they did not.

"What did you think would happen?" I thought of the two of us standing next to Gypsy V the day he set me free to go to San Antonio and find my sister. I didn't know how to drive, had never needed to since I'd had the ability to transport. In seconds, he infused me with the knowledge so I could get where I wanted to go. "You handed over the keys to the queendom, but didn't give me the knowledge to drive."

His brow knit in confusion and then cleared. If one thing was true, after so many years together, we understood each other better than either of us cared to admit.

"Do you want to learn?" he asked.

"It would be helpful."

"That is not what I asked," he said, closing the distance between us. "Do you want to learn to be the leader?"

Being the Wish Mistress had been nothing but frustration since the day he gave me his powers. It was much more satisfying to be to be a Guide and be directly involved with the charges and their wishes. But maybe that was just me being afraid to step out of my comfort zone after so many years.

"I'd like to try," I said. "I can't really know if this is what I want if I'm not given a fair chance."

"How would you like to proceed?"

Humpty was pushed, Dara had said.

I couldn't help but smile. "Gather all the queen's horses and all the queen's women and let's start picking up the pieces."

Chapter Twenty-Five

Robin

The next day was like the worst case of déjà vu ever. Certain things were the same as they had been in my game. Mom chattered at me all through breakfast. She toasted a bagel for me. I tried Irish Breakfast tea for the first time. She was thrilled. I asked her if I'd ever thanked her for making me breakfast every morning.

"That's not a red-flag warning," I said immediately. "I don't want to kill myself, I swear."

"That's good to hear." She still looked at me like I was a time bomb. "You do understand my concern though."

"I do. I promise you I want to make things better." I thought of the talk Desiree and I had. "I was thinking that maybe I can use what I went through to help other kids."

"Robin," she placed her hand over her heart. "I think that would be wonderful. It would help you heal, too."

I nodded. "So, thank you for making breakfast for me every morning."

She blushed.

"What do you think about Antonelli's for dinner tonight?" I asked.

She gave me a long, mom-stare. The kind that was full of love and made me believe what Desiree said about her being there for me.

"That sounds great," she said. "I'll call right away and make reservations."

Dad walked into the kitchen then.

"We should probably bring your husband," I said.

He looked at us suspiciously. "What going on?"

"Your son wants to take us out for dinner tonight."

"Yeah," I said. "Bring your credit card."

Dad gave me a thumbs-up. "Are you going to school today?"

"Are you ready?" Mom asked.

I didn't just spit out an answer. I analyzed my feelings first. Then I nodded. "I think so. If it gets too hard, would you come pick me up?"

She laid a gentle hand on my cheek. "Of course I will."

"If she's busy," Dad said quietly, attention focused on his coffee, "you can call me."

☮ ☮ ☮

At the bus stop, Zane and The Minions kept looking at me, laughing and saying things I couldn't hear. I stood up for myself in my game. Time to see how that would work in real life.

I took a deep breath and called, "Zane? Can I talk to you for a minute?"

He said something to The Minions, for which he got a fist bump, and then swaggered over to me.

"What's up, Tweety?" He nodded at my neck. "Looks

like you had a bit of trouble."

"I want you to stop now." My voice was firm despite my pounding heart. "I never did anything to you. Never once gave you a reason to treat me the way you do. I want you to stop."

His mouth pursed like he wanted to say something, but instead he shoved his hands in his pockets and kicked at the ground.

Then, I pushed my luck even further and said what I'd said to him in the game. "I don't know what kind of pressure your dad is putting on you, but you need to stand up for yourself. I'm sorry you're hurting, but you can't take that out on me or anyone else."

Fury was obvious on his face, but so was pain and a glimmer of what I hoped was appreciation that someone knew his secret. He didn't say anything, just grunted and walked away.

Once the bus came, I let everyone else get on first and took the empty seat next to Brianna. She started crying softly the second I did and I knew that what Jeremiah and Emily said about her was true. I said nothing, just took her hand while she cried all the way to school.

Mr. Service greeted us at the front door like always. Today he broke protocol and stepped away, pulling me aside.

"I'm fine," I said before he could ask.

"Glad to hear it," Mr. Service said. "I'd like you to go to the Guidance office. Ms. Sutherland is waiting for you. I'll be there shortly."

"Great," I said, "because there's something I'd like to talk to you about."

He blinked, surprised. "I'm anxious to hear it."

The discussion with Ms. Sutherland started a lot like the one in my game. She told me she knew what had happened and that she was available if I needed someone else to talk to.

"I'm so sorry, Robin. I understand what you're going through."

"Do you?" I doubted it. "Have you been harassed like this before?"

She sat straight hands folded on her desk. "Yes, actually."

"You were?" She looked like she would have been one of the most popular girls in school. No one messed with them.

"One of the girls in my college had been dating one of the big names on the football team. They broke up one weekend and the next weekend he asked me out."

I knew it. Cheerleader and the QB.

"The girl he had been dating spread a rumor all over campus that I slept with him." A look of pain and frustration darkened her face. I felt a twinge of camaraderie with her. "I never even knew him before he asked me out. Well, I knew him. Everyone knew him. We had one class together, but I'd never spoken to him. He said he thought I was cute and did I want to go to this party Friday night."

"What happened?" I asked.

"The other girl was at the party, too. She posted pictures of us dancing. She managed to get a few shots that made me look like I was drunk and hanging all over him. Those pictures got me kicked out of my sorority." She flushed, angry. "It was a sobriety and chastity sorority. You know, where we took a vow—"

"Yeah," I said and immediately pictured her drunk and naked. "I get it."

"Anyway, to make matters worse I found out that the guy only asked me out because I was a nobody and he thought that would make his ex furious."

What a jerk. "What did you do?"

"It was my senior year," she said. "I only had a few months to go until graduation so I kept to myself and did my best to not let the rumors get to me. A few people believed me but looking back, I should have defended myself better. My entire reputation for four years at college and high school before that was destroyed in one night."

"I'm sorry," I said. "That really sucks."

She nodded her thanks. "The point is, I survived it and you can survive this. I know you can."

Mr. Service walked in then. It was weird seeing him anywhere other than by the front doors, on the morning announcement video screen, or in his office.

"Good discussion?" he asked Ms. Sutherland.

She looked at me and I nodded.

"Wonderful," Mr. Service said and clapped his hands. "What did you want to talk to me about, Robin?"

"There's something I'd like to do," I said, "and I'll need your support to do it."

They glanced nervously at each other.

"What's that, Robin?" Mr. Service asked.

"I'd like to start a bullying support group." I held up my hand to stop them before they objected. "I know you tell people there isn't a bullying problem at this school, but you know that's not true."

Despite Mr. Service's squirming, Ms. Sutherland said, "I think it's a good idea."

Mr. Service didn't look convinced.

"We can call it something different if you're uncomfortable with the word bully," I said.

"It would appeal to more kids if we did," Ms. Sutherland said. "The Social Strength club or The Stand Strong club... something." She looked squarely at my principal. "We need to do this. It won't turn into some big sit-in, protest type group. We'll simply work on life skills so kids know how to stand up and defend themselves."

"It can't just be for the kids that are bullied, though," I said and thought again of Zane lifting weights at one in the morning. "The bullies need help, too."

Ms. Sutherland looked at me like I was an alien of some kind. But in a *that's so compassionate* way.

After a few more minutes of Ms. Sutherland and me

working on him, Mr. Service finally agreed.

"Start spreading the news," Ms. Sutherland told me. "I'll work on the logistics and specifics."

At lunch, I walked down the center aisle with my tray and stood by the Lunch Bunch. Only Jeremiah looked me in the eye.

I thought about everything I'd said to them in the game and part of me really wanted to say those words now. Instead I said, "I want you all to know that I forgive you. I'm still pissed. It was a supremely shitty thing, but so I can move on and deal with stuff, I forgive you."

Everyone, except Ivan, looked up. Emily fought tears. Tabatha picked at her nails. Pranav jutted his chin at me in apology.

"Ivan," I said. "Please look at me."

Slowly, defiantly, he did.

"I don't know what happened to you, man, to make you this way." My words came out strong. "I'm sorry for whatever it is. Ms. Sutherland and I are starting up a bullying club. I don't know when our first meeting will be, but if you'd like to show up maybe it can help."

Anger flashed across his face and I expected him to go off on me. Before he got the chance I said, "I'm going to sit in my old spot." I gestured over to the doors. "New start and all that. If any of you would like to join me, you're welcome."

I walked away then and sat in my spot. A shaky exhale escaped me. What had I just done? Was I starting over again with no friends? I placed my hand on my thigh. The peace stone was in my pocket. I liked knowing I could call Desiree, if I needed her.

The table shifted then as Jeremiah sat across from me. "Glad to see your face, Bird Man. Tell me about this group of yours."

Resources

If you need help, or know someone who does, here are a few places to try:

StopBullying.gov
SuicidePreventionLifeline.org
ItGetsBetter.org
TheTrevorProject.org

911
1.800.273.TALK (8255)
1-800-SUICIDE (1-800-784-2433)
TTY: 1-800-799-4TTY (1-800-799-4889)
LGBT Youth Suicide Hotline: 1-866-488-7386

A Parent
A Friend
A Classmate
A Neighbor
A Teacher or Principal
A Pastor
A Police Officer
A Doctor or Nurse

Acknowledgements

This was the hardest book I've ever written. It was originally going to be about bullying only. The more I got to know Robin, though, the more I realized it needed to be about more. To get into Robin's mindset, the mindset of someone who suffers from bullying and contemplates suicide as an escape from their pain, was painful for me. I can only begin to imagine what of those of you who live with this every day go through. I thought of you constantly while writing this book. I hope you know that things *can* get better. Know that I care very much about what happens to you. Please, talk to someone.

Rachael Dahl, I'm so sorry your family was touched personally by this topic, ironically while I was writing this book. Thank you a million times for your input.

Sue Duff, I am so very sorry for your loss.

Dakota Damschroder, I can't thank you enough for being my beta reader! Your insight was so helpful.

Bree Ervin, what would I do without your editing? To find someone so invested in my books has been invaluable. Thank you.

Paul and Eli, for listening to me obsess about this book, for giving me your honest thoughts on it, and for understanding the mind of the author in your home, thank you. I love you both with all my heart.

Connect with Shawn

Word of mouth is the very best promotion. If you enjoyed this book, please consider leaving an honest review with your favorite vendor or at Goodreads.

You can find Shawn on the web at the following sites:

www.Shawn-McGuire.com
Facebook: ShawnMcGuireAuthor
Twitter: @Shawn_McGuire
Pinterest: ShawnMcGuire1/

If you want to be the first to know about new releases and get all the latest information about Shawn's work, sign up for her newsletter! http://eepurl.com/V21k1

About the Author

Shawn McGuire is the author of young adult, coming-of-age novels that blend contemporary settings with a touch of fantasy and magic. She started writing after seeing the first Star Wars movie (that's episode IV) as a kid: she couldn't wait for the next one so wrote her own episodes. Sadly, those notebooks are long lost, but her desire to write is as strong now as it was then. She grew up in the beautiful Mississippi River town of Winona, Minnesota, the small town that inspired the setting for *Sticks and Stones* and *Break My Bones*. The Milwaukee area of Wisconsin (Go Pack Go!) was her home for many years and she now lives in Colorado with her family where she loves to read, cook and bake, craft, decorate her house, and spend time hiking and camping in the spectacular Rocky Mountains.

Made in the USA
Charleston, SC
10 June 2015